The Rest is Silence

an Edmond Holmes Novel

M. KATHERINE CLARK

ISBN-13: 978-0-9998708-9-1

Other works by
M. Katherine Clark

The Greene and Shields Files
> Blood is Thicker Than Water
> Once Upon a Midnight Dreary
> Old Sins Cast Long Shadows
> Tales from the Heart, Novelettes

Love Among the Shamrocks Collection
> Under the Irish Sky
> Across the Irish Sea
> On the River Shannon
> The Land Across the Sea, an Emmet O'Quinn Short

Love Among the Shamrocks Collection the Next Generation
> In Dublin Fair City
> Song of Heart's Desire
> Chasing After Moonbeams – Coming Soon

The Wolf's Bane Saga
> Wolf's Bane
> Lonely Moon
> Midnight Sky
> Star Crossed
> Moon Rise
> Moon Song, a Companion Guide
> Dragon Fire
> Heart of Fire
> Will of Fire – Coming 2021

Soundless Silence, a Sherlock Holmes Novel

The Rest is Silence, an Edmond Holmes Novel

Silent Whispers, a Scottish Ghost Story

Silent Night, a Scottish Christmas Ghost Story– Coming 2021

For my fans! I never thought Soundless Silence would have a sequel, but you wanted it! I hope Edmond's story fulfills all your wishes!

Prologue

1901. It was a difficult winter.

Her majesty, Queen Victoria died on January twenty-second and the empire was in mourning ever since. Her son, Prince Albert Edward, nicknamed Bertie, was to be coronated Edward the Seventh but not until the following year, as was custom. Until then, the country mourned and was perceived weak by other nations itching for war. There was always talk of some faction or other who caused unrest, but as the night fell on Victoria's reign, the wolves beat at the door and a new king, though advanced in age, was easy pickings if done correctly.

There were two things Bertie indulged in; women and cards, and more than once he was caught up in a scandal or two.

Chapter One

April 1901, Paris, France

A nudging at his booted foot, woke Henri from his post at the back door of *Le Chabanais,* the infamous brothel in France's capital. Waking with a start, his dark brown eyes assessed the men surrounding him. The rain fell in heavy drops, dripping into his eyes. But it did not prevent him from assessing the five men before him.

Henri took a deep breath, easing the gripping fear that took hold when he saw one man holding a lead pipe and another gripping a large knife.

"Wh... What do you want?" he called to them. One man, a particularly ugly one with a scar across his face, laughed.

"You were in the way," he answered. "Move it, boy if you know what's good for you."

His French was tainted by slang and an accent Henri had only heard in seedier areas of town. Henri pulled himself up to his full height, at eleven he stood a little under five foot three, much shorter than all but one of the men.

"Tell me what you want first," Henri stated. "This is my door, and I will not allow anyone through who will harm the occupants inside."

The men chuckled. "Oh, no, we won't *hurt* them, not all of them," the leader licked his lips, and another man grabbed the front of his trousers in a lewd gesture. "We're looking for a man. Calls himself a king."

Henri's eyes grew wide. "You're assassins."

"We prefer businessmen for hire," the leader said. "Now, step aside."

"He's not here," Henri tried again. "The English King left hours ago."

"Now, it's not polite to lie," the leader said as one of the men lunged forward and grabbed Henri by the hair. Yanking his head back, he held the knife to his face. Henri cried out.

"I'd hate to have to mar your pretty skin, but the problem is you lied and are in our way. We have it on good authority the king is still within."

Henri grunted in pain as the grip on his hair increased. His hands had grabbed the man's wrist to try to loosen his hold. The leader walked over to him.

"Hmm..." he observed his face. "Not one of mine, thank god. But can't answer for the rest of you. This bastard is too pretty for the likes of us."

"*Cochon*," Henri spat.

"Ooh," the leader winced jeeringly. "It's not your fault, boy. A whore's bastard never will have good manners. I think we need to teach him a lesson, boys." The leader gripped his jaw.

"You're pretty now, just wait until we're done with you. Every sewer rat in Paris will want a taste," the man holding his hair and knife to his face said.

Henri quelled the fear and pulled on his strength from years of begging for scraps and living on the streets. "You think I'm pretty? Too bad you're not three streets over. I know a place where men like you are celebrated."

"You little shit," he spat. "I'll teach you a lesson," the man turned him toward another with an even larger knife. "Go, Renard. Get it over with. We'll wait for you at the dock." He said to the leader.

Renard nodded and walked toward the door.

Henri struggled with his captor as the other walked slowly toward him brandishing the knife, a sick grin on his face.

"Let me go."

"Squeal, little pig," the man sneered.

"Never," Henri replied but the man's grip increased on his hair and chin and Henri failed to contain his cry.

"No one but the whores is going to miss you."

"Let him go," a voice from the shadows stated.

Henri and the men stopped and turned to look in the direction of the voice. The man holding Henri's hair and chin increased his grip. The eleven-year-old grunted.

"Leave now, stranger. This doesn't concern you," another of the men called out to the shadows.

The figure moved closer to the spherical glow cast by the dim flickering gas light illuminating the doorway. Henri tried to peer into the darkness but could only see the outline of what looked like a very tall man. Broad shouldered, wearing a dark suit, but the white of his evening shirt reflected in the light, even as his face remained in shadow. He was taller than all the others, standing a good head above the rest. Though Henri couldn't see detail, it looked like the man's hair was unfettered down to his shoulders. He was built like a warrior of old, like in the stories the *madam* had read to him as a little boy.

"I said," the voice spoke again. "Let him go." His French was flawless and with an elegant accent Henri had heard outside the more fashionable areas of town where the rich and foolish were easy pickings for a pickpocket of Henri's skill.

The leader, Renard looked toward one of the men playing with the lead pipe and nodded toward him. The brute moved into the darkness, but the stranger stayed motionless. The man moved further toward him. It all happened so fast. One minute the man struck at the stranger with the lead pipe but didn't hit him, then Henri heard what sounded like a loud crack, the man screamed and then there was another crack followed by a dull thud. It happened within a breath, but Henri felt the other man's grip on his hair and chin loosen more.

Another of the group of men raced toward the stranger. Again, it was over in a flash, but that time, there was no hesitation from the group. Another man raced toward the stranger and the man holding Henri released him and raced after.

"Look out!" Henri shouted to the stranger. The stranger didn't turn but his leg smoothly kicked behind him, hitting the man in the abdomen.

"Run, boy," the stranger shouted at Henri as the leader joined in the fray.

Henri slowly backed down the alley, but he didn't want to leave. There was no way the stranger could take all three men at once.

"Go!" the stranger yelled.

Henri looked around the area and dived behind some crates that smelled like they had come from the docks. Peering over the top, he watched as the stranger dodged and moved in a way Henri had never seen. The stranger did not move like a boxer Henri had snuck in to see the year before. He moved more like a cat. His strikes were hard but fluid. It reminded him of a snake.

Soon, all the men were on the ground except the leader who stood and stared at the stranger with fear in his eyes holding his broken arm. He slowly backed away but as soon as the stranger took a step toward him, the man turned and ran down the alley to the main street. The stranger drew out something from his inner coat pocket and put it to his lips. A shrill whistle echoed down the street and Henri wondered if the man was part of the *gendarmerie* police in Paris, but the whistle was not a police whistle.

Henri stared at the man's back. He barely breathed heavily but kept looking down the alley where the man left. After a moment, he lowered the whistle and placed it back into this pocket. Then, the stranger moved his head slightly to the right.

"I told you to run," he said in a low voice.

Henri held his breath. The stranger stood in the halo of light from the sconce and finally turned fully around. The face that met him was younger than Henri expected and yet there was an aura of age about him in how he carried himself and the slightly lighter, almost greyish hair at his temples. The face had a dark bit of scruff lining the square, pronounced jaw and upper lip. His long aquiline nose added to the fierce dominance of his face. But his eyes, those hooded light grey eyes seemed to pierce Henri's very soul and he knew more than one of the ladies within would jump at the chance to be with a man so handsome.

"Who are you?" Henri asked.

"Who I am is of no great importance," he answered.

"*What* are you then? Are you a demon?"

"And if I was? Would you run then?"

Henri shook his head, and the man breathed a chuckle.

"I don't know if you have either courage or stupidity," he said. Henri looked down. "What is your name?"

"Henri," he replied.

"Henri," the man repeated. "What are you doing out here on a night like this?"

"I usually sleep inside but with the English king in attendance, there is little place else to sleep."

"You do not like the English king?" The stranger asked.

"I have no opinion on the man, but the way he treats my ladies, leaves something to be desired," Henri said.

"Your ladies?" the stranger questioned.

"*Oui,* the women in *Le Chabanais* are mine to protect... one of them is my mother."

"Oh? Which one?"

Henri looked away. "I do not know. But one of them and I will protect them all."

"Brave words," the stranger stated. "Commendable action. Your father would be proud of you."

"I have no father."

"Everyone has a father even if they don't know him," the stranger said.

"They took me in from off the streets when I was a boy."

"You are still a boy."

"When I was younger, then," Henri replied. Oddly, he did not take offence to the stranger's tone. He was speaking in nearly monotone so Henri could not decide if he was supposed to take offense.

They said nothing for a moment, then the stranger took a step closer. "You did well, protecting the ladies. Now, I need to get inside."

"Why?" Henri looked up sharply.

"Because the king's life has been threatened and he needs to know and leave at once."

"Leave?" Henri stepped around the crates.

"Go back to London," he explained further.

"He will never leave. He loves it too much and Paris loves him."

"Perhaps, but the king did not ask my uncle to ask me to protect him on this journey if he did not know his life was in danger."

"Your uncle?"

"It is not important. If you do not trust me, you do not have to. But I *am* going inside."

"I just saw you murder four men. I will not let you go in."

He raced around the crates to block the door.

"Murder?" the stranger asked, then shook his head and nudged one of the men lying on the ground. The man moaned and Henri backed up until his back hit the crates.

The stranger watched him with an almost hawk-like expression. "How old are you?"

"E... eleven."

The stranger's eyebrows rose slightly. "Brave for one so young. Brave or foolish. Let's go with brave." The stranger turned to the door, clearly intending to enter. He pinned Henri with a stare. Henri froze, only letting out a breath when the man looked away.

"*Monsieur!*" Henri shouted over the din of music, laughter, and playful squeals. The stranger paused just inside and turned back. "Please... tell me your name."

The stranger stared at him for a long moment then finally, "Edmond, you can call me Edmond." Before Henri could respond, the stranger entered the brothel and the door closed behind him.

Chapter Two

Five Years Earlier

"Extra! Extra! Sherlock Holmes' secret revealed!" One boy yelled outside of 221B Baker Street. "The king of detection has a queen! Read all about Sherlock Holmes' secret family! Extra!"

Sherlock Holmes stood in Baker Street with a roaring fire listening to the paper being read by a strong, slightly French accented voice.

"'Sherlock Holmes shocked the world yesterday by announcing the arrival of four people no one ever thought existed. The great detective revealed he was by no means a confirmed bachelor when he introduced his wife, two sons, and daughter to London Society. This revelation comes after the close of one of the most brutal crime sprees since Jack the Ripper. Not much is known about his secret family except they were living on an estate in the south of France.

"'In a private interview with the family, the great detective revealed he had been married for nearly twenty-six years to Marguerite Holmes nee Moreau. Little is known about her, except she and Mr. Holmes met at her family's estate in Yorkshire many years ago before the detective's world-renowned career and association with Doctor Watson.

"'It is known the detective used an alias while over in France and his family used it as their last name. The name Maison is the French word for home. In the private interview, this paper was able meet his family, as it is not just his wife but his children as well. Mrs. Holmes is one of the loveliest women on earth.' Quiet so, mama," Edmond complimented quickly and continued reading.

"'Her quiet demeanor and attentive behavior had a way of putting everyone at ease. She is quoted to say she is very happy to finally be back in London and is thrilled to be with her husband after all these years of taking time when he could get away. "He is a wonderful man, and I knew when I married him, he would be an even better father and he has never proven me wrong." She stated.

"'Holmes and his wife have three children; Charles, Edmond, and Rebecca. His devilishly handsome eldest son; Charles Percival Holmes will soon have the hearts of all this seasons' debutants in his hands. He is a fashionable twenty-four-year-old and has an interest in politics. His equally handsome, though less fashionable younger brother, Edmond Weston Julian Holmes, twenty-three, is said to be a virtuoso on the violin, like his father. The youngest of the three is Rebecca Jacqueline Holmes who, the detective and his wife have confirmed, will be presented to society this season. She is said to be one of the loveliest debutants of the season at just seventeen years.' *Bien-sûr*," Edmond smiled at his sister.

"'This news comes as a shock to the nation but not to his friend, Doctor Watson who confirmed he knew about them but was sworn to secrecy. He has indicated he is looking forward to getting to know his friend's family better. Sherlock Holmes has confirmed he will still be taking cases in his private capacity until further notice.'" Edmond ended reading and listened to the conversation around him. He knew being in England would change his life. He was just not certain if it would be for the better. Either way, he raised the wine glass to his lips and observed his family seated in the main room of 221B Baker Street and smiled. It was the best of times.

Five Years Later
Paris, France

It wasn't the first brothel Edmond Holmes had ever been to, and he was fairly certain it wouldn't be the last given the king's propensity for the fairer sex. But *Le Chabanais* was elegant in a gauche way. The women were lauded for their beauty and every face Edmond saw confirmed the rumor. Though many of them greeted him as a lover, he was certain none remembered him. It had been nine years since he was last there. A foolhardy holiday after his time in China to rid his mind of someone long lost.

He gave none the impression he was there for himself, instead, he walked confidently through the throngs of naked and half naked women until he reached the stair. Two of his handpicked men stood as silent sentries on either side of the stair, unaffected by the images around them. Married for many years to two wonderful women, fathers many times over, and brothers, Yancy and Jakob were the only two he trusted to be inside the brothel. The rest of his men waited outside and down the street protecting from all sides.

Edmond gave them a nod and took the stairs two at a time. Reaching the King's suite, Edmond paused to listen. Once too many times Edmond had walked in on the sight of the king utilizing his *love seat* and Edmond would rather break his own bones than ever see that again. But as the sound of laughter and not other noises echoed through the door, Edmond knocked twice and entered.

"Holmes!" the king exclaimed with a beaming smile.

"Your majesty," Edmond bowed in his direction but did not look. The king was in his sphinx bathtub drinking a glass of champagne while watching two scantily clad women dance, another massaged his shoulders, and yet another handfed him cold cuts and grapes.

"What brings you to my chamber at this early hour?"

It was past midnight, but to the king it was early in the evening of delights.

"We need to leave, sire. Tonight. I have come to assist you," Edmond said.

"Leave? Whatever for?" he asked.

"Due to the fact an assassination plot was just thwarted, your majesty. And heaven only knows how many more might happen."

The king stared at him for a long moment. "Thwarted, you say?"

"*Oui,* majesty."

"Well, then," he cried jovially and accepted more champagne from the woman serving him. "I see no reason to leave. Why waste a good night? Let's celebrate!"

"Sire, I don't think—"

"No, no, come now. I don't mind sharing," he indicated the two women dancing. They stopped and hurried toward Edmond. "You are far too overdressed for this place, Holmes. Evening attire will get you nowhere."

Edmond pulled himself up to his full height as the scantily clad women threw their silk scarves over him and around his neck.

"Come man, enjoy life!"

"I am required at my post, highness," he bowed and took a step back.

"Stay!" The king said. "Champagne?"

"Thank you, *non,* I need to keep a clear head. Excuse me."

Edmond removed the silken scarves from his neck and handed them back to one of the pouting women near him and bowed out of the room.

"Damn, Froggie, doesn't know a good time when it's right in front of him. If I didn't know any better, I would think he was a molly."

Edmond sighed as he heard the king speak before the door closed. It wasn't the first time the king had called him the two derogatory names. French he may be, but one who finds pleasure with other men or in a dress, he was not, though he knew a few men on his detail who did enjoy that sort of entertainment. Edmond cared not, so long as they did their duty when needed. He was simply not ruled by his emotions and to someone who was, it was not easy to understand his disinclination to pleasure. Though no prude, as he did enjoy indulging occasionally in the women who worked there, he was not there for himself.

As he walked back down the stairs, he straightened his

dark tailcoat and tried to flick a spot of blood off his once pristinely white cuff. His brother would hate that Edmond got blood on one of his best dress shirts, but Percy had nearly a dozen more and one would not destroy his *ensemble*. As it was, Percy's manservant Braxton had to adjust the shirt for Edmond's build and need for a looser fitting shirt to practice his martial arts. His brother was not a small man, but Percy preferred his shirts tight fitting as was the style and his back was not nearly was well developed as Edmond's.

Thoughts of Percy invariably brought back thoughts of their current home in England. If Percy's letters were anything to go by, Edmond would be an uncle again soon and not just with Percy's wife Alexandra in the family way, but his sister Rebecca, Lady Hughes and her husband Cedric, Baron Hughes announced they were expecting their firstborn child two months after Edmond left with the prince. Shaking his head to clear it of nonessential work, he stepped off the last stair and glanced at his men.

Glad to see they were still unaffected by the women around them, he leaned in and whispered new orders.

"Remember Remember," he began the well-known English rhyme about Guy Fawkes. The men nodded and stood up straighter. The code of a possible assassination attempt had been chosen by Edmond at the start of the travels.

One last look at the debauchery around him and he sighed. This was the last and absolutely final time he did a favor for his Uncle Mycroft.

Leaving the main room to the back door, he took a deep breath of the rainy, putrid air. It was better than being choked by the overabundance of French perfume within.

He looked around honestly surprised not to find Henri waiting for him. The young boy had gumption, Edmond would give him that and loyalty. Part of him reminded Edmond of himself. The bodies of the group of men who Edmond had defeated had been removed and if the clear trod of police standard issue boot tread was any indication, his man down the way had gone for the police when Edmond had whistled.

Taking another deep breath of the Parisian air, Edmond always preferred the countryside over the big city, but Paris was like a home... of sorts.

Closing his eyes, he relaxed every fiber of his being. His heartbeat slowed, his breath grew lighter, his muscles unbunched. He was soothed. The art of meditation was more a Tibetan form, but Edmond had studied centering in China which was similar. To center the body would be to bring all other parts' attention to the epicenter of it all. It was something he could do for moments or hours but as he centered, he still kept his ear tuned to the area around him and... there... just to his left, a movement. A soft movement but movement, nevertheless.

The boy. Henri.

He hadn't left as Edmond first assumed. His father would be most displeased if he had told him. Sherlock Holmes always said, never assume. But part of Edmond was impressed. The boy was good at avoiding detection. No doubt hiding from the *gendarmerie*.

"The king is still alive," Edmond threw over his shoulder. "And in case you were wondering, your ladies are fine too."

Henri didn't reply immediately but after a beat, his cracking voice asked, "how did you defeat so many?"

"What do you mean?" Edmond turned. Henri's young face was filled with awe as he peered at him over the fish crates.

"There were five of them and one of you, though if I had gotten free, I would have been able to take two at least," Henri said.

Edmond found himself fighting a grin. "Oh at least, I'm sure."

Henri walked around from behind the crates and faced him. "Can you show me some of the moves you did?"

"Moves? You mean formations?"

"Is that what they're called?" Henri's brown eyes glistened with interest in the flickering light.

"*Oui,* that's what they're called."

"Where did you learn?"

"In China," Edmond replied.

"China? But you're French."

"I am French and British."

His nose scrunched up. "I don't like the British."

"Have you met any?"

"*Oui,* and they're all so arrogant."

"I agree, some can be."

They went quiet for a time.

"*Monsieur* Edmond, please, can you show me?" Henri finally begged.

Edmond observed the young boy before him. He could easily tell him no and make him leave, or he could indulge the boy and show him a few easy maneuvers. Before he even started debating with himself, he knew the answer. He had saved the boy from being injured or worse by the gang of ruffians, of course he was going to teach him.

Henri waited, holding his breath. He had asked *Monsieur* Edmond to show him some defense moves. When he was being held by the smelly man, Henri wanted nothing more than to know what to do to protect himself and his ladies. But he was weak and could not defend himself. Had *Monsieur* Edmond not arrived when he did, he would be dead or at least seriously injured and the king would be... he shuddered.

Monsieur Edmond tilted his head to one side, and again Henri was struck by how hawk-like he looked. Henri pulled himself up to his full height and kept his gaze on him. He was being measured and the last thing Henri wanted was to be found lacking. The more Henri looked at him, the more things he observed. *Monsieur* was a difficult man to decipher but he noticed two things. He was powerful but restrained and his last name began with an H as the signet ring on the smallest finger of his right hand indicated.

"Very well," *Monsieur* said. "Come here, Henri."

A smile split his face and he rushed over to him. *Monsieur* was unbuttoning his tailcoat and draped it over one of the crates. Then, he rolled up his cuffs. The shirt looked altered as if it originally was not cut for his broad frame, but the vest fit him well and fell over his shoulders down to a tapered waist. It was clear whatever *Monsieur* did, gave him an impressive figure. Henri had not seen someone who looked like him except in the paintings in the *madam's* rooms. Henri found himself thinking how fortunate he would have been had someone like *Monsieur* been his father.

"Which is your dominate hand?" *Monsieur* asked. Henri looked at him confused. *Monsieur* picked up a piece of broken pipe and tossed it at him. Henri grabbed it. "Good, right-handed like me, makes it easier."

Monsieur took a stance, his feet far apart, his right foot behind the left, his body sideways, his torso cheated out just a little, his arms level with his chest and his hands in a loose fist.

"Mirror me," *Monsieur* ordered.

Henri studied him for a long moment then imitated his stance. *Monsieur* nodded. "Now, hold," he said as he walked over to him observing the stance. *Monsieur* said nothing for a moment, then Henri felt pressure on his back foot. "Further back," his foot was nudged, and he complied. "Good." Then, *Monsieur* reached around him and squared his shoulders and turned his right hand out a little. "Better."

Monsieur walked around him and stood before him. "Now, this stance is one you can take before a fight if you have time and should be your primary form. Meaning whatever you do, you return to this form. If someone comes at you from the front and say has a knife or pipe like the men tonight, then you raise your left arm to block," he showed him. "And jab out with your right then back to your form. Now, show me."

Chapter Three

"Good," Edmond caught himself smiling as he saw Henri twist his way out of his hold once more and tried to swing his fist around to knock against his jaw. Edmond moved back when Henri's fist came a little too close. "Very good, Henri."

"*Merci, Monsieur,*" the young man beamed. For a moment, Edmond saw a shadow of someone he knew in Henri's face and it took him off guard to realize it was himself. For a span of a heartbeat, Edmond's hands grew clammy and the hair on the back of his neck stood on end. But then he remembered Henri was eleven, too old to be his, but the boy was fairly like him. His light brown hair and features looked so familiar, but his dark eyes cast the familiarity to the side. While so stunned, Edmond did not see Henri's fist and then pain exploded across his jaw, Edmond stumbled back. "*Monsieur?*" Henri shrieked. "I am so sorry, *Monsieur.* I thought you wanted me to attack. Are you all right? I am so sorry."

"I am fine, Henri," Edmond assured. His jaw was slightly tender, but he had been through worse. "You have a solid strike. But you must get stronger if you are going to take on men twice your size."

"I am sorry, *Monsieur.*" The poor boy looked to be hyperventilating. Edmond strode over to him in two easy strides and placed his hands on his shoulders.

"Enough, Henri. No harm is done," Edmond promised. Henri looked up at him, his face scrunched up and his lip trembled. "Henri, everything is fine." Tears filled Henri's eyes and before Edmond knew what to do, they overflowed, and Henri threw his hands up to cover his face. Without another thought, Edmond pulled the boy into him and held him tightly. Memories of his own father holding him as he wept entered his mind. "Shh, shh, it is all right, son. Nothing to worry over."

"I was so scared," he hiccupped.

"I know," Edmond soothed. "But I would never treat you poorly, you must know that."

"Not just that, *Monsieur,*" his voice cracked. "But everything. I thought... I thought I was going to die."

"Ah," Edmond breathed softly. "I understand," he soothed. "You are safe now, though. All is well."

"Thanks to you," he answered.

Edmond pulled back and looked at him. "And you will be able to protect your ladies now." Henri's eyes glanced to the back door then back at Edmond. "Now, go inside and get something to eat and a bed for the night. I'm sure the *madam* will have a place for you."

Henri shrugged but agreed. Shuffling to the door, Edmond watched him go. Turning back around, he locked eyes with Edmond and again something flickered across his face that Edmond recognized but could not place.

"Thank you, *Monsieur.* I owe you my life."

"You owe me nothing, Henri," Edmond said. "It was bravely done. Now go."

With a final brief smile, Henri entered to brothel and shut the door. Edmond let out a breath and leaned against the brick façade. Something about Henri was so familiar and yet, he could not place it. And there was a connection to the young boy he had never felt before. An entirely fatherly feeling overcame him as he listened to the noises in the street to his left. Had he not been absolutely certain in the age of the young man, Edmond could easily wonder if his short visit to *Le Chabanais* nine years ago had not produced such a wonder. But as it was, Henri was eleven, and even if his age was questioned, he looked on the cusp of manhood, eleven, ten at the youngest. But something...

Edmond took a deep breath and closed his eyes tuning out the light echo of rain on the empty crates beside him, the *woosh* of the gas lamps, the chatter and laughter from the men stumbling out of the brothel and into the streets. Though he blocked the extraneous noises, he kept his ear tuned for anything unnatural.

When he had calmed his body, mind, and soul as was his tradition, he took another deep breath and opened his eyes. He was in for a long night. The door opened and Edmond looked back. The *madam* stood there, one arm above her head, on the casing of the door.

"*Madame La Rue*," Edmond bowed slightly.

"*Monsieur Holmes*, a pleasure as always," she answered. "I trust the king is comfortable."

"With your hospitality, *madame*, how could he not be?"

"He is a good customer. My girls' only complaint is his excess weight. But that is to be expected. They all look forward to his visits. The champagne is endless and some of the girls enjoy the bubbles. He pays well too."

"I am sure he takes care of each of them."

"He is very generous. Which is why I would hate to have his visits marred in any way."

"What do you mean, *madame?*" Edmond asked.

"I have heard some strange and wonderful tales from Henri this evening."

Unsure how long he had meditated, Edmond glanced down and pulled out his pocket watch. Three quarters of an hour had gone by since he sent Henri inside.

"He seemed to believe there was an assassination attempt this evening and you are some kind of knight in shining armor come to the rescue for king and country."

"Henri has a vivid imagination," Edmond replied.

"So, he was mistaken?"

"He had nothing to worry about."

"That was not an answer, *monsieur*."

"*Oui, madame* but it is enough of one. The king is well and will doubtless be back soon."

"When will you leave?"

"We leave on the morrow."

"Well, then, perhaps a bite to eat and a glass of wine for you? I can recommend Marie, one of my best girls for your pleasure. She is highly praised and is sure to cleanse herself daily."

"I thank you for the generous offer, but I must refuse. I am to remain at my post, and I would not have any young woman out in this weather," Edmond explained though he would not mind a distraction, and it had been some years since last he indulged, he would not accept.

"Some wine then," she offered. "And I will have cook make you a sandwich. We brought in some chickens for his highness and they have not all been eaten."

"My thanks," Edmond bowed again to her.

"You will wait here?"

"I will be here," he confirmed.

"Excellent," she answered. "I shall return."

The door closed again, and Edmond hunched in the shadow of the doorway to prevent as much of the rain getting on his jacket as he could when it began to pour. It was nights like that he wished he had never accepted his uncle's charge. He could be back in his rooms at his uncle's flat in Pall Mall beside the fire, reading a book with a glass of cognac in his hand. But the thought he would never have met Henri, the idea the young boy could be lying in a puddle of his own blood, a flash of the king's slit throat in the sphinx tub, the red mixing with the golden color of the champagne, shook him from his misery. His duty was to bring honor to his family name.

The door opened again, and the madam offered a plate with some roast chicken between two slices of fresh bread, a type of spicy spread he could smell from where he stood, that made his mouth water. A few olives, a couple small tomatoes still on the vine, and a selection of cheeses filled the plate. The *madam* offered him the plate as she produced a bottle of wine and a glass. Once Edmond took it, she opened the bottle and poured a generous portion into the glass and handed it to him.

"Many thanks, *madame*," he said, his stomach twisting with its hunger. He had not eaten all day due to making plans and being at his post but as the smells tantalized him, he took her generosity and offered to pay.

The madam smiled at him but shook her head. "Anyone who stays out here out of devotion to their king on a night like this, deserves this free of charge. Enjoy."

She shut the door before he could reply and as it was, he had to bite his tongue. The first words he would have said were, "he's not my king."

Chapter Four

The morning brought with it a beautiful sunrise and as Edmond ached to perform his morning routine of Tai Chi Chuan to center himself and prepare for the day, he had no time. Standing guard at his post all evening, he stayed as warm as he could with the madam's wine and a cloak she offered around the three o'clock hour. As he stood waiting at the door, he heard someone shuffle over to him. His man, a valet his uncle had picked for him and the one he signaled to go for the police last evening came up to him.

"They didn't find the leader, sir," he announced.

"Dammit all to hell," he muttered. That would mean be extra vigilant and perform a thorough sweep of the king's ship before they departed. "Very well, any of the others talk?"

"Nothing concrete and they are giving up no names."

"You did well, Terrey," Edmond complimented. "Did you have a place to stay last night?"

"I stayed in a chair at the front, sir. Made sure everyone entering or leaving was supposed to be there."

"Is there such a thing at a brothel?" Edmond questioned.

"True."

"And how were Yancy and Jakob," he asked after his two men inside.

"Silent sentries, sir," Terrey confirmed.

"Good," he answered. Though Edmond needed no assistance from a manservant, his uncle convinced him to take Terrey on for security purposes. Terrey had been fully vetted by the Foreign Office and was of exceptional use when Edmond could not be everywhere at once. And Edmond considered him more a friend than a servant. "Then it is time to wake his majesty."

"Good luck with that, sir," he grinned. "Apparently, his highness was out cold from the alcohol and pleasure as of three o'clock this morning."

"Well, it wouldn't be the first time I received his ire. I am sure it won't be the last. Prepare the others. We depart *immédiatement.*"

"Yes, sir," Terrey answered and hurried around the corner.

The noises coming from inside the brothel were much more sounds of sleeping. Edmond took another moment to breathe in his favorite part of the day, dawn, and, pulling off the cloak, he entered the brothel, shaking his head at the sights before him. Bodies of drunken men and women lay around the area in different stages of dress. A couple women who worked there, were having breakfast at the small round table in the corner to Edmond's left. The *madam's* quarters were closed but sounds of doors closing upstairs preceded men trotting down the steps and across the dimly lit room. Yancy and Jakob stood at their post, no sign of tiredness in their eyes. They said nothing to him as he entered. Terrey came in from the main road and nodded to Edmond, saying the two at the front door, one across the street in a flat overlooking the road, and the two at various points on the side streets were ready and gathering out front.

Edmond reached the two Israeli men who stood by the stairs. Leaning over to Jakob, he whispered. "We leave soon. Join the others at the door, but do not leave in case I have need of you."

"Understood," Jakob answered and turned to his brother to give the message.

Edmond had met the two men at the Home Office and quickly saw a similarity in their movements to his. Following them once, he watched as antisemitic Englishmen attacked them just outside their residences. The gang of men were intent on ridding England of the *Jewish problem* as they said. Little did they know Yancy and Jakob were adept fighters and though Edmond saw a few moves he recognized, most of their style was completely different than his Chinese way. Meeting with them at a later date, Edmond learned they had been taught an ancient form of martial arts known as *Abir*. Since then, the two men were his close friends and chosen by Edmond to join the king's procession.

Taking the stairs up to the king's rooms, Edmond found the king's secretary and valet, sitting at the doorway just waking up. Seeing Edmond, he stood quickly and smoothed the front of his waistcoat.

"Mr. Holmes," the slight man said. "The king is not yet awake."

"Then he is to be woken," Edmond answered simply. "We leave now."

"Is... is there a problem?"

Edmond did not answer, and the secretary fumbled to the door. Knocking once, the secretary did not call out and Edmond tried not to roll his eyes. The man was little more than a mousy looking person with wisps of brownish hair, a small face, large dark eyes, and a figure that would look better on a scarecrow than in a suit. Calming his irritation, something so unlike him, he chalked it up to being damp, cold, and eager for a proper meal followed by a warm fire and his bed. Over the last week, one hundred sixty-eight hours, since they landed in Paris, Edmond had been awake overall for nearly one hundred and sixty hours of them, catching sleep when he could, but it had been over twenty-four hours without sleep, and he was drawing on every ounce of strength he had left.

When the valet did not knock again, Edmond stepped forward. The mousy man stumbled back as if afraid of him. Edmond found odd satisfaction in that, but he raised his fist and knocked loudly on the door.

"Your majesty?" he called. "It is time to leave, sire." He knocked again, louder that time. "Your majesty."

Grumbling from the other side of the door calmed him. Edmond could handle the king upset, he could handle him drunk, but forcing him out of *Le Chabanais* was going to be difficult. Something crashed to the floor that sounded like an empty champagne glass.

"Damn and blast it all," the king's voice grumbled. Edmond knocked again. "I'm coming, dammit."

Edmond waited and soon the door swung open. Edmond kept his eyes on the king as he was certain, without looking, the ruler of Great Britain and Ireland was standing before him... nude.

"What the bloody hell do you want, Holmes?" he demanded.

"It is time to leave, sire," Edmond answered. "*Monsieur*, if you would assist his majesty to dress, I will wait here."

He knew the valet's name of course, but something about the man irked him and he chose never to use it.

"Leave?" the king questioned. "Damnation, Holmes, I'm not going anywhere until I have properly awakened and had some sort of breakfast."

"I am sure your personal chef will have breakfast waiting for you on the ship, your majesty. But we do need to leave within the next twenty minutes," Edmond made a mental note to call down to Jakob or Yancy to have them tell Terrey to run ahead and tell the chef to prepare.

The king turned away from him muttering some scathing term and something derogatory about Edmond's anatomy, but he ignored it and stepped aside for the valet to enter and shut the door behind him. Edmond stepped to the top of the stair and whistled down to the door. Jakob and Yancy looked up and when Edmond motioned for one of them to come up, Yancy, closest to the steps, raced up the steps to meet him.

After giving Yancy his message for Terrey, Edmond waited by the door. Thirty minutes later, which led Edmond to believe the king made him wait ten minutes longer than necessary deliberately, the door opened, and the king stepped out properly dressed in the latest fashions. Edmond's peek into the room showed the four women asleep on the bed and one on the floor. Without another word to Edmond, the king slowly descended the stairs. It was clear the man was suffering from the aftereffects of too much alcohol the previous evening.

The madam waited at the base of the stairs. "I understand you are to leave us, your majesty."

"Aye, though not by my choice, *Madame La Rue.*"

"You are needed elsewhere, sire," she said. "We look forward to your next visit."

The king pulled out a pouch of coins and handed it to her. She curtsied and tucked the coins inside her bosom. Edmond nodded to her and mouthed a thank you as he walked with the king to the front door. The *madam* smiled softly at him and watched them leave.

Edmond stepped into the royal coach with the king and his valet. Jakob and Yancy rode on the back of the coach along with the footman. Another hackney carriage carrying the rest of the men were behind them. The king grumbled the entire way to the docks and Edmond felt a headache coming on. He was looking forward to his cabin on the ship where he had some of his oils, herbs, and rubs. He was also looking forward to a gentle easy crossing.

Chapter Five

The docks came into view and Edmond was never gladder to see the ship. Once the carriage came to a stop, Edmond turned to the king, who had ignored him the entire ride.

"I will go aboard, sire and make sure all is well. Please stay here until my man comes for you."

The king grumbled his consent and Edmond left the carriage. Breathing the salty air, Edmond filled his lungs with the cleaner scent than the back alley of the brothel as Terrey met him at the ramp.

"All well?" Edmond asked.

"Yes, sir," Terrey answered. "Chef has prepared a large breakfast for his majesty and the cabin has been prepared."

"Excellent," Edmond said as he boarded the ship. Greeting the captain, Edmond looked around the area. "Anything of note?"

"Nothing, sir," the captain replied. "All quiet here."

"Good, I will do a quick sweep to alleviate my curiosity."

"I assure you sir, everything is in order," the captain walked with Edmond.

"I have nothing but faith in your abilities to discern that, Captain, however it is my way and will ease my mind to do a final sweep before I allow his majesty to board. You understand, I am sure."

"Of course," the captain stated. "But I can assure you—"

"Who is this?" Edmond asked seeing a face he did not recognize amongst the captain's crew.

"Powers," the captain answered. "Bosun's mate."

Edmond observed the large man. Standing over Edmond's tall frame, and nearly double the size of the captain, the new Bosun's mate was a large intimidating man. He kept his eyes down but slowly looked up when Edmond approached.

"Powers," Edmond addressed him.

"Yes, sir," he answered.

"And how long have you been sailing?"

"All me life."

"What is an Irishman doing in France?" Edmond asked.

"Comin' back from the wars, sir. I wanted to book passage

to me family's farm in Cork but when I heard the king's ship was looking for crew, I wanted to do my duty, sir."

Edmond looked at him taking in all of the things his personage told him. He was the son of a farmer used to manual labor, second son but forth child. He was kicked in the shin as a young boy, his posture showed, no doubt a goat or something equal its height. He had been in war, artillery the man was a crack shot, and that concerned Edmond.

"Tell me, Powers," Edmond began. "You are sitting on a train between an old woman and a young boy. The boy is sitting on the aisle, the old woman by the window looking out at the countryside passing at an alarming rate. There are other seats available, but the boy cannot move, and the old woman does not move. Suddenly, there's a beautiful young woman demanding you move. What do you do?"

Powers looked at Edmond for a moment, then glanced around at the others standing near him. They all seemed unsure what Edmond was talking about.

"I give up my seat for the woman?" Powers offered.

"And where do you go?"

"To... another empty seat?" he asked.

"And yet the boy cannot move," Edmond stated.

"But I can."

Edmond said nothing but turned and headed across the ship, the captain and Terrey tailing behind.

"What the devil was that about?" the captain demanded.

"It was a test."

"Dammit all, man, I know it was a test but why and what does it mean?"

Edmond whirled on the captain and stared at him. His head cocked to one side. "Tell me, Captain, what would your answer have been?"

"Naturally, I would give up my seat."

"And you would be wrong. I do not want the bosun's mate alone or near the king and if he owns a firearm, it is to be confiscated for the duration of the voyage and placed in my care until the king disembarks."

"Dash it all man, speak the queen's English."

"I would rather speak the *king's* since he is the one who rules now, does he not," Edmond replied.

"What the bloody hell are you talking about?" The captain demanded. Terrey's lips twisted as he tried to prevent his smirk.

"Do explain it to him, Terrey," Edmond said. "I need to check the ship."

"Yes, sir," Terrey answered and turned to the captain. "You see the old woman is the previous monarch's England who refuses to change or move, and who watch the country without interest. The young boy is the current king's England in its infancy, weak, but cannot move, cannot change without help, he's also blocking you in. And the beautiful young woman is an outside power who lures unsuspecting men into a false sense of security to give up the seat in order to get closer to the boy who is helpless to move. You are protecting the young boy, you give up your seat, he's susceptible to her. And why would she demand you give up your seat when there's others nearby? Certainly, she wants your seat specifically, why? To injure the boy who cannot move."

"Well dash it, if I had all the information I would have chosen not to move."

"That's the point of psychological riddles, Captain," Terrey answered. "The correct answer is to point out to the young woman there are other seats or better yet, move the old woman, that way you are still closest to the boy and can keep an eye out on the young woman."

"Seems demmed ungentlemanly."

"There's little of gentleman in war," Terrey said.

Edmond had to admit he was proud of Terrey. He was the only man who had answered it correctly two years ago when Mycroft introduced them. Of course, it was the answer of many to agree to move for the woman, but that was the point of the riddle. A beautiful young woman can manipulate for her own gain and Edmond needed only those who understood that to be around the king at such a vulnerable time.

Leaving his valet to speak further with the captain, Edmond stepped down into the hull of the ship and further into the cargo bay. A quick cursory glance around told him all he needed to know. He hurried back up to the main staterooms and cabins. Checking each, including his own, he found nothing out of the ordinary. Finally, the kitchen and dining room were checked, and Edmond reappeared on deck. The men still lined up waiting for the king. Looking at Terrey, Edmond nodded, and his valet headed to the king's carriage.

"Powers' firearm, Mr. Holmes," the captain offered. "He surrendered it with ease."

"Thank him for surrendering it and let him know it will be returned to him when we dock."

"It's about damned time," Edmond heard the king say. "I swear, he yanks me out of bed and keeps me waiting in this cold, damp carriage. If he wasn't so damned good, I wouldn't keep him around."

Edmond almost hoped the king would release him from his duties. But as soon as the king's feet touched London soil, he would be free with a healthy pocket full of coin and a large deposit into his account at Ransom and Company in Pall Mall. But until then, he took his job seriously as it was not just the king's safety, but his father's name attached to the royal entourage.

The king ambled up the ramp and greeted the captain. As the captain welcomed him aboard and introduced the shipmates, Edmond stood silently, Terrey by his side. The king and his valet were shown their quarters and Edmond let out a sigh of relief when the ship cast off. A peaceful crossing. That was all he needed. He would be home soon.

Chapter Six

Terrey turned to Edmond once the king was settled in the dining room eating the breakfast the chef had prepared.

"Do you not partake, sir?" he asked.

"I will eat later," Edmond answered. They had been at the crossing for a half hour or so and Edmond needed to check on something in the cargo hold. "Perhaps bring a tray to my room?"

"Of course, sir," Terrey replied with a shallow bow.

Edmond slipped out of the stately dining room and made

his way across the ship to the stairs leading down to the cargo hold. When he entered, he was grateful for the sconces that had been lit on the walls. It was a damp, cold place. After the evening Edmond had, he was looking forward to a warm bath and a shave but there was something else he needed to do first. Sighing heavily, he sat on one of the crates marked grain and pulled at his necktie. Loosening the cloth and the buttons of his collar, he pulled off his coat and breathed deeply. He was unable to do his morning routine for the last few weeks and he felt the bubbling emotions coming to the surface. Usually, his routine was able to make him less susceptible to his very French emotions as his brother called them. But when he was unable to center himself, he felt them moving just under the skin and with the king's constant badgering, name calling, and downright despicable behavior, Edmond found he was more easily influenced by his emotions than he desired.

There were reasons he suppressed them, reasons he never let his true feelings surface. Since he returned home from the Orient ten years ago, he had done away with things he did not need. Emotions, feelings, and memories of that time... one particular time, were extraneous.

Closing his eyes, he gave in to the memories for a moment. Letting everything pour over him like molten lava, he embraced the pain and remembered when he first returned home to his parent's chateau in Montpellier, France.

He was home. The old Chateau loomed before him, the same as it ever was. Remembering how, for the first three years in China he had to visualize his home just to fall asleep, Edmond closed his eyes and took a deep breath in. The roses his father had brought on his mother's birthday nearly twenty years ago, bloomed in the shade of a tall tree. The English Rose's sweet smell brought memories of dinner parties, play times outside with his

brother, father, mother, uncle, and sister. The French Lavender lining the path to the house, a reminder of his mother's perfume. Hearing voices around the side of the house, he walked slowly. The staff he used was well worn, but his legs needed a break from walking so far.

His mother's voice floated on the wind and a newly invigorating feeling rushed through Edmond's body. Turning the corner of the house, he watched for a moment as his mother sat on the veranda watching his little sister play in the yard with a dog, one he didn't know. His heart hurt when he saw how grown she was. On the verge of being a woman. His brother was not there but he heard his mother speaking to the housekeeper and another woman.

Then the dog turned toward him, clearly catching his scent, and barked. Rebecca looked over and caught his eye. She raced to her dog and called for their mother, not having recognized him. Marguerite stepped off the veranda to see who it was. When her eyes caught his, she gasped.

"Get on out of here," a man's voice called from behind him. "Get on out, we have nothing for you. Get, before I let the dogs on you."

Edmond looked back at his mother who was running toward him, petticoat flying around her.

"Edmond!" she cried. Little did he know how much that sound would mean to him until he heard her say it. She didn't slow down, and he braced himself to take her in his arms. Reaching him, she threw her arms around him and held on tightly. "Oh, my boy. My sweetheart! Oh, I'm so happy to see you!" he winced when the scabs on his back pulled. "What is wrong, my darling? What happened?"

Squeezing his eyes closed to shut out the pain and screams he still heard as clear as if they were beside him, he took a deep breath and let it out slowly. Tears slid down his cheeks, but he felt his mother brush them away.

"Darling, come with me. Come inside," Marguerite said.

The memories still too raw, he opened his eyes and stared at the dancing gas light in the sconce on the ship's hull. Clearing his throat, he huffed a sigh and stood.

"You should be grateful I didn't drag you out of here when I first came down and carried you back to *Le Chabanais* myself," Edmond said to the empty room.

A moment passed and then he saw the movement from behind the king's cases of wine and champagne. Henri stood and looked at him.

"Why didn't you?" He asked.

"Because I was intrigued," Edmond answered. "Why are you here?"

"Did you tell the king?"

"No, and I do not intend to, but tell me why you are a stowaway on this ship?" Edmond questioned.

Henri looked down and used his booted foot to dig into a gouge on the wood before looking up at Edmond.

"I..." he looked away again.

"Speak freely, Henri," Edmond stated. "You are in no danger from me. I would have the truth."

Again, Henri looked up at Edmond. Walking over, he sat beside him with a huff.

"You saved my life," Henri said. "You taught me things."

"So, you could defend your ladies," Edmond reminded him.

"I know," Henri replied. "But I thought..."

"What? You thought what?"

"That maybe... maybe... if I had a father... he would be like you?"

Edmond's heart pulsed for the boy who never had the love of a father. A love that would hold no matter the sin. No matter the transgression. A love he experienced as a young man. A feeling he would wish for any who needed the love of a father.

"Perhaps I was mistaken..." Henri's small voice pulled Edmond from a memory of his father comforting him. Edmond looked over at him. Seeing Henri's dark eyes set in a face Edmond knew but could not place, he could never let the boy go. He would step into the role of Henri's father. He was uncertain as to why he wanted to do it, but he felt a pull to the boy as if he had to protect him.

"No," Edmond said. "You were not mistaken, Henri. God help me, but there's something about you..." he looked away and toward the shiplap of the cargo hold. "If anyone asks," he huffed. "You say you are Henri Holmes. You are my son. I will look after you when we dock in London. I don't know what I can do for you, but you will be safe on this ship."

"Really?" he questioned, and his innocence made Edmond smile.

"Really, Henri," Edmond stated. "Now, come with me. I must introduce you to the king for him to give permission for you to travel with us to London. Until I can return you safely to your ladies... if you so desire it, I will vouch for you and you will tell all you are my son."

"But... You cannot be my father. You are too young."

"Old enough to have fathered you. Make no mistake, Henri, all will be well. Do not contradict me."

"I will not, *Monsieur.*"

"Good. Now, come with me. We need to meet the king."

Chapter Seven

Henri followed *Monsieur* as he walked out of the cargo hold. It was a different reaction to him being a stowaway than Henri thought could or would happen. Still unsure if their ruse would work, Henri made no mention to his doubts to *Monsieur*. He simply followed him up to the main deck, wanting to stop and look around to see the opulence of the ship, but he did not let *Monsieur* get too far ahead of him. Rushing after *Monsieur's* retreating frame, he found him before a closed door and *Monsieur's* fist raised to knock.

"Say nothing," *Monsieur* cautioned before the door

opened. Henri nodded

The opulence of the room surprised Henri. He had lived in the most lavish of places but in that moment, he realized there was more than *Le Chabanais*. The room was stately, kingly. The dark wood furnishings complimented the white linen of the tablecloths and silver cutlery. The circular room with windows out to the starboard side showed the choppy waters of the channel. A brilliant chandelier hung in the center and a lone table was beneath. The man who sat at the table was larger up close than Henri thought. The king was not a tall man, standing just two inches taller than Henri but sitting, it was clear the king ate well and did little in the way of exercise. In fact, opposite *Monsieur*, the king looked old and very... German.

Henri had to bite his tongue to stop him from laughing at the funny looking man.

The king looked up from his plate to lock eyes with *Monsieur*. "Holmes," he grunted.

Monsieur bowed. "I hope you are feeling more like yourself, your majesty."

"Aye, demme, that champagne goes straight to my head. The morning after is never good until breakfast." The king sounded genuinely fond of *Monsieur*.

"I am glad to hear it, sire. You will be pleased to know the captain has informed me all is clear, and we should dock in London in time for tea," *Monsieur* said.

"I am pleased. Though I shall miss Paris."

"And I believe I can safely say Paris will miss you, sire."

The king nodded then just as he was about to return to his meal, caught sight of Henri. "Well, bless me, who is this?"

"Forgive me, sire," *Monsieur* started. "This young man is

attached to me and I hoped you would grant him safe passage."

"Attached to you? How the devil is this street urchin attached to you?" The king demanded. "And when were you going to tell me about this? A stowaway is not to be abided."

"No indeed, sire. Which is why I confess a sin to you and throw myself and him on your well renowned mercy."

The king sat back and tossed his napkin on the table. Standing, he walked over to him. *Monsieur* lowered his eyes and Henri saw how he hunched his shoulders attempting to make himself smaller than he was, a good half a foot taller than the king.

Henri stared in fascination. He had never been that close to royalty and yet, something about the man who was deciding his fate made Henri shiver. He stepped closer to *Monsieur*, hiding half of himself behind him. *Monsieur's* arm came around behind, shielding him.

"Damnation, Holmes whatever you get up to in your own time is yours but don't force my hand."

"Never, sire. This young man is, in fact... my son."

The king's eyes grew wide and he took two steps back. "What the devil?" He demanded

"*Oui,* sire I was as surprised as you when I found out."

"And just when did you find out?" The king questioned.

"Last night when there was an attempt on your life. Henri," *Monsieur* motioned to him. "Fought your five attackers nearly being killed but when I assisted, he told me his name and age and the woman in *Le Chabanais* who mothered him. The dates, times, and names added up. That and he looks much like me when I was his age. He carried a note from his mother, dead these many years ago, naming me as his father."

"If she was a whore then how would she know the father?"

"Please do not ask me for details in front of him, sire."

The king waved him off. "Does he speak?"

"He does, but only French I am afraid."

Though Henri wanted to tell him that wasn't true, and he understood English fairly well, he stayed silent.

"How old is he?"

"Eleven."

"Eleven?" The king questioned. "Damn it, man how is that possible? You would have been a lad yourself!"

"Seventeen, sire but you must remember I am French. They start us young over there."

The king shook his head. "I suppose I have seen that. And of course, you would not be as well adept of preventing conception at such a tender age." *Monsieur* said nothing as the king thought it over. "He foiled the plot to kill me?"

"He did. Without his assistance, they would have gained access to the back door."

"And where were you?"

"I regret to say I was derelict in my duty as I was distracted by Marie, one of *Madame La Rue's* best girls. Though my eyes only left the door for a moment."

"Hmm," the king muttered. "I see the truth is not something you wish to say. I have never seen you partake of the brothel's delights. Whatever the circumstances, he is your son and I owe him much. Very well, Holmes he stays but do not mistake my charity for forbearance. Your uncle will be hearing of this. And though I don't believe for a moment you of all people were distracted enough to lose your charge, he will be hearing from me how I do not appreciate stowaways nor a half truth."

The king sat with a flourish and took his napkin again. Stuffing the corner into his collar, he turned his attention back to the meal. *Monsieur* bowed low.

"I appreciate your majesty's understanding."

Monsieur turned to leave, pulling Henri with him.

"*Non*, sire please," Henri began, and *Monsieur* stiffened. "*Monsieur* is not at fault. He was not derelict. He was there. It was he who defended you, sire without him I would most assuredly be dead. I stowed away. It is my fault."

"Henri. That is enough," *Monsieur* snapped.

"Please do not place blame on him. *Monsieur* is loyal to you."

"Henri."

The tone of *Monsieur's* voice made Henri jump. Turning, Henri saw the look in his eyes. Hard. Upset. With him. Looking back at the king, Henri lowered his gaze when he saw the quizzical look in his eyes. But it was clear, Henri had overstepped.

"I'm sorry." He looked from one to the other. "I... Sorry."

Henri ran from the room, across the main deck, and down to the cargo hold.

Chapter Eight

Edmond had to consciously unclench his hand when Henri ran out of the room. On one hand, he appreciated Henri trying to speak up for him, but Edmond did not care one way or the other what the king thought of him. On the other hand, Edmond had told Henri to stay silent because he knew the king. One false move by a foreign boy and he could be... cruel.

"Majesty," Edmond began. The king held up his hand stopping him.

For the first time in his life, Edmond felt nearly helpless

looking at the King Edward. Henri's future was to be decided and there was little Edmond could do. Even though he just met the boy the night before, there was something familiar about him and Edmond felt an immediate kinship with him.

"Brave boy," the king finally said. "I can see a bit of you in him, Holmes. Not everyone would have the guts to speak to me like that."

"I can only apologize, sire," Edmond said.

"There is nothing to apologize for. He was right to tell me the truth of it. Still, I do not appreciate you not telling me everything."

"Forgive me, sire. I hoped to appeal to your fatherly nature. I only just got my son and when I found him on the ship in the cargo hold merely wanting to learn more about me and be near me, I was afraid of what you may want done with him." Edmond lied. He had not been afraid, for he would defend Henri, but it was better to make the king feel powerful.

"I would not harm your son. Nor you for wanting to protect him," the king said. "You could have kept him in the cargo hold for the few hours we sailed, but you brought him to me. I respect that. I respect you." He motioned to one of the other men in the room. "Prepare a cabin next to Mr. Holmes' for his son and send in my tailor." Looking back at Edmond once the man left to do the king's bidding, he continued. "It would do little good to have your son looking like an urchin when he steps off the royal ship."

"My sincere thanks, sire," Edmond bowed.

"Now, you have done your duty and done it well. I know I don't make things… easy for you, Holmes but I count you and your uncle as my good friends. Go. Get to know your son. I will not have need of you before we dock. Place one of the others on duty at my request. That way you can spend time with him."

"Again, you have my greatest thanks, majesty," Edmond bowed and just a twinge of guilt flared in his belly. When the king looked down at his food again, Edmond bowed once more and walked out of the room.

Crossing the main deck, he made his way to the cargo hold.

Henri sat on the same crate Edmond had used earlier. His head and shoulders hunched and his back rising and falling as he breathed heavily. He froze when he heard Edmond enter the room.

"Am I to be thrown overboard?" His small voice asked.

"Do you want to be?" Edmond asked.

The poor boy blanched and shook his head. "I can't swim. I don't want to die. Please?"

His small plea and sudden tears in his eyes tore at Edmond's heart.

"Then it's a good thing you won't be thrown over," Edmond said. "Instead, the king has made up a cabin for you next to mine and has called for his tailor to make you new clothes."

"New clothes?" He asked. Edmond nodded. "I've never had new clothes before."

"It is one of many new things you will have once we reach London."

Henri's eyes sparkled. "You aren't going to send me back to *Le Chabanais*?"

"No, not unless you so desire it."

"I do not," Henri replied. "I do not regret my life there but... since meeting you I have seen a new world and I want to find where I belong. I've always wanted to find my father, even though I know he's either dead or uninterested in me, I still would like to have a name. A surname."

Edmond sat beside him, his small smile lifting his lips as he took the boy's hand in his. "For as long as you want, you will have a name. The name Holmes is a strong, well respected name, especially in England. And though I am not your father, Henri, I can and will help you in any way you need."

Henri looked up at him and smiled widely. "I hoped... when I thought of the man who fathered me, I hoped he would be someone strong, trustworthy. I even thought perhaps he was some king of a far-off country, but what I found in you is better."

"You are a very sweet boy," Edmond patted his hand. "And I will attempt not to fail you until we find your real father. But now, come with me. Do you have any belongings?" Edmond stood from the crate.

Henri jumped down and hurried to the side of the hold. Finding a sack, he walked back over. "Small things I have... procured over the last few years."

"Henri," Edmond looked down at him. "Are they yours?"

"They are now," Henri replied, a light pink tinge coloring his cheeks. Edmond breathed a chuckle.

"Well, no more pickpocketing, are we clear?" Edmond questioned.

"*Oui, Monsieur.*"

"Good," Edmond answered. "Now, come with me. The king has given you a cabin next to mine. We shouldn't need it since we're set to dock in a few hours, but if you are tired, you can rest. I will need to eat and lie down for a little while. I have not slept."

Henri nodded and followed Edmond out of the cargo hold. Edmond ignored the looks from the crewmembers. Luckily, the men under his charge kept their inquiries to themselves. Yancy and Jakob stood outside the dining room door and only nodded once as he past. Reaching his cabin, he let himself in to find Terrey and another man standing before the full-length mirror.

"Sir," Terrey turned and bowed but the confused look in his eyes as he looked at Henri trailing behind him, confirmed the king's tailor had told Terrey the news. "The king's tailor is here. He needs to measure Master Holmes for a new suit."

Fortunately, Terrey was a consummate actor, and his voice did not betray his surprise.

"Excellent, thank you, Terrey," Edmond replied with a look that promised explanation as soon as they were alone. "Henri, this man is going to make a suit for you. Step up on the pedestal before the mirror so he can take your measurements."

Henri looked between the three men then back to Edmond. "Will it hurt?" he asked in French. Though Terrey knew the language, Edmond answered him.

"No, not at all. He will merely use the tape measure in his hand to take in the length of your arms and legs so when he sews your outfit it will fit you. I get it done all the time." A stretch of the truth since he had not had a new article of clothing tailored for him in over three years. Not since his sister's wedding.

Henri nodded and stepped forward. The tailor positioned him on the pedestal as Edmond turned back to Terrey.

"Could you be sure to bring some food for Henri and see to it I am not disturbed for at least two hours? I have not slept."

"Of course, sir," Terrey answered. "Let me help prepare you for bed."

Edmond always found being dressed or undressed by a valet unnecessary and would usually wave Terrey off saying he did not need his assistance, but whenever there were others with them, such as the tailor, both valet and master fell into their perceived roles. Edmond stood still as Terrey unbuttoned the collar of the shirt and pulled off the jacket. The tailor had finished measuring Henri and turned back to bow to Edmond.

"I shall have something done in a couple hours," he said.

"I appreciate your time and skill, master tailor. And the king's generosity," Edmond stated. The tailor bowed once more before leaving the room.

"What on earth is going on?" it didn't take Terrey long to inquire. Though he was his valet, Edmond classified Terrey as a close personal friend and did not require he tack on *sir* to every conversation. Being nearly the same age, they shared many confidences over a glass of cognac together.

"Henri, Terrey, Terrey, Henri," Edmond made the introductions. Henri stared nearly doe eyed at the two men. Something in the look in his eyes made Henri seem like an animal caught in a hunter's snare. "Henri was outside *Le Chabanais* and helped foil the plot to kill the king." Edmond continued to tell the story of what happened over the last eight hours. Between yawns, Edmond answered Terrey's questions and finally when he was satisfied, Terrey agreed to keep up the façade of Henri being Edmond's son and help in any way he could.

Edmond asked him to show Henri the cabin next to him and see he was fed.

"I need to sleep," Edmond said pulling off his shoes and waistcoat. "Wake me an hour before we dock, Terrey."

"Yes, sir," Terrey agreed. "Come along, Henri."

Henri looked over at Edmond, concerned. "Terrey will take care of you. I trust him with my life."

Finally, the boy nodded and walked to the door where Terrey waited.

"Thank you, *Monsieur*," Henri said to Edmond. "I am grateful for everything."

Edmond smiled at him. "Be sure to eat, Henri and get some rest if you need it. Terrey will make sure you are comfortable."

Henri sent an appreciative smile before he walked out into the hall and followed Terrey to the next cabin. Edmond watched the main door close after the boy and took a deep breath. Pulling off his shirt and trousers, he grabbed the *changshan* Terrey had left out for him. Pulling the traditional Chinese tunic over his head, he felt the familiar smooth material against his bare chest and with it, all the memories of China. The good and the bad. The sweet and the painful.

Edmond pulled out the oils he always carried with him. Opening one of the bottles, he inhaled the soft scent of eucalyptus. Two drops into the small cup on the lamp beside him and the smell permeated around the room. Closing the drape over the porthole, Edmond turned in the muted light of the single lamp and lied down on the soft mattress. The scent and feel of his tunic along with the rocking of the ship lulled him to sleep. He prayed the memories and dreams would stave off for just one night.

"Edmond, my boy, I must speak with you," Mycroft had said gently. Edmond immediately quelled the nerves that built in his stomach at his uncle's tone.

"Of course, Uncle, what is it?" Motioning for him to sit before the fire, Mycroft handed him a letter. "Ambassador Gemming has died."

Edmond looked up at him, the jade ring on his right ring finger suddenly very heavy.

"He wrote to you before he passed. His son-in-law sent it on to us. He writes his father-in-law was adamant he send it on and thanks you for your short friendship. He also invites us to pay our respects to him. He is interred with his ancestors in China. Think on it, lad. I will give you time to read his letter in peace."

"My thanks, Uncle," once Mycroft left, Edmond slowly broke the wax and opened the letter. It was written half in Chinese and half in English.

Like a mouse caught in a trap, Edmond was ensnared in the recurring dream of reading and rereading the letter from the ambassador. But as predicted, the letter changed to one he never wanted to read again. One bringing pain he hoped never to feel again. But since his short trip to China with his uncle two years before, the dreams merged into one and Edmond couldn't wake from it until it ran its course. Even then, he would wake up sweating, heart pounding, and body aching.

Sure enough, after his third time reading the dreaded letter in his dream, Edmond was forced awake. Looking into the grey eyes in Terrey's concerned face, Edmond took a deep breath to quell the memories.

"Again?" Terrey questioned apprehensively. "Edmond, when are you going to consult someone?"

Edmond shook his head. "I know what my dream means. And can it be truly classified as a dream if it is simply a memory replaying?"

"I have heard of a man, a psychoanalyst in Vienna. His work on dream interpretation is radical and avantgarde. Perhaps you can consult him?" Terrey offered.

"I would rather be whipped again," Edmond answered.

"But why?" Terrey demanded. "Why do you torture yourself?"

Edmond had no answer to give. "Where are we?"

Terrey huffed an annoyed sigh at his blatant change of subject, but let it rest. "You slept for three hours and a quarter." Terrey held up a hand when Edmond was about to protest at the length of time. "You needed your rest, Edmond. Do not think I don't know just how long you were awake. Henri ate breakfast and the tailor came in once more to check his arm length. I checked in with Yancy and Jakob. The king has retired to his study for a time, going through some paperwork with his secretary, Mr. Brown. Yancy and Jakob remain outside. The captain has informed me, we are on track to dock before teatime."

"Excellent," Edmond answered. "Help me dress? I find I am too tired still to look presentable."

"You could rest longer."

"No," Edmond replied. The thought of being trapped in his dream again was unappealing.

"Very well," Terrey said and went to the wardrobe pulling out a fresh shirt and jacket then turning back to Edmond to assist him.

Once shaved and dressed, Edmond left Terrey to make the final preparations and pack Edmond's remaining clothes. Knocking on the neighboring cabin door, Edmond walked in to see Henri being inspected in a new coat by the tailor. His medium sized frame looked wider in a tailored coat rather than the near rags he had been wearing. His face was washed and from the lingering smell of pine, Terrey had drawn a bath for him using some of Edmond's soap. Henri's hair, a light brown once clean, glittered in the candlelight but a shadow fell across his face.

"Master Tailor, you are a wonder," Edmond praised. "How do you feel, Henri?"

"Like a toff," Henri grumbled. "I would pickpocket men who looked like this."

Glad to see the tailor had no understanding for the French Henri spoke, Edmond raised an eyebrow at him and pursed his lips together to prevent the upturn of a smile.

"Does it pass muster, Mr. Holmes?" the tailor asked.

"It does indeed," Edmond complimented.

"I was unable to find proper footwear, but the king has sent word ahead of us via the telegraph to have a pair of patent leather shoes in his size rushed aboard before we disembark."

"His majesty is too kind. The very soul of generosity," Edmond lauded.

"Well, my job is finished here. I must go and see how the removal of a stain in his majesty's evening coat is coming," the tailor said. He nodded to Edmond as he walked by but said nothing more.

Henri looked at himself in the mirror, his brows furrowed. Edmond walked up behind him.

"What is it?" he asked.

"Is this what pretending to be your son is going to be like?" Henri questioned.

"Is something wrong?"

"I just... I don't feel like... me."

Edmond again had to quell his smile. There were too many times he felt the same way.

"Truthfully, Henri, this is a little much, but I will say there is no need to feel awkward in such an outfit. I learned that only a few years ago. My brother would try to dress me in his second-best dinner jacket. He would try to force me into uncomfortable collars and neckties but when I understood that society holds certain echelons to a standard, I realized my brother was trying to help me. It did not stop me from grumbling every time, but I understood why. For the time being, you are going to be viewed as a certain position in society and we must reflect that image in dress and carriage."

"I am nothing better than a bastard son of a whore. What position could I attain?"

Edmond stared at him. Never had he heard Henri speak so dispassionately about the ladies at *Le Chabanais*.

"What has you so upset, Henri?" Edmond asked cautiously. The boy huffed a sigh and looked away from the mirror. "I thought you cared for all of your ladies."

"I do," Henri replied heatedly.

"Then, what is it?"

Henri's shoulders deflated and he buried his head in his hands. Edmond placed his hands on the young boy's shoulders and waited.

"I am nothing. I am no one. Why would you want to help me? I don't deserve it. You claim the name of Holmes is respected and idolized wherever you go, so why would you want some undeserving street rat to have any claim on the name even for a short time?"

Edmond turned him around to face him and bent to be eye level with him. "You are not some undeserving street rat, Henri. Do you hear me? I will not hear you call yourself that again. You have made the best of a sticky situation and you flourished. You singlehandedly tried to protect your ladies and the king. You even tried to protect me when you called out and refused to leave when I told you to. I will not have you thinking you are anything less than an extraordinary young man. One I am pleased to know and am looking forward to getting to know better." Henri looked up at him, a soft yet sad look in his eyes. "You are brave, strong, and considerate. I never had children and I doubt I ever will, but if I had a son, Henri, I would wish him to be just like you."

Henri stared at him as a soft smile lifted the corner of his mouth. "Thank you."

Edmond drew him into an embrace and kissed the top of his head. "Now, enough of that. You may look like a toff but inside you are still you. That brave young man I watched challenge five men twice his size to protect all those he cared for and one he claimed he didn't care about at all. But you knew if the king was injured, it would mean pain for your ladies. That is the measure of man you are and the one I am proud to call my son, for however long you may wish to be. So, Henri Holmes, are you ready to wear these rather fine clothes just until we disembark?"

Henri grinned and nodded.

"Good," Edmond replied. "When we disembark, the king may or may not ask me to accompany him to Buckingham. If we meet anyone along the way, I will introduce you. Once I am dismissed from the king's service, we will need to go to my family. They must find out before the newspapers. To them, you will be as we truly are, but to the rest of the world, you are my long-lost son. Understand?"

Again, Henri nodded and looked out the small porthole in his room. "How much further is it until we dock?"

"Perhaps another couple hours or so," Edmond answered. "Have you ever journeyed to London?"

"No," he shook his head. "I have only ever been around Paris. I was born there."

"Were you born at *Le Chabanais?*" Edmond questioned.

"At a hospital, but I was placed in a home as an infant. I never knew my mother. I was simply told she was a… a whore and I should be grateful she placed me with the nuns. I never felt grateful when they would smack me over the hands with their rulers."

"How did you wind up at the brothel?"

"I ran away from the home when I was six. Me and a couple other boys. We made a living pickpocketing and became each other's family. That is until I pickpocketed *Madame La Rue.* She caught me and instead of turning me over to the *gendarmerie*, she offered me a place to stay."

"How old were you?"

"I'm not entirely certain but I lived through two Christmases while on the streets. I stayed with my ladies after that."

"But I still don't understand why you were sleeping outside if they took such good care of you."

"They did, but only when there was no important guest staying. The king, a marquess, a duke, an emperor. I was used to sleeping on the streets, so it meant little to me. The *madame* usually had a cot for me in the small dressing room off her rooms and she taught me how to read and write. I asked her once if I could be her son or if she knew my mother. She merely smiled at me and turned my attention to the volume of Rousseau I was reading so I never knew my mother's name. I suppose I hoped it was her."

"Rousseau is ambitious for one so young," Edmond answered.

"It contained stories about our glorious revolution and how we can never let royalty enslave us again."

"Do not talk such radical ideas in front of the king," Edmond winked.

Henri laughed but eventually sobered. "Can you tell me what London is like?"

"Of course, but let's go up on deck and get some fresh air," Edmond offered. "We may be able to catch a glimpse of Dover's cliffs."

Henri readily agreed and followed Edmond out of his cabin and up to the main deck. The spray of the channel caressing their faces as they stood by the railing and the fresh salty air with blue skies lifted Edmond's spirits considerably.

Chapter

Nine

Henri had never been on a ship. He had never left Paris in all his eleven years, but as he stood by the railing, he took a deep breath of the clean air and it made him feel light. He was on his way to a new world, a new life. Adventure, something he always hungered for, but was too afraid to do alone. As he stood beside *Monsieur*, he closed his eyes to feel the sun shining, the spray of the sea, and the calm *Monsieur* exuded.

"Did you sleep well?" Henri asked unsure of what topic to mention.

"Not as well as I will when I find my own bed," *Monsieur* admitted.

"Where do you stay in London?" He asked opening his eyes and looking out across the sea.

"With my uncle. Do not fear, there is room there for you as well."

Henri let a small smile lift the corner of his lips. "I do not fear much, *Monsieur*," he admitted. "And I do not mind sharing a room if needed. My cot at *Le Chabanais* was in a small room shared with two others who worked at the brothel. Sometimes one or both of them were not there."

"You shall have your own room, Henri," *Monsieur* stated. "There's no more need to share."

"I have never had my own room."

Monsieur turned to look at him. "Many things will change for the better, Henri. I promise you."

And Henri believed him.

Edmond never thought he would be so grateful to see the London docks. As soon as the king's ship lowered its anchor, Edmond went in search of Terrey. The rogue was found in Edmond's cabin, but it was the suspicious bruise on his neck that made Edmond's brow quirk.

"And just how many times does this make?" Edmond questioned.

Terrey had the nous to look sheepish as he gathered Edmond's case. "I cannot help it if the king employs such beauty."

"Let us hope Miss Sarah has no male family members. You may be in trouble," Edmond teased.

Terrey grinned. "She is an orphan, poor dear, but is also well aware of my wicked ways."

"I am certain she is."

With a chuckle, Terrey walked over to the main door where Edmond stood. "All look well, sir?"

"Indeed, you packed the sleeping oils?"

"I did, as per your instructions. I must say I did enjoy the scent. What is that compound?"

"Simply eucalyptus," Edmond revealed.

"I may purchase some from you for my mother, sir. She's having a difficult time falling asleep since my father died," Terrey said.

"No purchase, I would be glad to give you some," Edmond offered.

"My thanks." Terrey smiled and Edmond stepped aside for him to move out of the room. "Are you happy to be back?"

"In more ways than one," Edmond replied. "This is the last time I allow my uncle to dupe me into a favor."

"It did seem worse this time than ever before," Terrey agreed.

They met Yancy and Jakob outside of the king's study. Both men said nothing, not unusual for them. They were mostly seen and not heard, as Edmond gave orders for them to disembark and check the perimeter. Edmond knocked on the door and heard the king's permission to enter.

Standing before him, Edmond took in the complete transformation of the man from the night before to that morning.

All drunkenness gone and nudity covered, King Albert Edward, soon to be Edward VII, stood resplendent in his red coat, white breeches, jewels, and metals pinned to his chest.

"We have docked, sire," Edmond explained. "All seems to be well. We can leave at your discretion."

"Very well," he resigned, all thought of the carefree prince vanished in the face of the careful king who stood before him. Straightening his collar once more, King Edward walked to the door allowing his secretary to collect the papers still on his desk.

Edmond walked just a step behind the king as was custom for his station, but close enough to protect him if needed. There was something on the king's mind. Edmond had seen the transformation from playboy prince to leader of the greatest empire on earth before but this time... something else had happened.

"Sire," Edmond proceeded cautiously. "If I can be of any assistance, I do hope you will call on me. You most graciously allowed my son passage, if I can repay by offering an ear to listen, you know whatever is said is in the strictest confidence."

The king huffed a longsuffering sigh. "Sometimes I curse the Holmes name. You randy lads always seem to know when something is bothering me."

"It is a curse I accept, sire," Edmond tried to make light of his words but stopped for a moment, just shy of the main door to the deck. Turning to Edmond, the seriousness in the king's eyes seemed misplaced. Edmond waited.

"Did your father prepare you for fatherhood?" he asked.

Edmond schooled his features to prevent any emotion crossing his face. "Fatherhood?" he clarified. At the king's intent gaze, he nodded. "I would say yes, sire."

"Tell me how."

"Well, ehm…" Edmond thought a moment. "By being open and honest with me. Always showing he cared. He took an interest in me and furthered my dreams. All things I believe a father does for his son. When I needed his advice, he was there. When I needed a listening ear, he provided one. I can only hope to emulate him. Why do you ask this, sire, if I may be so bold?"

"My mother never prepared me to be king. She never involved me in decision making. Sometimes I feel a fraud."

The admittance of such a human feeling from the king made Edmond pause.

"I am wanting to name my son as my heir officially and involve him in matters of State so he is better prepared when he takes over, but I am being blocked."

"By whom, sire?"

"Everyone," he answered. "The Prime Minister does not think it is a good idea and even the queen is hesitant. I must admit I am worried about him."

Edmond said nothing for a moment as he thought about the king's predicament. The nation mourned the death of the king's first-born son Albert Victor a few years before. Prince George was still a young man and the king's second born son. He was never the one intended to have the throne.

"If I may, sire," Edmond began. "One thing I have learned from my father and my short stint as a father myself is that you must give your child every opportunity you were not afforded. Make the next generation better. Give them the ability to make a better world. That is all I want for my son."

"Even if there is a chance he may be killed? Or you may die before he is ready?"

Edmond studied the king's face. That was what was truly worrying him.

"You are king, sire," Edmond stated. "He will be too. You both know the risks as did your mother and her uncle before her. All of them back to the beginning. But there is one thing you have that none of the others had."

"And that is?"

"Me," Edmond replied with no false modesty. "Now what has truly happened? You would not be thinking like this if something did not happen."

"Merely thinking if you had not been able to foil the plot to kill me at *Le Chabanais* what could have happened. George is not ready for the throne. There is much I still need to teach him."

"Then, sire, teach him. He will not learn if you do not guide him." Edmond paused for another long moment. "There is something else. I can see it."

The king huffed. "You are all so damned perceptive. The lot of you would have been burned at the stake for being witches a couple centuries ago."

Edmond said nothing. For all the king's propensity to make Edmond's life hell, there were times where the king's affection for the Holmes family shone through. But it was also those times Edmond hated because it usually meant he was hiding something that would affect Edmond's security plan. But when the king pulled out a folded piece of paper from his inner breast pocket, and handed it to him, Edmond's hair on his neck stood on end.

Whatever that letter contained caused the king to worry. Edmond took it and first, observed the paper. Typical butcher's paper, a red wine stain in the corner, faint but there. A musty smell, and yet, Edmond took a deeper sniff, definitely some sort of fishy smell. Torn hurriedly from a larger piece, clearly just a scrap of paper. Flipping the note open, Edmond read the words and his blood ran cold.

Remember remember the 5th of November, gunpower, treason, and plot.

The code Edmond had used to warn his men of a possible assignation attempt and one only five men knew. Granted the saying was well regarded for the notorious plan by Guy Fawkes in the seventeenth century, but the coincidence was too great.

The handwriting was rough as if someone was not well versed in either English, writing, or someone pretending to be.

"Now, I don't blame the boy," the king said. "But you must understand my concern after last year."

Edmond's eyes shot up to his. "You cannot believe Henri would have anything to do with this."

"I make no judgement, but it was found on my desk and I do believe he had the run of the ship while you were resting."

"Sire, with all due respect—"

"You knew nothing of this boy. He just happened to show himself at the same brothel I am notorious for visiting. He claims to know you and produces a letter claiming you as his father? How many others had he tried it with before?"

"Sire, forgive me, but you are mistaken. Henri would not do something like this. The boy knows nothing of you nor in all probability of Guy Fawkes." Every fiber in Edmond's body was pulled tight. "And sire, might you be a little bit jaded due to the attempt on your life last year by a fifteen-year-old. Henri is not that boy. He is innocent of this charge."

"I hope you are right, Holmes, I do. For your sake, I hope his tales are true, but without corroborated evidence, how are we to know the truth?"

"There are other explanations. As my father says, one cannot theorize before one has data."

"He also says once you have eliminated the impossible whatever remains however improbably must be the truth. Do not think me ignorant of Dr. Watson's writings nor your father's cases," the king stated.

"I ask you, let me question Henri to put your mind at ease."

"I have no intention of either of us questioning him. He is a boy. And though it could cause great personal injury to me, I am not one to imprison children. He is free to go with you, and I do not want a scandal, you have been of great value to me. I owe you more than I will ever know, but hear me, Holmes, until this person is found, I will need you to watch the boy. I cannot have him come with you nor your uncle to Buckingham."

"Of course not, sire," Edmond agreed. "And may I have your permission to retain this note and discuss it with my father when I see him this evening?"

"Yes, granted," the king replied. "If it isn't your son, as either a practical joke or a menacing message, someone else placed it on my desk. Someone close to me. Someone who has access to my most inner sanctum."

"Have no fear, sire, soon you will be in the charge of the palace guards and my father and I will be working together. You have our loyalty."

"I never have doubted it, though I am grateful you have come 'round to the monarchy. For a while there, my sources told me you were nearly an anarchist with your ties to China."

"Never an anarchist, sire," Edmond defended. "Merely a freethinker. But my political opinions have no place in my work."

The king observed him for a long moment but then merely nodded and began walking down the hall again. Edmond folded the paper, placed it safely within his inner coat pocket, and followed the king up to the main deck.

Chapter Ten

Mycroft Holmes sat in his usual seat in the Diogenes Club waiting for news of the king's ship docking. In the Strangers' Room, he gazed out the window watching a young mother and her nurse pushing a perambulator. The poor dear didn't realize the nurse was having an affair with her husband. Mycroft tutted in dismay but that was the way of the world.

The door opened and the man announced his expected visitor. "Sir Charles Holmes to see you, Mr. Holmes," he announced.

Mycroft turned to see his eldest nephew, Percy to his intimates, stride confidently through the door, so like his father.

"Percy, my boy," Mycroft greeted him as the door closed and they were alone.

"Uncle," he grinned. "It is good to see you. I was pleased to receive your note."

"I am glad to have caught you at a time you were free," Mycroft gestured to the chair beside the fire and poured a glass of cognac.

"I will always make time to visit you, Uncle," he answered. "Afterall, I owe most all of my career to you."

"Nonsense, a simple word in the correct ear is not a debt," Mycroft offered the drink as Percy pulled out his cigarette case and struck the tobacco alight.

"It does not go unnoticed." Percy crossed one long leg over the other and stared at his uncle as he sat opposite him. "But these saccharine notes of wanting to dine with your nephew while your favorite is clearly across the Channel is suspect, even for your nefarious ways, Uncle."

"I do not have a favorite, you know that. And if I did, it would be your sister."

Percy chuckled. "I cannot fault you there. It is clear she steals the hearts of all she meets. If only I could carry a tenth of her abilities, ah, Uncle," he sighed. "These rumblings of war would never exist."

"There's always rumblings of war, Percy, it is nothing new."

"True," he smiled, then suppressed a yawn. "Oh, dear me. Forgive me."

"My grand-niece keeping you up at night?"

"Eleanor still does not sleep longer than predawn, and Alexandra is tired of late in her condition. It falls to me to rise early as I do not wish my wife to be stressed in this last month of her confinement."

"Indeed," Mycroft agreed.

"And of course, Phillipe is just of an age where everything is exciting," Percy spoke. "It is draining on us both."

"Still three children in four years is a blessing."

"Oh, I am not complaining, Uncle," Percy smiled. "And I would not change it for the world. Though I do believe we will hire a nurse for this last one. Alexandra is far too tired of late. It concerns me."

The image and deduction Mycroft had a few moments ago of the nurse and young mother, spurred his next words.

"Perhaps it would be best if an older nurse is hired instead of a young one."

Percy looked over the rim of his glass, a mischievous smile forming on his lips. "I will not stray if that is what concerns you, Uncle. My wife keeps me quite happy."

"I am glad to hear it," Mycroft answered. "But one hears of things."

"I will take your concerns under advisement." Percy took a long draw on his cigarette. "Now, perhaps you will explain to me the real reason for my visit?"

"I worry for Edmond," Mycroft stated.

Percy chuckled. "And yet, you claim no favorites," he winked.

"Percy," his tone was serious. Percy grinned and waved him to continue. "He is expected back today, and I worry he will fall into the same habits as before."

"And what habits have you so concerned? Waking before the dawn? Meditating? Assisting you in the Home Office? Or no, I know, playing the violin at two in the morning. Dr. Watson always talks about how irritating it was to share a flat with Father when he was in one of his moods."

"Damnation, no," Mycroft replied without heat. "Simply his reclusiveness. I am hopeful a dash of Parisian life has awaked him, and he will want to partake in London's finer offerings. Go to the theatre, the Season is coming soon, perhaps he could visit the *ton*."

Percy drew again on his cigarette, his grey eyes assessing. "What really is the reason you desire him to change so drastically? It would have nothing to do with the rumblings the king will be naming his son Prince of Wales and therefore his duties will extend to romancing the elite while on horseback in the Park?"

Mycroft stared at his nephew.

"I am not so ill informed, Uncle," Percy replied. "I have spoken to his highness myself on more than one occasion. What has you so concerned?"

"Concerned? No," Mycroft stated. "But there has been talk about the prince's suitability. He is nearly a recluse himself."

"Ah, I see, and you believe if you test your theory on one similarly inclined, then perhaps others will follow?" When Mycroft said nothing more, Percy went on. "The man lives modestly at best, for who indeed would retire to Norfolk? It is not as if any interesting people are from there. And though Sandringham House is very fine, each time I have been there the man is nowhere to be found. Obsessed as he is with his stamp collection."

"Many fine people have been born in Norfolk and perhaps even a future king or queen will be born there. You cannot disparage a place simply because you prefer the liveliness of the city, Percy."

"I can try," Percy muttered good naturedly.

"It would pain you to hear then, your grand uncle was born there."

"God forbid," Percy groaned.

"All I am saying is, I have a commission for you. Escort your brother around the *ton* for a week or so and take him to parties and balls. I need to see him... enjoying himself."

"There are always methods to your requests even if I do not understand them. You know I would do anything you ask, with all my heart for I know it is for the betterment of the Empire, but this? I cannot. Not with Alexandra in her condition, Uncle."

Mycroft wiped a hand down his face and sighed. "Damnation."

"But..." Percy started again. "I may have a solution."

"And that would be?"

"Tell him the truth. All of it."

"What on earth do you mean?"

"It is clear you received some sort of communique that has given you an overabundance of caution. Something that requires you to have a man about either the prince or the king. That man, naturally, is Ed. He is the perfect one for the position, but you worry he will not be able to show his affability and enjoyment of the tasks such as a ball or riding about the Park. You wanted me to take him about town to see how he interacts with the elite and if he is able to convince even the most knowledgeable of people when it comes to my brother. Me. But my advice is, Uncle, tell him the truth. All of it. You know he will not work well with half explanations or truths. Then explain what needs to be done. Much like our father, my brother is very capable of playacting convincingly. There is no need to further treat him as a boy. He is nearly thirty. And though we can never hope to be your equal, we are your nephews. Tell him the truth and he will do his damnedest to never let you down."

Mycroft nodded slowly but his mind traveled to every possible scenario of Percy's advice. On one hand, he knew Edmond would do well, always did. But on the other hand, how was he supposed to tell him everything when he himself didn't know everything. The scrap of paper he had received on his desk earlier that day said very little apart from the well-known rhyme of Guy Fawkes. But a threat, it was and as a threat it needed to be treated. But there had to be more. No information was written, hardly any clues were found on the paper. It was written on plain parchment, no letterhead nor watermark.

Pouring over the information, he sat smoking and drinking his cognac not hearing the page come in to tell him the ship had landed. But soon he felt someone shake his shoulder. Looking up, he locked eyes with his nephew, tired and worn thin but Edmond was there.

"My boy," Mycroft greeted him.

"Uncle, are you well? I called to you thrice without acknowledgement."

"I am, my boy, I'm sorry," he stood and embraced him. "I was merely thinking."

"Anything I can help you with?"

"In time," Mycroft stated. "Now tell me everything about your time with his majesty." Turning to the liquor cart in the corner beside the fireplace, he eyes lighted upon a young boy. Dressed in finery but a face he did not know. "Hello, who is this?" The boy turned wide innocent eyes up to him as he warmed himself by the fire.

"Uncle, this is Henri," Edmond began. "And for all intents and purposes he is my son."

Mycroft whirled around to face him. Waiting to see the joke at his expense. When no such feature crossed his face, Mycroft gaped.

"You better begin at the beginning, lad," he said sliding back into his chair.

"I can fetch you a drink, *Monsieur*," the boy offered in his native language.

Edmond shook his head and motioned him over. Sitting beside his uncle on the settee, Edmond waited until the boy, no older than eleven sat beside him.

"Well, where to begin," Edmond started. "Last night in Paris, the king's sixth night staying at *Le Cabanais*," Edmond told the tale in detail, without emotion as was his way with reporting after an assignment. But Mycroft's surprise faded as he listened and understood.

"And so it was I found him in the cargo hold and to prevent the usual punishment for stowaways, I claimed him as mine."

"And rightly so. I would have done the same," Mycroft agreed. "Do your parents know?"

"I was going to Baker Street as soon as my report to you was finished," Edmond said.

"I have need of you again, Edmond," Mycroft's voice did not betray his feelings on the inconvenience. There was no possible way they could spin the story to the papers in any manner to allow Edmond to companion the prince during the height of the season.

"I am at your command, Uncle," Edmond replied.

"*Monsieur*," the boy, Henri whispered. "You need to rest.

77

Can this not wait?"

"No, Henri," Edmond said, then turning back to Mycroft, continued. "Apologies, Uncle. Do continue."

"No no, the boy's right," Mycroft answered. "Fortunately, this is a local task and one you will not need to begin immediately."

"I am available," Edmond replied.

"I know that, lad, no need to try and prove anything to me," Mycroft said. "I know your worth and it is of the finest quality."

"My thanks for the compliment, Uncle."

"*Monsieur,*" Henri began. "I am hungry."

Edmond turned to look at him. "And I told you, we will have something to eat soon. Now, you promised me you would sit and listen. I need you to keep that, all right?"

Henri nodded with a large sigh and Mycroft had to prevent a grin. "Are you sure he's not yours in truth?" he teased.

Edmond looked back at his uncle with an exasperated expression and Mycroft lost his battle with a grin as it broke across his lips. Standing, Mycroft walked to the tray by the door. His luncheon with Percy had been cut short but the food Percy had not eaten was still under the warming lid. Though congealed gravy was not perhaps the most appetizing, Mycroft brought the plate over.

"Here, lad, enjoy," Mycroft offered.

Edmond looked at the plate before Henri began to devour the food and then back up to his uncle. "Percy was here?"

"Indeed, I asked him to luncheon with me but alas he was only able to be here a short time."

"While we have a moment," Edmond stated. "What does this new assignment consist of?"

"It is of the greatest importance, Edmond," Mycroft began. His nephew sat taller. "Similar to what you were doing for the king, but on a more personal level."

"A bodyguard?" Edmond offered.

"Just so," Mycroft said.

"And who am I to guard?"

"Ah," Mycroft shifted in his chair. "That is the part I don't honestly know yet."

"I do not understand."

"I will tell you all when the time comes but until then, I am afraid I will have to ask you to keep... certain things away from the press."

Edmond's quick glance at Henri who was enjoying his beef wellington too much to listen, told Mycroft he understood at least some of the delicacy of the situation.

"And another thing that I know you will not enjoy," Mycroft began. "But I promise is of the utmost importance."

"And that is?" Edmond's toneless question showed he was not judging before knowing all.

"Fashionable attire is absolute." The look in his nephew's eyes made Mycroft almost sorry he had mentioned it. "I would not ask if it was not—"

"Of the utmost importance, yes I know, Uncle," he answered. "It is not that I have an aversion to fashion, but you know if I am to be able to use all of my training I cannot be confined by a tight coat and tighter breeches."

"I do know that, Edmond, and I hope you will not have to be in this position for long nor do I hope you will need to use your training. But it is a threat to our nation's security."

Edmond's barely audible sigh was enough of a reply. "Very well. I will need to see a tailor."

"The very best will be waiting for you at our rooms tonight."

"Not tonight," Edmond asked. "My one desire is to see my family, introduce Henri, and then find my bed."

"He only slept for a couple hours," Henri offered.

"Henri," Edmond cautioned.

"No wonder I see exhaustion around your eyes, my boy," Mycroft said. "Get you to Baker Street. I do wonder about location. For this to be successful you will need to be perceived as an eligible bachelor."

Henri stopped eating and looked up then quickly turned to Edmond.

"But *Monsieur* you promised," he begged.

Edmond placed a gentle hand on Henri's arm. "And I will keep it, Henri. But perhaps once I start this new task, you could stay with my parents."

"I do not want to stay with your parents. I do not want to stay with anyone but you, *Monsieur.* Please do not make me." Tears gathered in the young boy's eyes and his lips wobbled.

"Listen to me, Henri," Edmond turned toward him and placed both hands on the boy's shoulders. "I am not going to forsake you. I think our friendship over the last few hours has proven that. Do you trust me?" Henri nodded emphatically and Edmond smiled. "Good, then trust me to know what is best for all of us. If I am needed to give off an impression for the sake of the country, then I will have to do so. But that does not mean I will forsake you to strangers. Besides, Mrs. Hudson's cooking is much better than our cook." He winked. Henri's face split in a grin.

Mycroft watched in awe. It was a far cry from last December when Edmond had told him what had happened in China and what caused him to be so resolute in never wanting children.

"We should take our leave," Edmond turned back to Mycroft. "I want to check in at Baker Street before three. Will you speak with the king regarding this situation? I do not want him, nor any on the ship to speak of Henri's presence since this new task requires certain delicacies."

"I will speak to him. And the crew are all under pain of imprisonment if they utter anything they hear to anyone. All will be well."

"Then we take our leave, Uncle," Edmond stood and took the nearly empty plate from Henri. The boy stood too and straightened to his full height, coming just to Edmond's shoulder. Offering his hand in a stiff handshake, Mycroft took it and shook once.

"A pleasure to meet you, Henri. I am sure you will keep my nephew on his toes more than he realizes."

"I am honored to carry the Holmes name," Henri said. "I will do it proud."

"I am sure you will."

"Farewell, Uncle," Edmond offered his hand too which Mycroft accepted. "I will see you tomorrow most likely."

"Sleep well, my boy," Mycroft said. "I will talk with you further in the morning."

Watching them both walk out of the room, Mycroft sat with a sigh. Edmond continued to surprise him. Mycroft couldn't prevent his smile as he thought of Henri. His nephew's life would change for the better and if he could help in anyway, he would. Another knock at the door roused him from his thoughts.

"Enter."

The page entered and bowed. "Sir, your visitor is here."

"Ah, thank you, send them in. Make sure we are not disturbed and bring us tea."

Again, the page bowed and stepped to the side. Mycroft stood as his guest entered. Greeting them, he motioned to the chair opposite and waited until they sat.

"I was happy to receive your note, Mr. Holmes," his guest said. "Have you thought of something I can do to prove to you my loyalty is to the king?"

"Your story," Mycroft began. "Is fantastical but knowing Moriarty like I do; I know it is well within his sphere of destruction. So yes, I do have something I think at which you would be useful."

"I am willing to do whatever it takes to take him down. As your brother aptly says, he is the Napoleon of Crime. I know him better than most. What is it you have in mind?"

Mycroft hesitated a moment, then leaned forward and began to speak.

Chapter Eleven

Edmond's fist was poised to knock when he heard his father's violin music drift down from the open window. The cool night air carried the soft notes to his ears, and he smiled. On tour with the king for nearly four months, he was glad to be home, glad to hear the familiar sounds, sounds that shaped his childhood and molded him into the man he was.

Knocking with a sharp tap, he looked down at Henri who was surprisingly demure beside him. The poor boy was overwhelmed and though Edmond had told him their visit to Uncle Mycroft was necessary, he knew the lad was tired and possibly hungry again. It had been many years since Edmond was that age and he had forgotten the constant desire for food. Feeling a little guilty for not getting him some lunch, Edmond placed a hand on Henri's shoulder. He smiled down at him.

"Just wait until you taste Mrs. Hudson's food, Henri. It is magnificent."

But the boy said nothing. Something was wrong. And Edmond knew what it was. He had promised him on the deck of the ship they would not be separated. The idea of staying with strangers away from his one friend in London was weighing on his mind. What Edmond wouldn't give to prevent going back on his word, but it was not his decision to make. He served at the pleasure of the British Government. And there was nothing he could do until he was guaranteed the king's coronation would take place and the empire his family called home, was safe.

They waited in uncomfortable silence until the door opened and Mrs. Hudson looked out.

"Oh, Master Edmond!" she cried excitedly and beamed at him.

"Mrs. Hudson, you are a sight for sore eyes," Edmond smiled back. It was good to see her. She had been his father's housekeeper for many years at 221b Baker Street and when Percy, Rebecca, their mother, and Edmond had come over to London from France at his father's urging, Mrs. Hudson took the news Sherlock Holmes was married with children in stride. And treated them like long lost grandchildren.

"Oh, come in come in," she gushed. "Your parents will be so happy to see you!"

Edmond motioned for Henri to go in first and Mrs. Hudson looked at him questioningly but no less enthusiastically.

"And who is this strapping young man?" She asked.

"Mrs. Hudson, this is Henri. We met in Paris a day ago. Happily, he's my charge," Edmond introduced. "Henri, this is Mrs. Hudson."

"*Bonjour*," he said softly.

"Oh, aren't you a charmer," she beamed.

"I was hoping you might have some food for him? I have been remiss in my attentions and I am sure he is hungry."

"Of course!" she cried. "You come with me and I'll get some food for you."

Henri looked at Edmond who smiled. "It's all right. Go on. I'll be right down to get you."

His shoulders hunched as he walked with Mrs. Hudson to the back of the flat where the kitchens were. Edmond watched them go wishing against hope he didn't have to leave him there. His uncle's task could not have come a worse time. Though his friendship with Henri was but hours old, he felt a connection to the boy as if something from his past niggled the back of his mind and he could not remember it. From the first moment he saw him, Edmond's beliefs he would never settle down and have a family nearly vanished. Henri could be his family. A son he never would have. Not that he was opposed to marriage, but with his history and his loyalty to his uncle, he could be called away on dangerous tasks in an instant. He could not leave a wife and children wondering if they would ever see him again. And yet, one look at Henri and the fatherly instinct he had suppressed in all his twenty-eight years, reared its head, and would not fade.

Shaking from his thoughts as Henri and Mrs. Hudson disappeared into the kitchen, Edmond took the stairs two at a time, following the violin music coming from the main study. He paused outside the door, which was cracked open, and peered through. The fireplace was lit, and the glow of the flames illuminated his father; Sherlock Holmes standing, playing the violin. His mother, Marguerite as beautiful as ever, sat on the settee watching. Love shone brightly from her eyes. For a moment, Edmond just watched, seeing his parents, a couple that was never supposed to be, a couple who had their ups and downs, a couple who survived no matter what life threw at them. He, his brother, and sister all owed the two people in that room so much over the years. Their father sacrificed watching them grow so they had a chance to live and have no fear of Moriarty, or any other who would use them to get to him. Their mother raised them practically on her own. They had servants, but Marguerite took her duty as a mother to heart and showered them with love, never letting anyone else step into the role. She saw her husband, the love of her life, very rarely during those years but she only ever showed her children love, strength, and happiness even if inside she was hurting.

When the king had asked him if he felt prepared to be a father, his initial response was no, but only because he never thought it would be a life for him. But if he could be even a tenth the type of parent his parents were, he knew Henri would want for nothing.

"Edmond?" his mother's surprised voice called. He looked back at her to see her standing, her eyes firmly fixed on him through the small crack of the door. His father turned and a wide smile lit his face. Opening the door entirely, he greeted at his parents.

"Mama, Dad."

"Oh, my boy," Marguerite squealed and rushed to him, throwing her arms around him, and holding tightly as only a mother could. "Are you well? You look well. A little tired perhaps but well?"

"I am perfectly well, Mama," he replied. "I apologize I didn't send word of my arrival. It was a rather sudden decision."

"You never have to send word, son," Holmes walked over and embraced him once his mother had moved to the side. "It is good to see you and have you home."

"It is good to be home, Dad," he answered with the informal address he used when they were alone.

"How was the empire?" Holmes asked as Marguerite hustled him into the room fully and into one of the armchairs by the fire.

"On edge," Edmond admitted. "There's rumblings of war."

"There's always rumblings of war," Holmes answered offering a cigarette from his cigarette case of which Edmond took one as Marguerite poured some wine into a goblet for him.

"Indeed," Edmond replied. "But this time... I am not certain. It is always a dangerous time when the monarchy changes hands."

"And with his majesty's propensities," Marguerite offered as she handed him his wine.

"Quite so," Holmes stated, lighting his and his son's tobacco. "You went to how many cities?"

"We docked first in Paris, then took the train down to Marseille. Crossing the Mediterranean to Tunis, then to Ibadan in Nigeria, then to the Gold Coast. From there we took another boat down to Capetown and docked there for a week touring along the coast. Then up through Rhodesia, Kenya, Sudan, around through Yemen and Oman. A ferry ride, docking in Mumbai for a week, then back across the Arabian Sea to the Persian Gulf into Basra. Up through Mesopotamia to Jordan to the port of Haifa. We took the boat from Haifa to Cyprus, then through the Mediterranean back to Marseille and up through Paris where we had been for about a week before landing in Dover today."

"Goodness," Marguerite sighed.

"Indeed, quite a few places," Edmond agreed. "All lovely in their own right. The king was greeted fairly and only a whisper of unrest."

"Did you have a favorite?" Marguerite asked.

"I wouldn't be able to pick, mama," he answered. "Though Capetown and Cyprus were most memorable due to the different but delicious foods. I also purchased these for you both." He pulled two packets out of his coat pocket. Handing one to his mother and the other to his father, he waited for them to open the small gifts.

"Oh, my," his mother breathed as she caressed the silken scarf he had seen at a bizarre in Yemen. "Oh, Edmond, it is beautiful."

"I'm glad you like it. I saw its bright colors and thought of you."

"Mm," Holmes sniffed the package of tobacco in his gift.

"It is a new tobacco for you, Dad, I think. I picked some up in Mumbai. It is very good."

"Smells like it," Holmes tossed his cigarette into the fire and began to roll the tobacco in the paper Edmond had purchased as well. Once lit, Holmes took a deep inhale. "Mm. this is excellent, Edmond."

"I am glad you like it. I had some of mine just the other night in Paris."

"Would you like some?" Holmes offered.

"No, no, I have my own. You enjoy," Edmond replied pulling out a cigarette case and lighting the tobacco.

"Your gifts are so thoughtful, *mon cher.* Thank you," his mother said.

"Of course," he smiled at her. "I was happy to get them for

you. I picked up a couple things for Percy, Alexandra, Rebecca, and Cedric as well. It helped me. I missed you all."

"We missed you too," she said.

"Indeed. How was Paris?" his father asked.

"Eventful," Edmond replied. "Which actually brings me to something quite delicate."

"What is it, *mon cher?*" his mother questioned affectionately.

"While I was in Paris," he began. "I met a young boy, Henri. He was a guard at *Le Chabanais,*" he shared a look with his father. Nine years ago, when he returned home and was trying to overcome his grief of losing the woman he loved, it was his father who insisted on taking him to the notorious brothel. Holmes did nothing more than sit and wait for him, but they both knew the history of the place. His father's keen grey eyes said enough, his mother knew, and Edmond was not sure how he felt about that.

"What happened to this boy?" his mother asked pulling her gaze from Holmes to Edmond.

"He was attacked by a gang of mercenaries sent to kill the king," Edmond explained. His mother's sudden intake of breath was loud in the quiet room. "He is well. I was able to assist him and he wanted to learn from me. But when I bundled the king onto the ship to leave the next morning, I found Henri in the cargo hold. He had stolen away and wanted to join me here. Of course, you know the penalty of being a stowaway on a royal ship."

"Overboard," Holmes answered.

"I could not allow that."

"Of course not, darling," Marguerite replied. "What did you do?"

"I claimed him as my son before the king," Edmond stated.

The room had gone quiet for a moment, only the snap of the fireplace and the noises in the street below echoed around the room.

"You… claimed him?" Marguerite asked.

"It was the only way to gain his majesty's favor. I claimed I had visited *Le Chabanais* as a young man, seventeen, and had unfortunately fathered a child."

"Seventeen?" Marguerite questioned. "The king thinks we would have allowed that to happen?"

"Mama, please, it is not what you think. The king understood."

"I'm sure he did," Holmes answered. "That would mean this boy is eleven?"

"About that, we aren't certain."

"And he is here?" Holmes asked.

"He is. Downstairs with Mrs. Hudson."

Marguerite blew out a sigh and leaned back on the settee. "Dear lord, what he must think of us. I mean, I know I met your father at seventeen and of course Percy had known a woman by then, but I never thought it would be discussed with the king."

"Please, Mama, I did not mean to make you think you were lowered in the king's eyes. Simply that it was the only way to save the boy's life."

"No no, of course, darling, and very admirable, but I just… well, never mind."

"Quite so, my dear," Holmes said. "It was admirably done."

"But there's another rub," Edmond admitted. When his parents said nothing more, he continued. "Uncle Mycroft has asked me to participate in another covert operation. One where I must give the appearance of being an eligible bachelor. I cannot have a son shown in society nor any hint of one. The king will be asked not to mention him, and Terrey knows the truth. But that means I will not be able to set him up with Uncle in Pall Mall."

"He can stay here," Marguerite offered.

"I had hoped that would be your answer," he smiled softly at his mother. "He is a courageous boy. He lived on the streets as a pickpocket from the age of six but the women at *Le Chabanais* took him in. He was not part of the men they use for other things, but he has never had a room of his own, nor a new suit before the king offered use of his master tailor on the ship this morning."

"I am sure he is a wonderful boy, or you would not have brought him here," Marguerite said. "But tell me, *mon amour,* why? What is it about him?"

"Honestly, Mama, I do not know," Edmond admitted. "There's something. A familiarity, a memory just out of reach. I do not know. But from the moment I first saw him shouting at the band of ruffians telling them he was to protect all within and how he showed no fear when they held him and threatened to kill him," Edmond shook his head. "There was... something."

"Then let us meet this something," Holmes stated. "He is with Mrs. Hudson?"

"He is," Edmond replied. "He had been complaining about everything earlier today, the noise, the cloudiness, the fact he was hungry even though he just ate a large breakfast on the ship, I had to admit to annoyance when we met with Uncle Mycroft. But then I remembered how it was being so young. Mrs. Hudson is feeding him."

"Let me go and make sure the upper room is presentable before you go get him, my love," Marguerite said standing. "I want to meet him."

"Of course, Mama," Edmond stood as she left the room.

Once they were alone, Holmes turned to Edmond and observed him. Edmond, used to that type of scrutiny from his father, waited.

"You care for the boy already, I see," was all Holmes said.

"I do indeed," Edmond admitted. "There's something decidedly... me about him, Dad. Had I not known for a fact the timing did not add up, I would have wondered if he was mine."

"Tell me," Holmes puffed on his cigarette before pouring them both more wine and giving Marguerite's glass a top off. "What is this new task Mycroft has asked you to do?"

"I am not certain of the details yet. I am to have breakfast with Uncle tomorrow morning. But I will say it must have something to do with another member of the royal household. Most likely the prince."

"Hmm," Holmes grunted. "And the fact the season is at its height does not help, I'll wager."

"Indeed, hence the need for a gentleman of leisure and an eligible bachelor."

"Quite so," Holmes stated. "Well, you know Henri is welcome here for as long as you need. Your mother will quite dote on the boy. She's been the most attentive of grandmothers to Percy's two and I'm sure will be to Rebecca's as well. Though it is difficult for me to think of the seventeen-year-old beauty I fell in love with so many years ago as a grandmother. Such is life, eh?"

"I am sure. Though of course, Mama is beautiful."

"The most beautiful," Holmes agreed with a wistful expression. Then, turning back to his son, continued. "You will be happy to know your sister-in-law is doing well in her confinement. I had a note from Watson just the other day to let me know she is progressing well, and you should have a new niece or nephew in but a few short weeks."

"I am glad to hear it," Edmond responded. "And how is Rebecca?"

"Glowing with motherly pride. She is due in three months."

"I am pleased. Have they withdrawn to Cedric's estate?"

"They did, two months ago."

They were silent for a short time as Edmond finished smoking his cigarette and tossed the stub into the fire.

"The king's life was threatened in Paris, I understand from your tale," Holmes began again.

"It was indeed," Edmond answered.

"Did you catch the perpetrators?"

"Some, not all."

"It is not..." Holmes left the name unsaid.

"No, at least I do not believe so."

The person he was thinking of, Professor James Moriarty, Edmond's grandfather, Marguerite's father was still at large. After the events nearly five years ago where Moriarty sold arms to both sides of the Boxer Rebellion in China and stirred up animosity for both English and Chinese from either race, and the possibility of Marguerite nearly being killed, Moriarty had not been discovered. Though Edmond was shot just after he was able to shoot the two men and his grandfather, Moriarty wore some sort of protective vest to prevent Edmond's buckshot from killing him.

Edmond could only hope the man died of his wounds or insanity long ago. But without word, his hope was thin.

"I will help you however I can, you know that," Holmes

offered.

"I thank you, dad, and I have a commission for you." Taking out the note the king found on his desk and handing it to his father, he waited while the great detective came to his conclusions.

"And the writing? Besides the obvious," Holmes questioned.

"It was a code I used with my men if there was a possibility of a plot or attempt."

"A code?" Holmes' tone showed Edmond he knew exactly what he meant but was gathering more data.

"If there was a plot any of us had heard of or a possibility, such as what happened in Paris, we would tell each other *remember remember.* It was a way for us to know what it meant quickly and to take action."

"And no one but yourselves knew of that?"

Edmond nodded. "Five of us. But of course, the nursery rhyme is well known."

"Indeed," Holmes answered. "But it is curious."

Edmond let him think for a moment. Holmes then turned back to him. "Your thoughts?"

"Besides the obvious, it bears no marks as typical butcher's paper, no indication of where it came from, the red wine stain in the corner, the faint but musty smell, and yet, had been near fish? I see it was torn hurriedly from a larger piece, clearly just a scrap of paper. And yet, sir, this was found on the king's desk in his private quarters onboard."

"You have checked your men of course?"

"Indeed, and I vouch for them all."

"So, who else would have access?" Holmes asked.

"No one. We kept the code a secret."

"Clearly someone knew. This is not just the well-known rhyme, son. It is a deliberate mockery of you and your security team."

Edmond nodded. "I had thought of that."

They heard Marguerite's step on the stair and Holmes flipped the note closed, handing it back to him. "Let us meet at breakfast to discuss this further with Mycroft and we can see what he knows."

"Agreed," Edmond stated as Marguerite entered the room.

"Ooh, such secrets, Sherlock," she teased seeing them standing close and whispering.

"The only secret here, my love is how you remain so beautiful."

Her tinkling laugh made Edmond smile.

"You are a flirt, Sherlock Holmes. But for now, let us greet Henri. The room is ready for our guest. Please, Edmond, bring him up so we may meet him properly. And then you will stay for a light refreshment?"

"I would, Mama, but I am exhausted. Perhaps I could come home tomorrow and join you then?"

"We look forward to it," she smiled, and Edmond walked out of the room, down the stairs, and to the kitchens to gather Henri.

Chapter Twelve

London was a dirty, smelly, and thoroughly disgusting place, Henri decided. The only saving grace was *Monsieur* was near and the food set before him was delicious. He attacked the plate with ravenous intent and thanked the odd-looking older woman with sounds of appreciation. The thought of staying there instead of with *Monsieur* was not as upsetting as Henri thought it might be if he would be able to eat like that. Still, *Monsieur* had promised him. On the deck of the ship, *Monsieur* said he would not leave him. And now he would.

Henri huffed.

"What's that sound for, lad?" Mrs. Hudson questioned, turning back from where she washed a plate.

"Nothing," he answered. The *madam* had made sure to teach him English, but it wasn't his favorite language.

"Now now, none of that, lad," she said then sat across from him at the table. "That huff was deliberate. Is the food not to your liking?"

"No, it is very good."

"Then what is it, pet?" she asked.

"*Monsieur* promised something and isn't going to keep it."

"That sounds very unlike Master Edmond. But perhaps he was unable to keep it?"

"*Oui,* but still, he promised."

"Now, don't you worry your little head about it, dear," she said. "He promised something but if circumstances had changed then perhaps it's for the best."

Henri pursed his lips but said nothing more as he ate and drank some tea. They sat in silence for a little while, Mrs. Hudson stood and walked back to the dishes that needed cleaning. Once the plate was empty, Henri stood and walked over to her.

"I can wash it myself, if needed," he spoke in a soft voice.

"Nonsense, love," she smiled at him. "I would be happy to do it."

"I am not used to being waited on."

She turned to look at him with a comforting smile. "Well, then, we'll have to remedy that, pet. There's no reason for you to worry anymore about what to do. You're with the Holmes' now and a greater family there never has been nor will be."

"A fine compliment, Mrs. Hudson." Henri whirled around to see *Monsieur* in the doorway.

"I speak the truth, Master Edmond."

"And how we love you for it." *Monsieur* turned to Henri. "My parents are anxious to meet you, Henri. I do believe my mother is as excited as when she was to be a grandmother for the first time." *Monsieur* grinned and motioned for Henri to follow.

Henri turned back to Mrs. Hudson and smiled softly. "Thank you for the food. You are a marvelous cook."

"Well now, I will have to keep making you food to prove it," she beamed. "Go with Master Edmond and meet Mr. and Mrs. Holmes. They will love you."

Henri wasn't so sure. He never had much love in his life before. Even the *madam* at *Le Chabanais* had taken her hand to him when he touched a figurine in her room. He fell in step behind *Monsieur* and walked up the stairs, his stomach rolling over and over with a strange sort of fear and excitement. The two people behind the door in front of him would decide his fate. Would they send him back to Paris without *Monsieur* knowing?

Introducing Henri to his parents was easier than expected. His mother put Henri right at ease immediately by greeting him in French and his father spoke to him in a soft voice he had heard him use on his sister, Rebecca. When Marguerite showed him the way up to his new room, Dr. Watson's old room, Edmond said goodnight and took his leave. The look his father gave him as he glanced back was determined. They would meet the next morning with Mycroft to go over the note left for the king.

Edmond nearly stumbled into Mycroft's set of rooms in

Pall Mall. Taking his coat off in the lobby and thanking the butler, he headed up the stairs nearly running into his uncle's maid Rachel.

"Oh, sir," she gushed in her Scottish accent. "It is so wonderful to have you home safe and sound."

"Thank you, Rachel," Edmond answered. "Or I suppose I should say Mrs. Yardley now. My best wishes for your life together."

A tinge of pink colored her cheeks as she curtsied. "Thank you ever so much, sir. We are very happy."

A few years ago, when Edmond first arrived at his uncle's, Rachel had formed an unfortunate infatuation with him. Not wishing to hurt the younger woman, he found ignoring her only worked so far and soon had to sit her down and tell her he did not want to hurt her but there was nothing he could do. She cried but they were better for it. When Edmond heard she was to marry the butler, he wished her all the joy in the world.

"I am very glad to hear it."

"Should I bring fresh linens for you? I can ask Mr. Yardley to bring hot water if you desire a bath."

"No, thank you, Rachel, I fear I simply want my bed. I am dead on my feet."

"Very good, sir," she smiled sweetly and curtsied.

Reaching his room, he found Terrey unpacking. "Sir," he turned and bowed shallowly. "How are Mr. and Mrs. Holmes?"

"Very well, thank you, Terrey."

"And Henri?"

"Safely ensconced," he explained. Terrey had waited for Edmond and Henri while he briefed his uncle in the Diogenes Club and knew of the plan to take Henri to his parents while he went straight to Pall Mall to unpack.

"Excellent, I am nearly done," he showed. "Should I get you some hot water?"

"No, I merely wish to sleep," Edmond said.

"Then let me help you," he offered, setting a shirt back down on the case and walking over to Edmond.

"I thank you. My eyes are crossing as I stand."

"Not to worry, sir, you'll be safely tucked in, in a moment," he teased.

"Oh, I should tell you, Uncle has invited a tailor to come in the morning to measure me for a new set of clothes. You will get your dearest wish, a master who actually cares about fashion."

"Words cannot express my delight," he stated drolly. Edmond chuckled. "And is this for a new mission, sir?"

"It is, you do not think I would choose that of my own free will, do you?"

Terrey grinned. "I wanted to make sure I was speaking with *Edmond* not Sir Charles Holmes."

"Oh, very funny," he teased. But his exhaustion was winning and as he swayed on his feet, he was grateful for Terrey's steadying hand. Without more words, Terrey grabbed Edmond's *changshan* and slipped it over his head.

Terrey walked back to the travelling case as Edmond finished removing his shoes and socks. Once in the state of dress he preferred for sleeping, Edmond shuffled to his bed. Terrey turned down the sheets and Edmond slid between them. Thanking Terrey for walking over and dropping two drops of his fragrant oil onto the warming lamp, Edmond rolled to his side, shut his eyes, and was asleep before he heard the door close behind Terrey.

Chapter Thirteen

Sunlight streamed through the closed curtains and a warm fire was lit in the grate as Edmond slowly woke. Disoriented by the bright light, he turned to check the time on his pocket watch. Blinking away sleep, he saw nearly ten o'clock in the morning. The door to his room opened and Terrey walked in silently with an extra linen for a bath but when he saw Edmond awake, he bowed.

"Sir, it's good to see you up. Your uncle asked me to wake you if you had not risen. Your father is in the breakfast room and the tailor should be here in forty-five minutes."

"Dear god, Terrey, did I truly sleep for fourteen hours?"

"Indeed sir, but that is to be expected. You hardly slept for months."

"I have no time to perform my routine, do I?"

"I would say not, sir, unless you can do so, shower, let me shave you, and be downstairs in twenty minutes."

Edmond shook his head. He hated days where he could not perform his ritual of Tai Chi and meditate in the back-garden Mycroft had made especially for him. But he was up, out of bed, and into the bath, head back and face primed to be shaved for the day, before he could even think. Terrey was a master at the straight razor. Though Edmond was not a fan of being taken care of by anyone, let alone having a manservant, Mycroft had insisted two years before and from the dozen applicants wanting to position, Terrey was by far the most intriguing candidate.

Educated at Eaton and Oxford, Terrey was the youngest son of an untitled nobleman. When his father died three years before, the bulk of the estate went to his eldest brother, but the debts alone nearly buried them. His second brother joined the clergy. As a rapscallion, Terrey had no desire to join the military's notoriously strict principles. Instead, he decided to try his hand at being a manservant. With no experience and little references, Edmond liked how Terrey did not hide his true personality but there was always something new and surprising about him daily. It was clear the man's reputation and ne'er-do-well persona hid an intelligent, dedicated, and sometimes overly ambitious person. Equals in nearly every way, Edmond hired him on the spot, and they became fast friends.

"Did you sleep well?" Terrey asked.

"I did, thank you. I hardly remember anything after changing."

"That's because you passed out and weren't to wake for love or money," Terrey teased.

"Passed out?"

"Mmhmm," Terrey stated. "I would know, believe me. I've passed out many a time after a night out."

Edmond held in his chuckle as Terrey's razor stroked just under his jaw. "I daresay you have."

"I was always the life of the party at Oxford."

Edmond could hear a slight twinge of nostalgia in Terrey's voice. Though Edmond could claim neither to have gone to Oxford nor indeed to any university, he understood the friendships and memories that were made.

"Do you speak much to your friends from there?"

Terrey paused for a moment then went back to shaving Edmond's right cheek. "No. Once my father's mismanagement of funds came to light and I was penniless, the *friends* I thought I had, were nowhere to be found."

"I am truly sorry. I know that happens."

"They were not my friends. They were merely a means to an end. It brought my own shallow feelings to light. Had what happened to me happened to others, I doubt I would have been so welcoming if they showed up on my doorstep."

"You would," Edmond answered. "You're a caring person."

"Not sure if you're still asleep, sir," Terrey replied a teasing edge to his voice. "But we are still talking about me, are we not?"

Edmond chuckled feeling the razor lift from his skin as Terrey cleaned it.

The conversation stale, Edmond stayed still as Terrey finished. Once his shave was complete, Edmond soaped up a scrap of linen and washed his body quickly. Drying and changing into his usual clothes, without a coat, he thanked Terrey and walked out of the room, trotted down the stairs, and opened the door to the breakfast room to see his father and uncle at the table, a cup of tea at their elbow and a small plate of food before them.

"Good morning, forgive me for sleeping in so late," he greeted them both.

"Not at all, dear boy," Mycroft said. "You needed your rest."

"You slept well, Edmond?" Holmes asked.

"I did, Dad," he smiled. "I am very refreshed. Though I find the thought of food is making my stomach growl in expectation. The last I ate was dinner two days ago."

"There's plenty there, lad," Mycroft stated. "Help yourself."

"My thanks, Uncle." He added a few items to his plate. His uncle was kind enough to always have his preferred items for breakfast and a pot of hot water for him to make his own tea. Edmond never could stand the taste of black or brown tea. He much preferred the lighter taste of his Chinese blend. After making up a plate and grabbing the pot for tea, he spoke to his father. "Was Henri an admirable houseguest, Dad?"

"He was indeed," Holmes answered. "Your mother quite dotes on him already. They went out this morning to have him fitted with more suitable clothes at my tailor."

"I am grateful she has taken him under her tutelage," Edmond sat beside his father to eat.

"The king's tailor will be here shortly, Edmond," Mycroft revealed, and Edmond had to consciously prevent himself from groaning in frustration.

"Terrey will be most pleased to hear that," he grumbled.

"Indeed," Holmes grinned. "Do be sure to stop by when

you are dressed like a toff. Percy may faint from the shock of it."

"Speaking of Percy," Mycroft began. "I asked him 'round to discuss what is expected at court."

The food on Edmond's plate was instantly unappetizing. Not that he didn't love his brother. Percy and he were closer than twins, but to be lectured in courtly appeal by his elder brother was not how Edmond wanted to pass the day."

"Could Percy not step into my shoes? He knows tradition and already has the clothing. He could easily…" Edmond's voice trailed off.

"No, lad," Mycroft sighed. "I understand your dislike and I would never force you into something that would make you uncomfortable, but I will reveal, Percy was my first choice for this. Not that I question your worth, Edmond but I knew how difficult this would be for you."

"And Percy refused?" Edmond asked.

"With Alexandra due in three weeks?" Holmes offered.

"Ah," Edmond replied. "I had forgotten that." He paused and forced himself to eat a little more. Then, looking back up at both his father and uncle, he nodded. "I suppose, this is for the best then."

"I know how difficult this will be for you, Edmond," Mycroft began. "But it is absolutely essential for the safety of the realm."

"Then I will do my utmost, Uncle. Before we get into the details, I wanted to speak with you. I went to Baker Street last night with Henri and asked Dad to take a look at something. We both agreed it was far too important not to bring it to you." Edmond pulled the scrap of paper out of his pocket and handed it over to him.

Mycroft took it and after a moment of observing the paper, flipped it open and froze.

"Is something wrong, Uncle?"

"Where did you get this?" Mycroft questioned.

"It was left on the king's desk on his ship," Edmond explained.

"You've seen it before," Holmes provided.

"Not this exactly," Mycroft corrected. "But..." he paused and pulled out another piece of paper from his inner breast pocket. "*This* was left for me yesterday."

Passing it to Holmes, Sherlock leaned toward his son so Edmond could see it too and unfolded the paper. Almost immediately, Holmes and Edmond snapped their gazes back to Mycroft.

"Interesting," Holmes said. "You questioned your secretary?"

"I did. He saw no one," Mycroft revealed.

"Nothing to show the paper manufacturer. No distinguishing marks," Holmes stated.

"Indeed, so you see my urgency to have you take up the position," Mycroft replied turning to Edmond.

"And the details of this position?" Edmond questioned finishing his tea.

"The new task is to befriend the soon to be prince and use your newfound position to keep an eye on him. We have had threats to his highness' safety ever since Albert Victor died."

"Will the prince know of my true motives?"

"He will indeed but the household will not," Mycroft

explained.

"And being the height of the season, Edmond will be expected to attend balls and soirees with the prince," Holmes provided.

"Exactly so," Mycroft agreed.

No use in wallowing, but Edmond was not enthusiastic. There was nothing he hated more than balls and soirees. Mindlessly talking about mindless things to mindless people. Not his idea of a good time. But the task was for the future of England and her monarchy. He had seen how many times the life of the king was threatened in the last four months.

"And this new personality," Edmond began. "Am I to have a new title, name?"

"It would be difficult," Mycroft answered. "Since Sherlock is in the public eye and ever since you all came over from France, *The Strand* and other papers have run with photographs of you. No, you are to keep your persona, but the king has been consulted and for all your hard work throughout the years, he has offered you a knighthood."

"Oh, dear lord," Holmes sighed softly.

"*Oui,* my sentiments precisely," Edmond answered. "Uncle, I cannot express my appreciation and thanks more to you for all you have done for Percy and me, but I do not desire a knighthood."

"Desire is not in question, Edmond," Mycroft stated.

"Then let it be a fake one," Edmond offered. "I do not want to go through the rest of my life as Sir Edmond Holmes. I am honored to carry such a weighted name, Father," he went with a more formal title for Sherlock than *dad* in order to express the seriousness of the situation. "But I cannot. I will not."

"Indeed, which is why I thanked his majesty on your behalf and politely refused. You will be known as Sir Edmond Holmes for the duration of this task but in pretense only."

"Oh, *mon dieu, merci,* Uncle." The door opened and Terrey walked in and bowed. "Terrey?"

"Forgive me, sir, but the royal tailor is here," he announced, a glimmer in his eye that Edmond knew he would never live down.

"Thank you, Terrey," Mycroft announce. "Mr. Edmond will meet him in the parlor. Please be sure to meet with him and bring Edmond's box of cufflinks. We may need to purchase flashier jewelry."

Edmond looked over at his father, gaining strength from the look in Holmes' eye. He knew how much Edmond hated the fuss... just as much as he did. Leaning over to his son, Holmes whispered in his ear.

"Your mother would say something about how likeminded we are, Edmond," he stated. "I know how much you hate the prospect of having to be dressed in the latest fashions, but just know it is for a determined amount of time and will be over after the season."

"I do not despise fashion, Dad," he answered. "You know how difficult it is to perform my routines and mode of protection when I am wrangled into tight shirts and breeches. Percy has yet to forgive me for the time I ripped one of his shirts down the back simply by removing that perpetrator at the Christmas party three years ago."

"I know, son," Holmes replied. "I know. If I could change it for you, I would."

"I know you would. And my apologies for being dispirited. I will do as required."

"You have no need to apologize, Edmond," Holmes said. "And I know you will do whatever is asked of you. You honor this family."

Edmond thanked his father, sighed, and stood. "If you would forgive me, I will get this started quickly."

Walking out of the breakfast room, his head beginning to pound with the start of a headache, he crossed the hall and entered the parlor.

"Master Tailor," he bowed slightly in greeting. "A pleasure to see you again."

"And you, Mr. Holmes. Let us get started. Your man went to fetch some of your cufflinks. I do believe we shall begin by taking measurement of your torso and then see what sort of links you currently have."

"I feel I should warn you, sir, my selection is minimal and understated. My uncle believes we will need to pick out new ones, but I do not have the eye nor taste for such. Will you instruct me?"

"It will be an honor, Mr. Holmes. But may I ask why you have decided to pursue this if your heart is not in fashion?"

Edmond decided to try out his new persona and see if the tailor was convinced. Considering the man travelled with them, he doubted it. He pulled himself up to his full height and looked down his nose at the man.

"My brother, as I am sure you are aware is Sir Charles Holmes. Due to his wife's current condition, it has fallen to me to step into his shoes as it were and romance certain ladies at court," the tone of his voice changed as he channeled Terrey's haughty timbre.

"Of course," the tailor replied. "I must say, I am delighted to start. Your figure is one I have not sewn for before and am looking forward to seeing how my articles look on a man of your stature. Please, remove the waistcoat but you may keep your shirt on as we begin."

Though Edmond disliked what was happening, he admitted to himself the tailor was an expert and remained quiet. A trait he appreciated.

Terrey knocked and entered carrying the ornate oriental box which housed Edmond's cufflinks and rings. Sherlock had given both of his sons a signet ring to be worn on the fifth finger of their right hand with the engraved *H* on their fifteenth birthday, and the large jade ring from Ambassador Gemming was in a secret compartment. Terrey set the box down and waited. Once the tailor was finished measuring Edmond's arm, he turned to the box and Terrey opened it.

The tailor hemmed and hawed as he looked through the modest looking gold and silver studs. "Well, this will not do. This will not do at all."

"Indeed not, Master Tailor which is why I took the liberty of bringing a few of my own." His brother's voice from behind him made Edmond sigh then grin. Turning to see Percy, dressed in his latest suit looking as though he were lord of the manor, standing in the doorway, a wry grin on his face.

"Percy," Edmond breathed. He had missed him.

"Brother," Percy teased. "I could not let the opportunity go by without coming 'round to see you. Words cannot express my appreciation to you for taking on this... ordeal for me."

"It is my pleasure," Edmond matched his tone and saw Terrey snicker out of the corner of his eye.

Percy entered the room fully and offered his collection of cufflinks to the tailor, who immediately and excitedly picked out three gaudy pieces. Percy stood near enough to Edmond to feel each other's heat but not near enough to speak without others hearing and it certainly would not be appropriate to embrace his brother in front of the king's royal tailor. It would not be proper, not very English.

Nearly three quarters of an hour later, once the master tailor was finished and swept out of the room, Edmond fell into one of the wingback chairs and covered his eyes with his hand.

"Dear lord, Ed, never did I ever think I would have the pleasure of seeing you dressed in the latest fashions," Percy teased. Edmond grunted then pushed himself out of his chair.

"Not by choice, I guarantee you." He embraced his brother.

"What sort of mission are you doing now that forces you into uncomfortable neck ties and dreaded tailcoats? Uncle only told me to thank you for taking over for me."

"As if you don't know," Edmond replied seeing the telling grin on his brother's face.

"Only that you will be protecting the prince or king again."

"Indeed. During the height of the season."

Percy slapped Edmond's arm. "It is a difficult thing for you, I see."

"Especially as I am to be knighted."

"Well," Percy cheered. "We must have a ball in your honor, Sir Edmond."

"I pray you, do not."

"It would be the fashionable thing to do. My younger brother appearing among the gentry," Percy grinned.

"Your uncle thought you could assist your brother with the ins and outs of polite society since you are so keen not tease him," their father's voice came from the doorway. Both brothers turned and greeted their father and uncle who stood behind Sherlock.

"Awe, but I enjoy teasing him," Percy agreed. "What sort of brother would I be if I didn't tease him when I could?"

Edmond chuckled. "If only everyone in this room was teasing."

"Not to worry, brother mine, you will be in the very best form when I'm done with you." Percy turned to Terrey. "Will you assist me, Terrey?"

"I am at your disposal, Sir Charles," Terrey bowed.

"Excellent, could you have cook bring up some tea? We must first break him of the habit of wincing every time he drinks the king's tea."

Edmond groaned internally and Terrey glance his way, an apologetic look on his face.

"Once we have that down, we will continue with the etiquette of paying calls, the promenade, the different ways to act when there is either a country ball versus a fashionable dinner. How to wear your gloves and when to remove them. Then of course there's the hunting, the shooting, and the general gaiety of an evening. Thank the good lord for Terrey's knowledge of which waistcoat is to be worn at the opera, a ball, or a stroll along the Park."

Edmond fell back into a chair, his head aching.

"Percy," Holmes called. "A word."

Edmond covered his eyes with his hand willing the pounding to go away. He felt rather than heard everyone leave the room but when Terrey's comforting hand rested on his shoulder, he opened his eyes. Terrey crouched down in front of him.

"If I could do this for you, sir, I would," he said.

"I know, thank you Terrey. You are a very dear friend."

The corner of his mouth ticked up. "I'm grateful to hear that. Not many men would consider their valet a friend."

"It was always my intention," Edmond confided. "But... I just don't believe I can do this convincingly."

"Of course you can," Terrey urged. "Of any man walking the earth currently, it's you, Edmond."

"Your faith in me is humbling," Edmond answered. "I just feel disgusting. I'm becoming someone I'm not."

"No, sir," Terrey shook his head adamantly. "You are always who you are, what you wear, say, and do is no matter." When Edmond said nothing, he continued, shifting on to his haunches. "Wasn't it Montaigne who said *a wise man never loses anything, if he has himself?*"

Edmond blew out a breath and nodded. "You know it was," he smiled slightly. "He's my favorite author. My section of the library contains his complete works."

"I do know that," Terrey teased.

"You are nearly as bad as a brother, Terrey," Edmond chuckled. "Manipulating my favorite author's quotes to serve his purpose."

"Glad to see I have not lost my touch," Terrey grinned. "Now, here," he offered a small vial to Edmond. Recognizing it as his oil for headaches and other ailments, he gratefully took it. Placing his finger over the stopper, he twisted his wrist, topping the bottle once to let a drop of the oil drip on his finger. Pressing his forefinger to his temples, he rubbed the mint scented oil on either side of his head. The ache nearly vanished, and he took a deep breath, smiling slightly as he let it out.

"Thank you," he stated.

"Of course," Terrey answered. "Now, my advice, sir, listen

to what your brother has to say. There are times you listen to something once and have perfect recollection of what was said months later. Do the same here. You can also pretend not to listen if that helps."

"I am becoming far too transparent to you, Terrey, or you are becoming too observant."

"We'll go with me becoming observant," he winked playfully. "It's not difficult to do when one is surrounded by the family of Sherlock Holmes."

Edmond chuckled but shook his head. "Be so kind as to inform my family I am ready for their torture... I mean, education," he corrected.

"Oh, I know exactly what you meant, sir." With a laugh, Terrey stood and headed to the door. Once open, Edmond knew he was in for a long day. Holding to Terrey's words of encouragement and most importantly Montaigne's message, he turned to his brother and listened as Percy began explaining the expected behavior of gentlemen in polite society.

Chapter

Fourteen

Several hours went by and Edmond's headache was still nonexistent thanks to the oil rub he used earlier. His own concoction of peppermint and lavender, he kept a lasting supply as the English weather caused his head to throb. He almost found his brother's instruction interesting and humorous. Percy seemed to explain not only what to do but giving a hilarious and often times inane reason as to why it was done. Their father and uncle sat on the side of the room playing chess while Terrey ran back and forth getting the things Percy needed for an example.

Edmond found he was quite enjoying himself when Percy

finally said. "Now, let us discuss how to speak to women."

Edmond nearly spat out the tea he was choking down. Looking up at his brother as he wiped the tea from his lips, Edmond laughed outright.

"You're not serious."

"As serious as ever, *mon frere,*" Percy stated.

"I know how to speak to women, Percy," Edmond answered.

"Indeed?" Percy questioned. "And of the two of us, who has a wife?"

"You know I am not opposed to marriage, just no woman would want me as I currently am. My life is not one to settle."

"That is nonsense," Percy replied. "And it is mostly because you hide in the back of the room hoping not to be noticed."

"No, I hide in the back of the room to watch everything around me. To make sure all is as it should be."

"Very well then," Percy motioned him to stand and looked around. Seeing Terrey, he beckoned him over. Percy maneuvered Terrey to stand before Edmond. "Speak to Terrey as if he were a debutant. Impress me."

Edmond could not contain his laughter at the surprised and uncomfortable look on Terrey's face. "Sir? Perhaps I am not the best... to play a debutant?"

"Hush now, Terrey, you simply have to stand there. Pretend to be a woman, enamored with my brother."

Terrey's face contorted in dislike. "If it helps any, Terrey, I feel the same," Edmond said.

"It's not that I do not care about you, sir, of course but

playing a woman and enamored with a man? Not something I have ever done."

"I understand completely," Edmond began. "Percy, let's not do this."

"This is highly important, Ed. You have made little effort to speak with a woman. Sometimes I wonder, brother dear, have you ever been with a woman?"

"Percy," Holmes' voice came from the armchair where he and Mycroft sat. "That is not something you should ask you brother."

"It determines what I am working with," Percy replied. "If he is a virgin, I understand—"

"Yes, Percy, the answer is yes. I have been with a woman," Edmond huffed. "Now can we get this over with?"

"Truly?" Percy's brow furrowed. "When?"

Edmond's headache was returning. "Does it matter? It has happened more than once and with more than one woman. So, can we skip this part and maintain poor Terrey's reputation and dignity?"

"Uh," Percy replied. "Of course. I did not... Forgive me."

"Nothing to forgive, brother," Edmond answered.

Their relationship was always close. Growing up together, not even a year apart and unable to tell any outsiders who they were, Percy and Edmond were best friends. But over the past few years, since Percy and Alexandra married and they both grew busier with their prospective careers, their relationship grew strained. Edmond had also never told Percy the true reason he left China.

"Ehm," Percy cleared his throat. "So, for a ball, to ask a woman to dance... Do you remember how?"

"To dance?" Edmond prompted. "I do indeed. My brother taught me."

Percy smiled and nodded. "I did."

"And to ask a young woman to dance, I offer my hand and ask her *may I have this dance*. The rest follows."

"Perhaps then, it is time for us to take a break?"

"I will see how luncheon is progressing," Terrey offered and nearly ran out of the room.

"Poor man," Edmond laughed. "Spare him his dignity, Percy."

"It was necessary," Percy replied slapping him on the back. "I must say, Edmond, I never knew that side of you."

"I am far from a prude, brother."

"Clearly," Percy grinned. They sat together on the settee and Holmes and Mycroft joined them. "So, when does this assignment start, Uncle?"

"As soon as the tailor finishes your clothing," Mycroft answered.

"So, a week then?" Edmond offered.

"About that, yes," Mycroft agreed.

"And when am I to meet with his highness?"

"I have arranged for us to meet Prince George at Sandringham House Monday next. There he and his secretary will go over his obligations and calendar with you."

"And will I use this flat as my home address?"

"No," Mycroft answered. "We have set you up with more fashionable lodging in Piccadilly."

"Piccadilly?" Percy looked impressed.

"Your clothing will be delivered there. I have asked Mr. and Mrs. Yardley to assist you during this time. I will function perfectly well with cook and our scullery maid. Mr. Yardley has offered to find you a cook, a maid, and a footman. Terrey will continue on as your valet of course."

"Of course," Edmond answered. Then, looking from his father to his uncle and back again. "Any further ideas on the notes?"

"At the moment, we need more data," Holmes said. "We cannot theorize until then. But I will caution you further, son. Someone close enough to the king and your uncle left those. Be on your guard. And anything, and I mean anything worrisome, call upon me as soon as you can."

"If not me, then I will send Terrey."

"Good, Excellent," Holmes agreed.

"Well, then, for the time being, I would like to visit with Rebecca and Cedric and call upon Alexandra," Edmond said.

"You are always welcome, Ed," Percy replied. "In fact, if you are free after luncheon, we can head to Cavendish Square."

"I would be delighted."

Terrey entered the room with a sharp knock and bowed. "Luncheon is served in the dining room, sirs."

"Thank you, Terrey," Mycroft replied and stood. "Demme, I could eat a horse."

Edmond followed his uncle, father, and brother out of the room to the dining room. The fate of the prince rested on his shoulders and for the first time in a long time, he was nervous.

Chapter Fifteen

The carriage rumbled through the streets of London as Percy and Edmond sat together. After luncheon, they had sent for a carriage and headed to see Alexandra.

"How are my nephew and niece?" Edmond asked.

"Phillipe is a little hellion," Percy started with a proud smile.

"He takes after his father, I perceive," Edmond stated.

"He does indeed. And of course, my little Eleanor is

perfection itself."

"Clearly she takes after her mother."

Percy chuckled. "Indeed, she does."

"How has this confinement been for Alexandra?"

"She's tired but claims it is the easiest. I tell you, being a father is the greatest joy, but each time her pains begin, I worry greatly for my wife's safety."

"I understand. But Alexandra is strong, she will have no complications, of that I am sure."

"I pray you are right." After a pause, Percy continued. "Ed, I wanted to apologize for my... assessment earlier. It was wrong of me to assume. I did not mean to embarrass you nor speak of things I know nothing about. I just... I was surprised is all. We used to tell each other everything. And the thought you kept something so important from me, I should not have, but I grew jealous."

"It is not that I kept it from you deliberately, Percy," Edmond started. "It is a... very painful memory for me and I did not wish to relive it."

"And I would never wish you to relive something so distressing. But can I just ask... Did you love her?"

"I did. Very much."

"What happened to her?"

"She died," Edmond looked out the window. Percy took his brother's hand and squeezed.

"I am so sorry for it, Edmond," he said softly. "Was it in China?"

"Yes," Edmond replied.

"If you would confide in me, your trust would never be

betrayed."

"I know that," Edmond replied. "It is not that I do not want to tell you, Percy, it is more I do not want to relive it."

"I understand." Percy looked back out the window and Edmond sighed harshly.

"When I was in the Orient," he began. "I... fell in love. She was my master's daughter. Whenever I was injured, she would be there to help me heal by mixing the oils and tea I needed, always alongside her mother or father. From the first moment I saw her, when I returned after a short trip home, my love of her grew every day. I was sixteen, she was fifteen and had just returned from her mother's family finishing her training. I know she felt the same for me and one night, when I was delirious with pain and opium after breaking two ribs in training, we kissed for the first time. Though I had been giving opium laced tea, I still remember it vividly. We had to keep our feelings a secret. Her status in society called for her to marry someone of higher standing, not to mention her brother watched her every move and hated me to such an extent he was the cause of many of my injuries. He claimed to believe I was taking his rightful place by his father's side. Even among all of that we found ways to be together. Meeting in the Peony Gardens or the Willow Trees.

"She turned seventeen and was soon betrothed to a man thirty years older and thrice widowed. He was a lecherous old fool. One night, I found him forcing himself on one of the servant girls and pulled him off her, breaking his nose. I would have killed him, but my master stopped me. The man demanded I be flogged. I told him I would gladly take that as punishment but to give me just two minutes alone with him first and he would never be able to force himself on another woman again. Unfortunately, I was not allowed to carry out my threat and I was given ten strikes from a bamboo pole. Hardly a punishment. Afterward, I begged my master to break the engagement. I could not see her married to a man like that. My master agreed but told me he would have to go to the city since it was a royal decree. He had no choice but to leave his son in charge.

"The wedding was still set for the end of the month just after she turned eighteen. We had a letter from her father saying he had arrived but nothing after that and as the weeks flew by, I barely slept. I stayed up every night making sure the man and her brother were passed out drunk and unable to hurt any of the women. One night, I retired earlier than my usual time after a long day training. But as I lay awake, unable to sleep worrying about the women in my care, my worst nightmare came true. She ran into my room, her gown ripped, face an angry red with a man's handprint across her cheek, and tears streaming down her cheeks. I rushed to her and she fell into me, telling me what happened. Her betrothed had tried to force himself on her, but she escaped before he could do more than slap her. My blood boiled and I nearly went to finish what I started only a couple weeks ago, but she held me back begging me to just hold her. She was trembling, my beautiful warrior maiden was shaking like a leaf.

"We lay on my pallet together just for comfort at first but soon things took a turn. We made love, both of our first times. Afterwards, I asked her when her father returned if she would have me as her husband. She agreed, telling me she loved me. But she was still worried and, though she was not ashamed of what we had just done, she was concerned her brother would find out. I promised her..." his voice cracked, and he turned away from his brother. "I promised her I would not fall asleep." He continued when his voice was level.

His shoulders heaved with a deep breath. "I'll never forgive myself for failing her, but I was so very tired. We both woke the next morning to shouts and her brother grabbing her by the hair, yanking her out of my bed. I tried to defend her, but he had five men with him. Usually not a problem for me but I was sluggish and vulnerable in my nakedness. They easily overpowered me, and we were both dragged out on parade for all to see. He threw his sister down in the courtyard and named her a whore, a disgrace to the family. He threatened to kill us both, but the man she was to marry stopped him, saying he still would still marry her since now she knew the act, he didn't have to be gentle with her. He only wanted her dowry and a son. She refused to marry him, but one of the men held a knife to my throat and her brother threatened to kill me if she refused again. I told her to refuse, my life wasn't worth the rest of hers married to the brute. She wept but agreed to marry him. They were to be married that day, but he wanted her to see my punishment first. I was to be whipped. Forty lashes. Tied to two posts, my arms stretched but to my sides, no clothing was granted for all was to see my shame. The punishment was rendered. You have seen my scars.

"I woke lying on my stomach, an aroma of incense and the sound of soft running water beside me. I was so weak, the pain... unconscionable but I felt someone laying strips of linen on my back. Slowly looking over, my sifu, my master, was sitting beside me taking care of me, his face grim. Immediately, it all came back to me and I tried to get up, but he stopped me. Once I calmed, I asked him where she was, but he shook his head. And it was all my fault."

"What happened with the brother?"

"The master disowned him. Last I heard, he had died in war. I tried to go and rescue her, but I was found out. I was given an ultimatum by the emperor's men. Life in prison or leave. My master chose for me. As much as I cared for him, I could never cause dishonor on his house. As he escorted me down the Tranquil Mountain, I vowed never to return. Then years later, when we first joined father and uncle here, I received a letter from my master letting me know she had... died."

"How?"

Edmond didn't want to say considering Alexandra's

condition, and Percy's expression changed when he understood.

"Was the child yours?"

"No, it was her husband's son. I never had a chance to say goodbye and never will."

"What was her name?"

Edmond shook his head. "I cannot say it. Please, do not make me."

"I am so very sorry for you, Ed. But thank you for telling me."

"Thank you for not pushing me," he replied. "It is over now, and I hope you understand. I have not been a monk since she died, in fact Father took me to *Le Chabanais* when I returned home, and he saw how I was handling it."

"Does Father know about her?"

"He does," Edmond confirmed.

"And does that... hinder you from looking for a wife and settling down?"

"In a way," Edmond answered.

Percy paused for a long moment before continuing softly, "I stopped at Baker Street to see if Dad wanted to go with me, but he had already left. I met Henri. He seems like a nice boy."

"He is. I would be grateful if you welcomed him into our family."

"Already done," Percy said. "Mama introduced us, and he knows to call me Uncle Percy."

"I appreciate it, Perce, I really do," he replied.

"Of course! Now, let us go in and meet with Alexandra."

Edmond looked out the carriage window to see they had arrived at Percy's home. Smiling at the thought of seeing his niece and nephew again, he followed his brother out of the cab and up the steps of the townhouse.

After meeting with Alexandra, embracing his nephew, and holding his little niece, Edmond felt better than he had for a long time. They had tea and talked of Edmond's travels. When Alexandra grew tired, Edmond excused himself and headed back to Baker Street to check in with Henri. The boy looked well. Marguerite and Mrs. Hudson were doting on him. Henri graced him a large smile and he was glad for it.

Heading back to his uncle's rooms, he enjoyed his last few days of freedom by performing his morning routines every sunrise and joining his family for dinner every evening.

Finally, Monday morning came around, and as Edmond stared at himself in the mirror, he didn't recognize the man staring back. His hair was trimmed shorter than he'd had it in decades. His shoes were shined. His morning coat fit snuggly over his broad shoulders. His light tan waistcoat and shined gold buttons glittered in the morning sunlight. Terrey walked around him, his eye critical of any speck or thread out of place. When he slowly nodded, Edmond knew he looked the part.

"Yes, I think this will do nicely," Terrey stated.

The rooms in Piccadilly were well appointed in the fashionable area of town and Edmond's household staff consisted of five. Not unusual for a well to do bachelor but for Edmond, who had never lived on his own nor managed his own estate, it was different.

"Everything running smoothly?" Edmond asked.

"Indeed," Terrey replied. "Mr. Yardley runs the household well."

"Good," Edmond took the lavender gloves from Terrey and held them in his hand; the signet ring shined and glistening on his left fifth finger. One more glance in the mirror and Edmond took a deep breath.

"You can do this," Terrey encouraged. "We all have faith in you, sir."

"Thank you, Terrey. Just know this is an act. I do not believe we can be considered friends out in society. If I speak roughly to you, please know our friendship has not changed. I consider you my brother."

Terrey's face morphed into surprise. He held himself up a little straighter.

"And I you, Edmond," he answered. "I was lucky indeed you needed a valet. Not many gentlemen would treat their inferiors so well."

"I have never thought of you as an inferior because you are not one," Edmond admitted. "Now," Edmond's entire countenance changed. He pulled himself up to his full height, puffed out his chest, schooled his features and looked down his long thin nose at him. "Please tell the others I am ready."

Terrey bowed and left the room. Edmond pulled on the lavender gloves and put away everything that made him who he was. For the duration of this assignment, he was Sir Edmond Holmes, friend of his highness, the prince, and the most eligible bachelor in London.

"Well, I never thought I'd see the day." A female voice came from behind him and he turned. His sister Rebecca, heavily pregnant stood in the doorway.

"Becs," he breathed, and for a moment his façade fell as he

hurried to embrace his sister.

"It is wonderful to see you, Edmond," she said into his shoulder.

"Forgive me for not making it over to Hughes Manor, sister. I was unable to leave London for any length of time."

"Nonsense," she waved him off. "Cedric and I do understand but I wanted to see you before you started your newest assignment. I have missed you."

"And I you, you look well," he glanced down at her six-month swollen stomach.

"I am well," she beamed. "Cedric is the most loving and extraordinary husband. I am truly blessed."

"I am glad for it, *ma Cherie*," he said.

Cupping his face, she stared into his eyes. "You seem unhappy."

Shaking his head, he disagreed. "Prepared."

"As I am not due for another three months, I have asked Cedric to be with you. He will never interfere but there will always be a familiar face at social gatherings."

"But what about you?"

"Mama is coming to the countryside with me," she announced. "And when I visited her, I met Henri? He is a wonderful boy. Excited about a trip to the country but said he must speak with you first to make sure it is well with you. What is the relationship between you, brother?"

"As far as the king knows, he is my long-lost son," Edmond explained.

Her eyes widened then twinkled. "You would have been young indeed."

"No younger than you were when you began courting Cedric," he teased. Rebecca blushed but held his gaze. "But the truth is, I care for him like a son. And when this is over, I am hopeful to be able to adopt him. He is an orphan, the child of a prostitute, but he is intelligent and eager to have guidance."

"You have grown soft, brother," Rebecca's smile was endearing. "I am glad to have a nephew. And I am glad to have the opportunity to get to know him better. Now, let us go downstairs. Everyone is waiting to send you off."

Edmond nodded and turned to the door, offering his arm to her. They left his room and walked down the stairs to the drawing room where his family gathered. His father, mother, brother, uncle, sister-in-law, brother-in-law, Dr. Watson, and Henri all turned to look at him. Henri's face contorted as he held in his laugh and Edmond grinned, gestured to his outfit, and rolled his eyes causing Henri to laugh even more. His brother and uncle nodded in approval as they took in his clothes. Rebecca walked over to her husband and took his arm. Cedric raised his hand in greeting as he stood by the fire.

"Thank you all for coming to send me off," Edmond started. "I doubt I will have a chance to see you anytime soon. But have no fear, if there is necessity," he looked pointedly at his sister-in-law Alexandra, "I will be there. You are all my priority and I love you."

"There won't be any need, Edmond," Holmes said. "You do not need the added worry. All will be well. You have our love and good wishes."

"Thank you, Dad," Edmond replied. "Please keep me informed?"

"Of course," Holmes agreed. "Now, clear your mind and go with your uncle."

Edmond went around the room embracing his family and taking their whispered blessings to heart. When he reached Henri, he embraced the young boy but once he pulled back, Edmond cupped his face and spoke low.

"Stay with Mama and help where you can?"

Henri nodded. "I... I am sorry, *Monsieur*," he started. "I did not mean to be angry with you earlier. And *Madame* is very generous. I understand now, what it is you do."

"There's no need for an apology, Henri," Edmond replied. "Now, I may not be able to see you very often, if at all, but know I will be thinking of you and am happy to have met you. I also was hoping you might consider..." he glanced up at his sister who nodded in agreement. "I would very much like to adopt you properly, Henri. Would you consider becoming my son?"

Henri stared up at him, his brown eyes large, then he nodded enthusiastically as he threw his arms around Edmond's waist. His family applauded but as Edmond pulled back, he wiped the stray tear that had fallen down Henri's cheek.

"I'm glad you will," he smiled then stepped back. "Mama will you—?"

"Of course, *mon Coeur*," she answered walking up and placing her hands on Henri's shoulders. "I'll look after him."

"*Merci*," he looked up at his family once more and then, embraced the person he was expected to be. He was sure they saw the transformation in his posture, the empty look in his eyes, the haughty way he lifted his head. "Now, I must go," even his voice held a disinterested lilt and a much stronger English accent to hide his slight French.

Turning to leave, he reached the entryway before he heard, "*Monsieur, Monsieur*, wait!"

Looking back, Henri raced out of the drawing room. "What is it, Henri?" He hoped the boy took no offence to his exasperated tone.

When the boy pulled out a folded piece of paper and handed it to him, Edmond took it, curious as to what it could be. Unfolding the parchment, he froze, his heart in his throat as he stared at the charcoal drawing of himself.

"So you don't forget me, or who you truly are," Henri said.

"You drew this?" he breathed. Henri nodded. Swallowing against the lump in his throat, he embraced the boy again. "Thank you. And I could never forget you."

Henri pulled back and tried to smile. "Be careful?"

"I will," he promised winking to lift the mood. "Now, go on back, have fun in the country."

Henri beamed but did as he was told. Edmond stared down once more at the portrait seeing himself as Henri had. The boy was talented. Folding it once more, he pulled out his pocketbook and tucked it safely away, then turned to see his uncle by the door.

"Our carriage is ready. We ride to the station then to Sandringham," Mycroft said.

"Let us go then," Edmond replied once more embodying the London gentleman he was expected to play and leaving the house and everyone he loved within.

Chapter Sixteen

The carriage ride to King's Cross Station and then the train ride to King's Lynn and the final carriage ride to Sandringham House was as Edmond had expected. Decidedly uncomfortable in his clothing, he allowed that frustration to inspire his character. Mycroft fell asleep shortly after the train departed the station leaving Edmond alone with his thoughts. Retrieving his small case Terrey had packed for him, he dug to see if it contained anything to pass the time. Pulling out a couple books, he laughed softly when he saw his well-worn copy of Montaigne's *Essais*. Flipping through it, a bookmarked page opened easily. The author's longest essay, *Apology for Raymond Sebond*, glared back at him. Reading, he nearly chuckled at the irony of it when his eyes lightened upon Montaigne's infamous saying *que sais-je?* meaning *what do I know?* That seemed to be the summary of his near future.

Sitting back, he read and dulled his mind for a precious few hours until the porter announced next stop was King's Lynn. Mycroft roused and checked the time on his pocket watch.

"Nearly there," he mumbled.

"Yes, Uncle," Edmond replied returning to the mindset of his character. "What do I expect when we get there?"

"We will be greeted by the prince's secretary and will meet the prince in his study. I'll introduce you two and we'll have luncheon. Then, we will make plans. The prince is traveling back to London with you tomorrow afternoon. You have a ball that evening which he must attend."

"And after that, will his highness stay at Piccadilly or will I stay with him at Buckingham?"

"Neither," Mycroft answered. "You will meet him at the engagements he has."

"Uncle," Edmond replied. "How am I expected to watch his highness if I am not with him at all hours?"

"You are not," Mycroft stated. "The prince only needs security when he is in public. When he is at Buckingham, he will be in the hands of the house guards."

"Someone is close enough to the king to place the note on his desk. Someone is able to get near enough to you to plant another. How am I supposed to protect the prince from someone inside the king's employ?"

"Again, you are not," Mycroft stated. "That is not your

place. Your task is to attend events with the prince. This is not the same as last time."

"Uncle," Edmond huffed.

"Edmond," Mycroft snapped. "Enough. This is how it is."

The hair on the back of his neck stood on end and his ire rose. "I do not appreciate how the details have been kept from me."

"Details will be revealed."

Edmond said nothing as the train slowly came to a stop at the King's Lynn station. They said nothing more as they disembarked the train. Out of the corner of his eye, he saw Terrey step out of second class. Without another look, at his valet, Edmond walked with his uncle, his borrowed swordstick clicking on the cobblestones. Percy had insisted on lending him his second favorite, stating *every gentleman at leisure has one.*

Finding the carriage emblazoned with the royal crest, Mycroft and Edmond entered, Terrey riding on the back beside the footman.

"Uncle," Edmond tried again, setting his persona aside for a moment. "Forgive my outburst."

"You were in character, Edmond," Mycroft replied. "And I tested you. You passed."

"But your answer is still the same."

"It is," Mycroft stated. "You trust me, Nephew?"

"With my life."

"What about with England's?"

Edmond stared at him for a long moment. "*Oui,* Uncle. Especially with England's."

"Good, then trust me when I say all will be well."

Edmond bowed his head in indication. "I do."

Uncle and nephew sat back for the six-mile carriage ride from the station to Sandringham House. When the gates opened to reveal the Jacobethan architecture, Edmond's breath left him in a soft gasp. It was beautiful. Eager to learn more about the history of the place, he exited the carriage as soon as it came to a stop, much to Terrey's dismayed look.

"Sir, I would have been happy to open the door for you," Terrey said in a manner that made Edmond realize his mistake.

"Yes, well, I am not in the habit of being kept waiting," Edmond answered and saw the subtle glint in Terrey's eyes at his perceived slight. "Next time, act quicker."

"Sir," Terrey bowed in apology.

Mycroft got out of the carriage and walked up beside his nephew as an older, stately gentlemen stepped out of the archway and into the sunlight.

"Mr. Holmes, Sir Edmond," he bowed. "It is wonderful to meet you at last. I am Howards the butler at Sandringham Estate. His highness asked for you to be shown into the Drawing Room. He will meet you there. Rooms have been made ready for you."

"Thank you," Mycroft said. "We are grateful for his highness' hospitality."

"My man will need a room prepared," Edmond indicated Terrey.

"Indeed, Sir," Howards agreed. "I will see to him. If you follow me, I will show you into the drawing room."

Edmond and Mycroft followed him into the manor, but it wasn't until after they cleared the entry that Edmond turned to look for Terrey. He was not behind him. Somewhere in the back of his mind he remembered Terrey explaining why but he could not remember exactly. Once they were shown into the drawing room, Howards bowed and spoke again.

"His highness will join you shortly. I will see your luggage is brought up."

"Thank you," Mycroft replied.

Edmond said nothing. Once they were alone, he spoke to his uncle. "Why did Terrey not join us?"

Mycroft looked at him as if he had grown another head. "Because he is a servant. He is not allowed to walk in through the front door."

"Classists," Edmond muttered. "I could not remember. Thank you," he said louder. "Now, does his highness know yet or will you be telling him now?"

"He knows." And Mycroft's words were confirmed when the doors opened and a man who could only be the prince, entered the room.

"Mr. Holmes," he greeted Mycroft as if he were an old friend. "It is good to see you again."

"Your highness," Mycroft bowed then took the prince's hand in a warm shake. "Allow me to introduce my nephew, Edmond Holmes."

The prince turned his frighteningly intelligent light eyes to Edmond. The prince had just turned thirty-six a couple months ago but he already looked so like his father.

"Your highness," Edmond bowed.

"I am pleased to meet you, Holmes. My father speaks highly of you and your family. And your brother Sir Charles, I count as a friend."

"The pleasure is mine, highness," he said.

"Now, you must be hungry. I have asked cook to prepare some cold cut sandwiches and the ale from these parts is excellent. Join me?" the prince offered.

"Indeed, we would be delighted," Mycroft said.

"Do you play backgammon, Holmes?" the prince asked Edmond as they walked out of the drawing room and into a dining room. Though Edmond was certain it was the smaller dining room, it still had enough seating for twenty-five people.

"I cannot say I have not, sire, but I have no understanding of the game," Edmond admitted. "And would make a terrible partner."

"Ah, so chess it is, then," the prince said.

"I can heartily agree with that, sire," Edmond replied.

They sat at the table and Edmond was pleased to see it was not a six-course meal. He would be able to keep his training for another day. The sandwiches were lovely and Edmond, though not usually an ale drinker, enjoyed the crisp taste.

"Sandringham is home for me, you see, and I am not one to linger in London," the prince said in answer to Mycroft's question which Edmond had not heard. "That is why these obligations to appear even after my marriage at these soirees and balls is so tedious. My father is the social one, not I."

"But surely the enjoyment of the Season is enough to coax you away," Mycroft offered.

"The Season is exactly the time I do not like to be in London," the prince chuckled. "But I do look forward to having you with me, Holmes," he looked at Edmond.

"I look forward to it as well, sire," Edmond forced.

"I'm sure you do," the prince's eyes twinkled. "My wife and her companion will return from the village later this afternoon. Perhaps when we are finished here, we can discuss business and join them for tea."

"Indeed, sire," Edmond offered. "My man has my social engagement schedule. If he could join us as we discus."

"Of course," the prince looked to Howards who stood stoically by the door. "Is Sir Edmond's man settled?"

"He is preparing Sir Edmond's afternoon attire, sire," Howards replied.

"Have him join us in the drawing room in a few minutes and call for Travers. We will discuss my social engagements."

Howards bowed and with a "yes, sire, right away" he left the room.

Prince George raised his ale in a toast. "To new friends and beneficial partnerships. I appreciate all you have done to be here, Holmes."

"The honor is mine, sire," Edmond lifted his ale in a toast.

"Tell me about yourself," the prince began after he drank and turned back to his luncheon. "My father has spoken well of you, but I would like to learn more."

"I am an open book, sire," Edmond lied. "Ask what you will."

The prince locked eyes with him, and Edmond knew the look. He was trying to discern more about him. As a Holmes, Edmond was frightfully good at hiding who he truly was. But found it endearing the prince would try or want to know him. Fortunately, the prince was distracted by Howards entering the dining to announce both Terrey and Travers were waiting for them in the drawing room.

Chapter Seventeen

Edmond requested to freshen up in his room after discussing the prince's social engagements. He and Terrey walked up the stairs and down the hall following Howards. They said nothing as the butler showed them the way.

Finally, they reached a closed door and Howards opened the heavy oak, stepping to one side, his arm extended into the room.

"Please let me know if there is anything else you may require, Sir Edmond."

"Yes, thank you," Edmond retained the haughty expression.

"If you desire me to show you to the drawing room when her highness and Lady Berkley arrive, please ring."

"Thank you," Edmond said again and stepped into the room. Terrey closed the door behind him.

Once they were alone, Edmond deflated and sat on the bed. Being someone he wasn't, drained him. He pulled out the drawing Henri had made for him and stared at the face of the man he truly was. That little moment of reprieve was enough to help him. The wardrobe door opened as Terrey looked for the afternoon torture devices, he would wrangle him into in just a few short moments.

"Help me out of this coat would you, Terrey?" he begged.

"Of course, sir," he walked into the room and helped Edmond pull off the tight material. Edmond took a deep breath as if it was the first one he had in hours.

"Thank you. I hope you understand... about earlier after the carriage came to a stop."

Terrey gave him a sardonic look.

"Good," Edmond smiled slightly.

"What is the plan?" Terrey asked. "I heard from the servants, the prince leaves on the morrow."

"We all do," Edmond explained. "He has the ball he... *we* need to attend."

"The first of many," Terrey replied. "May I ask, sir, is there anything you need me to do? I would be happy to try and infiltrate each place you go. If I recall correctly, those grand houses always try to bring in extra help especially when the prince is coming."

That added knowledge jolted Edmond out of his thoughts. He turned to Terrey who was brushing his coat on the hanger.

"They do?" Edmond asked.

Terrey looked over. "Well, yes," he answered. "Several of my friends always complained about it when they returned to Oxford after the summer holidays. I even remember attending my dearest friend's house, Hugh Manson when he had his majesty, our current monarch when he was a prince, to dine and celebrate the Queen's birthday. Hugh begged me to join them since it was going to be decidedly dull for him. He was not one for parties. I knew everyone in that household and there were several faces I didn't recognize."

"What is the hiring like?"

"I would imagine not very strict."

"Even when the monarchs are there?"

"Security is not up to the hosts, or so they believe. It is up to the king's guard," Terrey revealed.

"Dammit all to hell," Edmond huffed. "How the blazes am I supposed to keep him safe when I don't know the particulars? There's no way to forbid it. So, yes, Terrey I will need your eyes and ears."

"They are at your disposal, sir," Terrey replied.

"I will get you a list of the balls and parties we will attend. What else would you need?"

"A letter from my current employer stating you know I am taking these temporary assignments and a summary of my duties I have performed. I can write it up for you. Also, we may want to use your brother's name or someone unrelated to you. I would not want it to become awkward for either of us if someone connects the two names."

"Indeed, I will see to it you have the paper and pen you need. I will council with my uncle and see what name we can use."

"I will begin writing it as soon as I have the implements needed."

"Thank you, Terrey. I am not certain what I would do if you were not here to help me."

"I am glad to be of service, sir," he smiled and offered the coat again. "And I am happy to help my friend."

"And your friend is ever grateful," Edmond replied standing and shrugging into the coat Terrey offered.

Turning, Edmond allowed Terrey to inspect the coat and its fit. "Tell me, what is the atmosphere like in the servant's hall?"

"Content," Terrey replied.

"Any gossip?"

"None I have heard yet," he answered. "But I've only been here a couple hours. There is a very pretty chamber maid though." His eyes sparkled.

Edmond chuckled. "Try to keep it in your pants, Ter," he said.

"I would do nothing to embarrass you," Terrey winked. It was moments like that with Terrey, Edmond missed his brother and their camaraderie. Back in France they were so very close even after years apart when he was in the Orient. He couldn't help but worry he was losing his brother now they both had relatively no time for each other.

"You look distant, sir," Terrey's voice brought him back. "Is there anything I can help you with?"

"No, Terrey, thank you. Just memories," he answered. "Now, let us finish up here and I'll return to the prince and my uncle. Come with me and I'll ask for stationery for you to write the letter you need."

Terrey said nothing more as they walked out of the room and down the hall to the stairwell. Finding his uncle and the prince in the music room, Edmond's eyes were drawn to two women sitting on the settee together. One he recognized as the princess, the prince's wife, but the other… he paused as their eyes met.

She was stunning.

"Beautiful," he heard Terrey whisper behind him, awed no doubt by the same woman.

"Edmond," Mycroft greeted him, standing, and walking to the door. "Come in, come in, let us introduce you to her royal highness, the Duchess of Cornwall and York and her companion The Marchioness of Berkley."

"Your royal highness, Lady Berkley, my nephew, Sir Edmond Holmes," Mycroft's use of the title told Edmond the two ladies before him did not know the truth.

"Duchess," Edmond bowed. "Lady Berkley. It is an honor to make your acquaintance. His highness speaks very fondly of you, your grace."

"And of you, Sir Edmond," the duchess said. "My husband was just singing your praises."

"His royal highness is most kind."

"How long have you known the prince, Sir Edmond?" Lady Berkley asked.

Edmond glanced at Mycroft but continued with the first lie he could think of. "His Highness and I met when my brother was knighted, Lady Berkley."

"Oh yes, Sir Charles," the duchess stated. "You would love him, Arabella. One of the handsomest men."

"I have seen Sir Charles, your grace," Lady Berkley, who looked no older than Edmond's twenty-eight years, said. Then turned her attention back to Edmond. "But I have to disagree with you. For I find it is his brother who is by far the handsomest of the two."

Edmond prevented his face from warming at the compliment. Lady Berkley was exquisitely beautiful. Her dark brown nearly black hair was piled behind her head in a stunning coiffure. Her mocha-colored eyes danced between innocence and wickedness and her graceful countenance both intrigued Edmond and made him cautious.

"I thank your ladyship for the compliment," Edmond bowed.

"It is not a compliment if it is my opinion," she smiled, and the room lit with her beauty.

"Dear god," Terrey murmured dumbstruck. His words shook Edmond out of his stupor.

"Forgive me, your grace, my lady, but my valet and I have need of my uncle for just a moment."

"Of course," the duchess agreed, and Edmond turned to hurry out of the room.

Once alone, Edmond and Terrey exchanged a look and Terrey blew out a breath between puffed cheeks.

"Damn," he sighed. "You lucky, sod."

Edmond chuckled but was just as stunned as he was.

"What is it?" Mycroft asked.

"Nothing," Edmond answered quickly but Mycroft raised an eyebrow. "Lady Berkley is a beautiful woman."

"I meant about why you needed to see me, Edmond,"

Mycroft's droll voice said.

"Oh, ehm, right," Edmond began.

Mycroft rolled his eyes. "Do not let a woman lead you around by the cods, Nephew."

"Never, Uncle," he answered. "Terrey and I have discussed it and he is going to infiltrate the homes where we attend parties and soirees. He says large houses always hire more staff for the time. I have the list of the parties his highness is planning on attending, but we need a few blank pieces of paper where Terrey can write a letter of recommendation from his current employer. We also need to know if there is another employer he should use instead of my name since it may draw suspicion."

"Capital idea," Mycroft stated. "Use the title Lord Murray, Duke of Kent and have the forwarding address be mine."

"Yes, sir," Terrey replied bowing and leaving the area.

"I will retrieve paper for you and drop it off while you dress for dinner," Mycroft promised. "Now, come, we are to take tea with their highnesses and Lady Berkley."

"Lady Berkley, Uncle," Edmond began. "Who is she?"

"The widow of Marquess of Berkley, late of the Second Boer War and lady-in-waiting to her highness. Why?"

Edmond cleared his throat. "Curious, I suppose."

"Nephew, now is not the time to be led by other parts of yourself. You need the brain in your *head.*"

"I simply am surprised by a lady's beauty and wonder as to her intention. You should know, Uncle, I hold women in regard, but I am suspicious of everyone until they give me reason not to be."

"I am glad to hear it though you have no reason to be

suspicious of Lady Berkley," Mycroft stated.

"But Uncle—"

"Enough, Edmond," Mycroft snapped.

Edmond stared at him in surprise but stood to his fullest height and nodded. Mycroft led them back to the music room where he steeled against the beauty of the Marchioness and focused on his persona.

Chapter

Eighteen

Edmond stood staring at his reflection in the mirror of his bedroom. Terrey looked through the waistcoats hanging in the wardrobe. It was freeing to be out of his morning coat and waistcoat, but standing in his dress shirt and white tie, waiting for the white waistcoat and black tailcoat, his thoughts wandered back to Mycroft's uncharacteristic behavior earlier.

All thought of his conversation left him as soon as they were back in the music room with the prince and Edmond's eyes were drawn instantly to Lady Berkley. The ladies spoke of the prince's children and how well young Edward, the eldest and second in line to the throne after his father the prince, was maturing at his young age of seven.

Once it was discovered Edmond played the violin like his father, the duchess asked both he and Lady Berkley who was accomplished on the pianoforte, to play a duet. After Mozart's Sonata in G was chosen, Edmond was pleased to be presented the violin from the collection of instruments in the music room. His own violin was back at Pall Mall, but the Stradivarius played like a dream and Lady Berkley accompanied him beautifully. Sharing an intimate moment when he returned the violin to its case, Lady Berkley spoke of how well he played, and Edmond complimented her but sensed his uncle's eyes on him.

As he stood waiting to be dressed for his first royal dinner, he wondered. If she was a threat shouldn't his uncle be aware? And if she wasn't, what harm did it do to speak with a beautiful woman? It had been far too long since Edmond had been able to or desired to make a woman laugh and Lady Berkley's tinkling laugh lightened his soul.

"The diamond cufflinks, or the engraved ones, sir?" Terrey questioned from Edmond's jeweled box.

"Uh, the diamond."

Terrey said nothing only brought it over to him and fixed the cuffs. Once Edmond was dressed for dinner, Terrey confirmed he would write the letter and have it ready for Edmond to sign with the name and title Mycroft had given him. Edmond thanked him and opened the door to his room, heading down the hallway.

A door shutting to his right made him look over. Lady Berkley walked down the hallway but stopped when she saw him.

"Sir Edmond," she smiled.

"Lady Berkley," Edmond answered with a bow. "Might I say how lovely you look."

"Thank you," she replied. "And your *ensemble* is very fetching. I had no idea you were so adept at fashion. From what I had heard, you were no patron of the Royal Tailor."

"You do not strike me as a lady who listens to gossip, my lady."

"Oh, a lady always listens to gossip. One never knows when it will reveal something... intriguing." She offered her hand to him. "Escort me to the dining room?"

"With pleasure," he stated, tucking her hand into the crook of his arm. "I was saddened to hear of Lord Berkley's death."

"Yes, well, my late husband was not built for war. And at his advanced age, he should never have accepted the commission."

"He was a patriot and wanted to serve his country."

"He was an old fool who thought little," she answered gently, almost fondly. "But I was much aggrieved when he died."

"As any doting wife would."

"Ours was not a love match," she revealed. "My papa owed him money and I settled his debts."

"I am sorry you were placed in such a precarious position."

"Oh, 'tis no matter. He was not cruel. I grew genuinely fond of him."

"I am glad. And did he have an heir?" Edmond knew she had not had a child, that much he was able to discern from her personage.

"I was his second wife. Yes, his son is currently serving the rest of his father's military term. But you knew that already, did you not Sir Edmond?"

"My lady?" he questioned.

"I am much apprised of your father's exploits and I am sure his gifts of insight and deduction are hereditary."

"I can only plead guilty, my lady. But my skills are of no use in my current position."

"Oh, on the contrary, I believe they will be of very great use."

They entered the dining hall to see many more people than Edmond expected. The suddenness of being thrown into a dinner party and Lady Berkley's observations made the hair on the back of his neck rise. He released her hand as they were announced and bowed to her. She smiled at him and walked over to the duchess.

"Demme, that was a beautiful sight, Holmes," the prince walked over to him and slapped him on the back.

"Your highness," Edmond bowed in deference but when he rose, he looked at him confused.

"It's been far too long since I have seen that sort of twinkle in my wife's companion's eyes. She is a beautiful woman, is she not?"

"She is, of course, sire. A man would have to be blind not to see her virtues, but my time here is to watch out for you."

"Still, does not mean you cannot partake of life a little," the prince slapped him on the back again and reached for two glasses of champagne. Offering one to Edmond, the prince clinked his crystal to his. "Let it not be said anyone in mine or my father's employ lacks a chance to live."

Edmond said nothing more, knowing it would only encourage the prince. But he would clearly need to watch Lady Berkley. There was something... unnerving about her sharp eyes and even sharper mind.

As Edmond stood behind his designated chair, next to two people he did not know, waiting for the prince and duchess to sit, his hands grew clammy inside his white gloves. Though he had participated in many formal dinners previously, all eyes would be on him as it was his first royal dinner. The multiple utensils surrounding his place setting intimidated him. He could pretend to know what he was doing at his brother's or even at slightly larger events, but with the nearly thirty guests, all of whom Edmond had never met, apart from his uncle, the prince, duchess, and Lady Berkley, he hoped eyes would not scrutinize his every move.

A glance at the head of the table told him his uncle would be of little help as he sat beside the prince, a good five chairs away and on the same side as Edmond. He was on his own. Taking a silent deep breath, he already felt eyes on him, but he pulled on his brother's training.

Best rule for utensils is to start from the outside and work your way in with each course.

Counting the utensils, it was clear they would be having a feast. Usually content with eating very little, Edmond worried the inside of his cheek. His ginger and mint remedy for stomachache was in his room, and he knew beyond a shadow of a doubt, he would need the medicinal herbs that evening.

Once the prince and duchess were seated, Edmond followed protocol and waited until the ladies were settled before taking his chair in hand and pulling it away from the table. The menu at his place, showed a ten-course meal and almost immediately, bile filled Edmond's mouth. Though he was not particular when it came to food, he would eat what was placed before him, he was not one to indulge in gluttony.

"You look about ready to lose the contents of your stomach, Sir Edmond," the woman beside him said. He forced a smile and looked over at her. A countess if he remembered correctly. Her husband was a personal school chum of the prince and sat across from her.

"Forgive me, your ladyship, I hope I did not distress you," he said.

"Not in the least," she replied allowing the footman to place her napkin on her lap. "I have not eaten this much since the last time we visited Sandringham."

"Do you visit often?" he asked.

"Indeed, whenever the prince and duchess are in residence, we are happy to receive their invitation. My husband played cricket in school with his highness."

"A capital game," he lied. He never did understand the rules, but his persona of Sir Edmond would be expected to love it.

"Indeed, do you play, Sir Edmond?"

"Poorly, I'm afraid," he replied reaching for his wine glass. The sweet taste of Madeira was one he never truly enjoyed but the smooth taste of caramel and hazelnut along with the sweetness of peach and orange peel complimented the flavors.

"I understand you are rather new to this lifestyle, Sir Edmond," the man on his left spoke as he leaned back for the liveried footman to pour his soup.

"I am, sir, but not to the delicacy of court."

"I am glad to hear it, it would be dash awkward to sit beside someone unsuitable."

Edmond forced a smile at the insult. "I can assure you, Sir Thomas, I am far from unsuitable."

The man said nothing more and Edmond was glad for it as he ate his soup. The smooth taste of peas was one he enjoyed as a boy in France.

"Are you married, Sir Edmond?" the countess questioned beside him.

"Unfortunately, not as yet, my lady," he answered.

"Pity, and will you be attending this Season?"

"I have that great honor."

"Oh excellent, perhaps then we will be able to meet again."

"I would look forward to that, my lady."

"My daughter is newly married to the Viscount Milton. Are you familiar with him?"

"Not as such, my lady, but may I offer my best wishes to the happy couple."

"Indeed, such manners, you may, Sir Edmond with my thanks."

The footmen returned to remove the empty bowls and wine glasses though Edmond's and the countess' were still half full. Edmond drank from his water goblet as he waited for the next course. According to the menu, it was his choice of trout or whitebait. Forcing to remember what whitebait was, he waited to see what it looked like before he answered. Once the small fish were shown, he decidedly went with the trout and his white wine was poured.

After mindless chatter, five courses, four glasses of wine and one glass of champagne, Edmond was surprised at how well he felt. The soup and fish were excellent, the small fowl and torte was surprisingly light and the lamb and salad he chose, complimented each other perfectly. Grateful for the option at lighter fare, he found he was enjoying himself more than he thought he would. He was almost sorry when the excellent Chambertin wine was removed from his place setting.

Still five courses to go, Edmond took a moment to observe the rest of the room. His uncle sat beside the prince enjoying his fifth course and engaging conversation. The duchess spoke quietly with one of the other ladies in waiting. But the din of conversation and utensils quietly clanking and scraping against the fine bone china, was a soothing almost lullaby for him.

The footman came around to remove Sir Thomas' plate and refill his water glass. The man beside Edmond looked decidedly flushed with alcohol and overindulgence with food.

Edmond felt what was going to happen before it did. When the footman moved to replace Sir Thomas' water goblet, the baronet jerked to the side bumping the footman's arm. The crystal slipped out of his fingers and would have crashed to the floor had Edmond not reacted by striking his hand out and catching the glass.

"Sir, I can only apologize," the poor footman gushed.

"No harm done," Edmond offered the glass back to him. "Just glad I happened to catch it."

"What a heroic act, Sir Edmond," the countess said from beside him.

"I did not get any on you did I, sir?" the footman looked nearly scared to death.

"Demme you might have ruined my dinner jacket," Sir Thomas nearly shouted.

"I am so very sorry, Sir Thomas," the footman said.

"You should be, dammit," Sir Thomas replied.

If Edmond had not already disliked the man, he would have hated him even more.

"Yes, well," Edmond replied pulling on his persona but also injecting a little of himself in the coming reproach. "At least some of us have the grace to know their limit, Sir Thomas. The man was only doing what he was asked to do. You can find no fault in that. Well done, lad." Edmond nodded to the footman who looked almost on the verge of tears. The young man, no older than seventeen locked eyes with Edmond, as a relieved smile entered his eyes. "Now, perhaps you could set the water down at Sir Thomas' place and fetch me another glass of that delicious Bordeaux. My lady, can I have him get something for you?"

"I will have some more of the champagne, Sir Edmond, with my thanks," she said.

"And another glass of the champagne for her ladyship," Edmond said.

"Thank you, sir," the footman sighed in relief as he set the glass down and scurried to do his bidding.

The countess leaned in and whispered. "You play a persona, Sir Edmond most of the time, but that was the real you. I must say, in a society filled with men like Sir Thomas, you will find yourself endeared to all, servants and masters alike."

"All are men and women, my lady and isn't it in the scriptures that all men are created equal in the sight of God?"

The countess smiled softly and winked. "I do wish my Agnes had met you long before her husband. You do yourself a great service, Sir Edmond. I hope we shall meet again soon for you are quite intriguing."

"My thanks, my lady."

With that, the countess pulled back as they waited for the next courses and their drinks to arrive. Edmond looked toward his uncle to see if he noticed the incident but instead of Mycroft's eyes on him, he caught Lady Berkley watching him with shrewd interest.

Chapter Nineteen

The next morning, Edmond woke at his usual time and, though he could not go outside, he performed his routine in the comfort of his room in Sandringham. Twenty minutes later, Terrey was shaving his face and picking out the morning travelling attire. They were to have breakfast and then catch the eleven-fifteen to King's Cross. Terrey was at the wardrobe while Edmond buttoned his shirt.

"The lavender waistcoat, Terrey."

"Lavender?" he questioned. "Hmm..."

"What?" Edmond's reply was sarcastic.

"Nothing, Sir Edmond," he teased. "I just never thought I'd see the day when my master specifically asked for the *lavender* waistcoat."

"Oh Terrey, I'm nothing if not unpredictable," Edmond winked.

"More like trying to impress a certain Marchioness."

"That will do, Terrey."

"Yes, sir," Terrey's twinkling eyes didn't fade as he brought over the lavender waistcoat. "The cream-colored jacket would look well with the color of choice."

"For travelling? No," Edmond shook his head. "The grey will do better."

"Very well, sir," he replied. "And the grey and lavender striped pants?"

"Yes," Edmond answered.

Terrey grinned then pretended to sniffle as if crying. "I'm so happy. You're actually considering fashionable choices."

Edmond gave him a sardonic side-eye. "Oh, enough, enough," he teased.

"Who would have thought it? A woman catching your eye was all that was needed for you to care about how you look." Terrey helped Edmond into the waistcoat as he pulled on his trousers.

"Lady Berkley has absolutely nothing to do with my choices in wardrobe."

"Oh, indeed," Terrey nodded mockingly.

"Have I ever told you, Terrey, you are an *emmerdement?*"

Terrey grinned. "Every day, sir."

Knowing his term was used in jest and that Terrey knew what it meant being fluent in French from an early age, Edmond laughed and shook his head.

"Finished?" Edmond asked as Terrey helped him with his coat.

"Nearly," Terrey replied. With a critical eye, Terrey brushed the back of Edmond's coat to make sure there were no wrinkles and pronounced him ready. He actually said; "ready to go sweep said lady off her feet." But it meant the same to Edmond.

Edmond left the room leaving the packing to Terrey and headed down to the morning room. After a light quick breakfast, the prince and Mycroft spoke with Howards and made sure the carriage was ready. The ladies had not joined them for breakfast as was customary but as Edmond placed his top hat over his light brown hair and took his walking stick from the footman, who also held his overcoat, he caught movement out of the corner of his eye.

Lady Berkley walked toward him, dressed in a mint green *at home* gown, the cashmere glistening in the sunlight from the windows. Her high-necked vest looked to be made of Oriental silk, a beautiful fabric Edmond knew firsthand felt like the gentlest water between his fingers. Her dark brown hair was pulled up to the top of her head in a morning fashion and her eyes, the large dark orbs were lined with some sort of lighter color though it was faint it drew his attention. Her decidedly floral scent wafted over to him; sweet night blooming jasmine mixed with the earthier scent of rosemary. He had not smelled jasmine since he had left China and the scent brought with it wonderful memories and yet, the painful ones were still there.

Shaking himself out of his stupor, he turned and bowed to her. "I take my leave of you, my lady."

"Do you?" she questioned pleasantly.

"I am leaving with his highness on the eleven-fifteen train to return to London," Edmond explained.

"Dear me, what a coincidence," her voice told him there was no coincidence at all.

"My lady?"

"Come now, do you truly believe two people as in love as their highnesses would want to be separated?" She paused but continued without waiting for a reply. "They have taken their rooms at St. James' Palace and I shall be with them. Her highness and I travel to London by the same train."

"Indeed? Well, I am delighted to hear that."

"I hoped you would be," she looked up at him with a devilishly seductive look that had him floundering for a moment.

Percy had taught him what to say while dancing with a stranger, but that moment seemed far too intimate. He needed to flirt. He had never needed to flirt before. He didn't *need* to, he amended. But something about Lady Berkley made it impossible not to *want* to. Still, Edmond was guarded but his new persona would not be. Drawing on the numerous times he had seen Percy flirt before he married, Edmond smiled at her.

"I am indeed. Will you be attending the ball tonight?"

"If her highness wishes. It is at the Duke of Pembroke's home. I would imagine she would join since she and the duchess are such good friends. But I will not know until I see how the train ride has wearied her."

"Of course."

"But if we do arrive, would you seek me out?" She questioned.

"Would you like it if I did?" Edmond asked.

"I would. I would be interested to know how someone with your catlike grace and reflexes would be on the dance floor."

"My lady?" he queried for no one was to know of his martial arts background.

"Come now, I saw how you saved the water glass from falling and didn't spill a single drop. Or how you move about the room. You watch people Sir Edmond. And I am curious what it is you see."

"Everything. I see everything, my lady. The good, the beautiful, and the evil."

"Surely no evil is done under their highnesses' roof."

"One would hope, my lady. But perhaps you would do me the honor of saving a dance for me if you do join us?" He changed the subject.

"I would be honored."

He bowed to her, she curtsied quickly. "Until tonight, if I am so lucky," he said.

"Luck will have nothing to do with it." Again, the look was back in her eyes and Edmond had to prevent his reactions. It was not easy as the attraction was strong, and it had been a long time since he had felt such longing.

Edmond bowed his head once more and turned.

"Oh, Sir Edmond?" He turned back. "That color lavender, is quite fetching. It brings out the lavender in your grey eyes."

Edmond stared at her for a long moment. Part of him, the human side wanted to smile, flirt, kiss and perhaps see where their clear chemistry would take them. The other part of him, the machine side, calculated. What and why, how and who. What did she mean and want? Why did she do as she did? How did she see what he was? Who was she? Truly.

"Until tonight, Lady Berkley."

"It will be a pleasure, Sir Edmond." With that promise ringing in his ear, he bowed once more, shrugged into his overcoat, and walked out the door where the carriage, his uncle, and the prince were waiting.

Never in his career with Edmond Holmes had Palmerston Terrey ever seen his master and friend so besotted. It was quite endearing. But Lady Berkley was stunningly beautiful. Terrey could see how any man would find himself at a loss for words whenever she was present. As he assisted Edmond into his formal ball attire for the first of many soirees, Terrey watched him out of the corner of his eye. Edmond could not be considered nervous, nor could he be considered excited. But there was something about his countenance that made Terrey pause.

"Everything all right, sir?" he asked as he helped button Edmond's white waistcoat.

"Hmm?" Edmond questioned. "Oh, ehm, yes, thank you, Terrey."

"You seem... distracted."

Edmond looked down at him and took a deep breath. "I am."

Terrey paused fixing his white tie. "I may tease you, Edmond, but I am genuinely concerned about you. If there is something I can help you with, I am here."

"I know. Thank you, Terrey. But I'm just not sure what is going on with me."

"Could it be you're attracted to Lady Berkley?"

"Any man would have to be blind not to find her beautiful."

"That's not what I meant, sir," he replied.

"I know that's not what you meant, but that's all there is to it. I am in no position to woo a woman. And besides, my knighthood is a sham. What would a lady, a marchioness at that, want with someone like me?"

"You sell yourself short, Edmond. You have much to offer."

"No, Terrey," he shook his head. "I cannot allow my head to be turned by a beautiful woman. Not while I'm on a case."

Terrey said nothing more as he helped Edmond into his dress coat. Ready for the ball, Edmond asked Terrey to hail him a cab and once the hackney was ready, Terrey helped him into his overcoat and handed him his top hat and white gloves.

"I shall be home late," he called over his shoulder as he got into the cab and drove off.

Terrey stood in the entryway as the door closed behind Edmond. There was something far deeper at work. He had never seen Edmond so distraught. Whatever it was, Terrey was ready to face it head on.

Chapter Twenty

The home of the Duke and Duchess of Pembroke was elaborately beautiful. Every window was lit with light to where it poured out onto the streets. Edmond stepped off the hackney and straightened his hat, taking a moment to allow Sir Edmond's persona to fall over him and root itself firmly into his mind.

Striding up the walk and steps, he entered the house, handed over his overcoat and hat and was ushered up the stairs to the ballroom in a matter of moments. The announcer looked at him and bowed.

"Sir Edmund Holmes," he shouted.

Edmond prevented his eye roll. He knew his name and pronunciation was French and sometimes difficult for English people to pronounce, but to deliberately mispronounce his name... he shook his head and plastered a smile on his face. Heading to the Duke and Duchess of Sandringham to greet them, he waited in the line of guests. Edmond's gaze searched the room. Taking in the faces around him, he focused his thoughts and blocked out the spousal arguments, the clandestine relationship between a debutant and a footman, the furtive glances between married women and their lovers, who were not their husbands, and the general buzz someone trained in observational skills clearly saw.

Not seeing the prince and duchess standing in the line with the Duke and Duchess of Pembroke, he breathed a little easier. Having arrived somewhat early, he wanted to make sure he scrutinized the area and servants before the prince arrived.

"Sir Charles Holmes," the announcer called. Edmond looked over his shoulder to see his brother walk in and scan the crowd. They locked eyes and Percy nodded to him. He was there to assist if needed.

"Baron Hughes." Again, Edmond heard the announcer and saw his best friend Cedric walk in and stand behind Percy in the line.

No time to think any more on the other guests, Edmond was next to greet the hosts and he straightened, embodying the person he was meant to portray. Stepping up to greet the hosts, Edmond bowed slightly.

"Your grace," he addressed the Duke. "Sir Edmond Holmes. It is a pleasure to be here."

"Sir Edmond," the Duke of Pembroke greeted. "I don't believe I've had the pleasure before."

"Just recently in the service of his majesty," Edmond explained.

"Ah, capital!" the duke offered his hand which Edmond took in a shake. "A pleasure to meet you then! May I introduce my wife."

"Your grace," Edmond bowed low as the duchess curtsied.

"Sir Edmond," she greeted. "Welcome to our home."

"It is lovely. Thank you for the welcome, your grace."

"May I present our son, The Marquess of Dorchester, and our daughter Lady Penelope Creighton."

"Lord Dorchester, Lady Penelope." Edmond bowed.

"We follow your father's exploits with great interest, Sir Edmond," Lord Dorchester said. "We are pleased to have you here."

"The pleasure is mine, my lord. Never have I been surrounded by such... beauty," Edmond replied, his eyes turning to Lady Penelope. She was not what Edmond would call a beauty in the eyes of society, but he always knew beauty came from within.

"Are you interested in finding a beauty of your own?" the marquess asked.

"Indeed, my lord but with all these lovely ladies, it is difficult to decide who to pursue."

The marquess chuckled. "Believe me, Sir Edmond, I understand entirely."

"Would it be impertinent of me to request a dance from your lovely sister?"

"I do believe Penelope would be happy to accept. What say you, sister?"

Lady Penelope curtsied. "I would be honored to accept, Sir Edmond."

"Capital," Edmond replied. "Then, I shall keep you no longer. But I look forward to claiming my dance with you, my lady. My lord," he bowed to the marquess and stepped away from the receiving line.

Again, scanning the area, he watched the footmen and other servants moving about. Terrey had not been able to infiltrate the house since it was such a short time after returning to London. But it gave Edmond a chance to see what he was in for. The room was beginning to fill and as the herald continued to announce attendees, Edmond was sure the room would warm quickly. Grateful for his training, he was well versed in using his mind to overcome his body's perceived heating.

"Their royal highnesses Prince George and the Duchess of York and Cornwall."

Everyone in the room turned to the door as one and bowed or curtsied as the prince and princess were announced. The prince looked regal in his royal uniform and the princess was resplendent in a royal blue silk gown, reflecting the lights around her with the gems and beads sewn into the dress.

"The Marchioness of Berkley."

Edmond's pulse began to pound, and his hands grew damp in his white gloves as she glided into the room as if floating on a cloud. Her eyes met his and a sly grin appeared on her lips. He looked away quickly, feeling like a green boy of Henri's age in the presence of a beautiful woman. Someone walked up beside him and another on the other side.

"Well, it appears you have the manners down pat, brother mine," Percy said. "I wonder what a wonderful teacher you had."

"Yes, indeed," Edmond answered. "I must thank mama for

all those years of training."

Percy chuckled into his champagne glass.

"It helps that your best friend is a baron," Cedric supplied on the other side of him.

"Of course, dear brother-in-law," Edmond teased. "Though you may be assured I will never call you *my lord*."

"It'll only go to his head," Percy agreed.

"Very well, very well, if I didn't love my wife so much, I would leave you two jackanapes to your own devices," Cedric teased.

"I say it's a very good thing you love your wife so much and leave it at that," Percy replied with a wink. "You know what we'd do if you didn't."

"You may want to try and scare me, Percy, but that only works if there's a doubt in my mind. And there is no doubt in my mind how much I love Rebecca."

"Glad to hear it."

Edmond didn't reply as his eyes were on Lady Berkley.

"And who is that beauty?" Percy questioned following his brother's gaze. "And why does my brother look like he just swallowed an insect? Tell me true, brother... has some lady caught your eye?"

"And even if she had, Percy," Cedric replied. "Is he not allowed a little privacy?"

"None," Percy answered. "You know how long I've waited to see my brother fall over himself when a woman is concerned?"

"I am here to protect his highness," Edmond whispered. "Nothing else matters."

"Oh, of course," Percy winked. "But if that *nothing* turns your head? You cannot stay in the shadows."

"Enough," Edmond breathed low as the prince and duchess walked over.

"Well, if it isn't the Holmeses and yes, Lord Hughes I consider you one of them since you are married into the family," the prince said.

"I consider myself one as well, your highness," Cedric answered after they all bowed.

"It is a pleasure to see you again, your highness," Percy replied.

"And you, Sir Charles, how is your lovely wife?"

"Has her time come yet?" the duchess asked.

"Any day now, your grace. I thank you for remembering her. She truly misses the opportunity to be here and speak with you," Percy replied.

"Please give her my best," she said.

"I will indeed. My thanks, your grace."

"Darling, I need to speak with Lady Berkley. I will leave you to your rounds," she said to her husband.

"Of course, my dear," Prince George kissed her hand and let her go. Edmond watched but he told himself it was not to get a glimpse of Lady Berkley.

The evening passed in a bit of a blur. He danced with Lady Penelope and another two ladies he did not know. Blending into his surroundings, he kept his attention on the prince. When the orchestra took a rest for a few minutes, Edmond carried around his second glass of champagne, not drinking. As he reached the refreshments table looking for a cooling glass of water, he was accosted by three older ladies, all of whom he had never met.

"Sir Edmond," one lady offered her hand to him. "It is wonderful to make your acquaintance. I am Lady Biddlesbe, this is Lady Longtree, and Lady Pike."

"My ladies," Edmond bowed over each of their hands. "To what do I owe such a great honor?"

"It is our... unofficial duty you see, to welcome any new member of the aristocracy."

"We are the welcome committee, you understand."

"And we find that you have not been properly welcomed."

"Ah, Lady Biddlesbe, Lady Longtree, Lady Pike, it is an honor to be welcomed to robustly."

"I have heard Sir Edmond, that you did not care for the frivolities of females. And a ball was not a place one would find you," Lady Longtree said.

"Yes well, my lady, one does not want to outshine one's elder brother. Now that he is happily settled and married, it is time for me to consider such... interesting prospects," he explained.

"And has anyone caught your eye yet, Sir Edmond?" Lady Pike asked.

"Not as yet, my lady. But that is perhaps because I have been assisting my dear friend, the prince for so long with his collection."

"Collection?" Lady Longtree questioned.

"Indeed, he is an avid stamp collector. The man has sent me all over the British empire for his stamps. Now, he has turned his pursuits closer to home, so have I."

"How fascinating," Lady Longtree replied. "You are home for good?"

"I am indeed, unless of course duties at court prevent me."

"And you are a close friend of his highness?"

"I have that great honor."

"Well, how exciting," Lady Pike said. "Perhaps you will take tea with my daughter and I tomorrow? We would love to hear more about your travels."

"I would be delighted, Lady Pike."

"And, of course you are most welcome to join *us* for supper, Sir Edmond," Lady Biddlesbe said. "My Elizabeth is quite accomplished on the pianoforte."

"That is most welcome news, Lady Biddlesbe. I find few things the equal of a well accomplished woman playing the pianoforte."

"I have heard that you play the violin, Sir Edmond much like your father," Lady Longtree stated.

"I dabble, Lady Longtree," Edmond replied.

"Well, then we must have a concert! My Victoria has a beautiful singing voice. In fact, the prince himself heard her and said heaven is missing an angel in the form of my daughter."

"That is praise indeed, Lady Longtree." Edmond's eyes lifted when he saw movement behind the three women. Lady Berkley walked over to him, a suppressed look of amusement on her face. "Lady Berkley," he bowed low. The other ladies parted, pursing their lips at the intrusion.

"Sir Edmond," she dipped in a shallow curtsy. "I do believe I am owed a dance."

"Of course, my pleasure, my lady," he said. "Do forgive me, I promised Lady Berkley a dance when we met yesterday at Sandringham. But I look forward to tea and supper."

"Tomorrow? Three-thirty," Lady Pike offered. "Number ten just off the high street."

"And perhaps eight o'clock?" Lady Biddlesbe stated. "Sixteen, Arlington Street."

"My honor, ladies," Edmond bowed to each of them. "Lady Pike, Lady Biddlesbe, Lady Longtree."

Edmond offered his gloved hand to Lady Berkley and they walked to the dance floor as the orchestra struck up a moderate waltz.

"You looked like you needed saving, Sir Edmond," Lady Berkley said.

"I thank your ladyship for the consideration," Edmond replied.

"And you already are the talk of the ball," she teased.

"How so?"

"Do you really not know?"

"I do not believe so, my lady."

"The cut of your suit is quite fine, and you along with it."

Heat spread up Edmond's neck under his collar. He cleared his throat. "I am pleased to be blessed with certain... attributes."

"Indeed, and every lady who sees those attributes can bless the good lord for his gifts."

Edmond said nothing.

"You are shocked," she teased. "You do not believe a

woman of my standing should speak to a man like that?"

"Indeed, my lady, I have no opinion on the matter."

"Liar," she grinned. "I do hope you know, Sir Edmond, as a widow, I have no reason to be a blushing debutant fiercely guarding her virtue."

Edmond nearly tripped but recovered quickly. Any other aspect of his life, he was in control to the very minutia of his being. Even when dancing with the other ladies, he was careful to guard who he was and play the part assigned to him. But with Lady Berkley. Something about her wound him up.

"You have no need to fear me, my lady."

"Fear you?" Lady Berkley's tinkling laughter floated around him. "Good lord, no. In fact, Sir Edmond, I am quite certain it is you who should fear me."

Edmond looked down at her, searching her face for her true meaning. "Whatever you intend, I hope you will keep me informed."

"You will be the first, Sir Edmond," she replied. "For I intend all sorts of wicked things for you."

"You are quite the coquette, my lady," Edmond answered. He needed to get hold of his emotions when it came to her. He had given in to his feelings once and it ended in misery.

"And you are quite the bounder," she offered.

Edmond's body tingled. A bounder was a pretender, a person who reached above his station. In his case, bounder was the exact definition of what he was doing. Surely, she did not know. His uncle would not have told anyone. Even the princess didn't know. There was no reason she would know. And yet...

The music ended and Edmond was glad of it. He needed to focus on his persona. It was slipping and he could not stop it.

They bowed to each other but when he escorted Lady Berkley to her chosen place on the side of the room, she squeezed his arm.

"Until next time, Sir Edmond. I enjoyed how very... vigorous you were."

Edmond bowed again. "My lady, I hope I did not tire you."

"Oh, it takes more than once to tire me, Sir Edmond," she replied.

Edmond stared at her. Though he knew it shouldn't, her unladylike behavior is what drew him to her. When he considered what he admired, a stalwart lady was high on the list. But something about Lady Berkley fascinated him. He wondered again, just who she was and what she knew about him. Deciding to no longer participate in the dancing, he took his leave and sought out the prince. Grateful to see he was standing beside Percy, Edmond made his way over and caught his brother's eye. The prince and Percy looked over with a wide grin on their faces.

As soon as Edmond reached them, he was slapped on the back and the prince spoke; "Demme what a grand sight that was. You and Lady Berkley are well matched in both looks and mind."

"Indeed, Edmond," Percy agreed. "She is a beautiful lady and to see you two together did my heart well."

"If I may be so bold, sire, what exactly is her story?" Edmond asked refusing to feel jealousy creep through his body when she was asked to dance by another.

"She married a friend of her father's and mine. She and my wife got along well and when Lord Berkley accepted a commission with the royal navy, she came to stay with us since she was all alone in Berkley Estate and townhouse. My wife enjoyed her company."

"And she is... of English descent?"

"She is, hearty English blood," the prince said. "You could do far worse, Holmes."

"I am sorry if I have given his highness reason to consider Lady Berkley and I in a romantic entanglement, but I can assure you, sire that is not my intention. I am here as your guard."

The prince laughed, then turned to Percy. "Speak to him, Holmes. He clearly doesn't understand what we all saw. If you need me, I will be at the refreshments table."

Edmond turned to his brother. Percy sobered for a moment, then a soft smile lifted his lips.

"You were... magnificent, Ed."

"Thank you," he replied. "And to think you were worried." He grinned.

But instead of making Percy laugh, his brother's expression darkened. "What is it?"

Percy shook his head. "Have I ever really known you?"

"What do you mean?"

"I see you and I don't know which is the real you. I don't know if you even find Lady Berkley attractive. If you are interested in pursuing her or not. Have I been a horrible brother to you?"

"Percy," Edmond breathed. "How can you possibly think that?"

"I feel our friendship... is declining. And I don't know what to do because I don't know who you really are."

"Percy, of anyone you, dad, and Uncle Mycroft know about what happened in China. I keep things close. It's not for nefarious reasons, it's who I am, my studies, my history. What I learned. How I lived. China. Everything. But you are my best friend. And yes, I find Lady Berkley... wildly beautiful, funny, and mysterious.

Would I want to be with her? Yes, I am a man in my prime. But I don't know who she is. She could be anything sent to distract me or get close to me in order to hurt the king or the prince. I don't know. So, I have to be detached from that sort of physical need."

"And if she is just as she appears? A beautiful woman who is interested in pursuing you?"

"No one is as they appear. You know that. Father taught us better than that."

"Tell me something then."

"Anything," Edmond said knowing he may regret it.

"Tell me her name."

"Whose?"

"The woman you loved in China."

Edmond stared into his brother's eyes seeing an earnestness he had never seen before.

"If it truly means something to you..." he hesitated, took a deep breath, and plowed ahead. "Lei. Her name was Lei."

Percy said nothing for a long moment, then brushed his hand over his brother's clearly wanting to embrace him but knowing it was not done in polite society.

"Thank you," Percy said. Then, pulling back, he placed a very visible mask over his features with a wide grin. "Now, his highness was correct. Everyone saw you and Lady Berkley. All I am saying is, see what happens. Have you spoken to Father or Uncle about this?"

"Uncle says I have no reason to be suspicious of her, but he did not tell me why."

"Then trust our uncle. Do you want to see her again?"

"It is not that simple, Perce," he replied.

"Yes or no."

"Yes, all right, damn you."

Percy grinned. "Then do it. You deserve to be happy, Edmond."

"I have a job to do," he replied.

"Oh, very well, but you're going to see her quite a bit as she is with the duchess and you with the prince. Who knows what could happen in those darkened little rooms, behind a curtain, you both thinking you were alone, close quarters," he widened his eyes suggestively, and bounced his eyebrows.

"Enough," Edmond laughed but couldn't ignore how his body tingled at the thought of it.

Percy leaned in and whispered. "Think on it. Just because you court a lady does not mean you ignore your duty to the crown. You are expected to woo as it is the season, and you are an eligible bachelor. Have you forgotten your cover?"

"Percy, there are times, though I love you and would do anything for you... that I absolutely hate you."

"No, you don't," Percy muttered with a wink. "You'd be miserable without me."

Edmond huffed a sigh. "I have accepted an invitation to tea and dinner from two separate ladies trying to pawn their daughters off on *Sir Edmond.*"

"It's a start. I had seven after my first ball, but I am the older and devilishly handsome brother."

"You are never going to stop quoting that newspaper article from five years ago are you?"

"Never," Percy agreed. "Oh, looks like you might have a

third invitation soon." He looked over Edmond's shoulder causing Edmond to look back and step to the side.

"Sir Charles," a man no older than thirty greeted Percy.

"Lord Beaumont, a pleasure," he replied.

"Indeed, indeed," the average looking man said. "It was dashed good of you to let me share your cab the other day outside of the Carlton."

"The pleasure was mine," Percy stated. "May I introduce my brother Sir Edmond Holmes."

"Sir Edmond," Lord Beaumont said, and the men bowed. "This is my sister, Lady Grace."

"Lady Grace," both Edmond and Percy bowed and took her hand.

"Pleasure," she said in a soft voice, her eyes glancing furtively to Edmond.

"Is this your first season, Lady Grace?" Edmond asked.

"In a way," she replied.

"Mine as well," he smiled. "At least when it comes to the attention being on me."

She beamed. "I could readily believe you are used to the attention, Sir Edmond. Such bearing is wantingly needed in gentlemen these days."

"Your ladyship pays me a great compliment," Edmond said. She was sweet looking. Perhaps just twenty, and when the light caught her hair, it looked as if it was strings of gold. Just as Edmond was going to offer a dance, as was expected, the orchestra stopped playing and the gong rang, indicating dinner was served. His eyes rose, scanning the crowd. He denied he was looking for Lady Berkley but, in his heart, he knew that was a lie. Not seeing her, he turned back to Lady Grace. "Might I have the honor of escorting you into dinner, Lady Grace?"

"I would be honored, Sir Edmond. Thank you."

Edmond offered his arm to her and Percy fell into step behind him walking with her brother.

Chapter Twenty-One

The dining hall was just as extravagant as the ballroom. Two long tables were set with the best china, gold utensils, and the finest crystal for wine and water goblets. Edmond found his seat and offered to assist Lady Grace. After seeing her to her chair, Edmond sat beside her.

"How elegant," she oohed at the setting.

"Indeed, but I had little doubt after seeing such a lovely ballroom," Edmond said. Looking across from, him he froze. Two dark eyes danced directly before him. Lady Berkley.

"Are you well, Sir Edmond?" Lady Grace questioned.

"Forgive me, my lady for startling you. Yes, I am perfectly well. The heat from the other room has caught up with me."

"Oh indeed, it was quite warm," she agreed. Edmond smiled at her, glad to see the prince was seated at the head of the table to his left so any conversation with Lady Grace would turn his head in that direction.

They spoke very little apart from the weather London was experiencing in recent days while the first and second courses were presented. Edmond found Lady Grace's conversation sweet and simple but hardly engaging. He maintained the expected interest and conversed with her, but as the third course was being served, the hair on the back of his neck stood on end as something did not feel right. Glancing over at Percy across the table three people down from him, he saw his brother lean back, his usual gallant expression suddenly rigid and guarded. He locked eyes with Edmond and nodded slightly. They both felt something.

Edmond sensed Lady Berkley's eyes on him, but he did not acknowledge her.

"Is something wrong, Sir Edmond?" Lady Grace asked.

He looked over at her and forced a smile. "Forgive me, my lady, a... bout of indigestion."

The diners were unaffected by what the two brothers felt. But soon, their senses were proven correct. A side door opened, and Edmond looked over. A young footman stumbled into the room. The butler hurried over, no doubt to reprimand him for interrupting and being above stairs when he wasn't supposed to be. But the butler didn't make it in time. The young man fell to his knees and then down to his stomach. Some of the diners began to notice and murmurs started.

"Hitting the sherry a bit too hard," one of the noblemen

said. Another agreed but Edmond blocked the voices out. There was something unnatural about how still the man was. The butler was standing over another footman who tried to shake the man awake to no avail.

Percy locked eyes with Edmond and shook his head. Something wasn't right. Edmond leaned over to Lady Grace and spoke in a low tone.

"Lady Grace, please forgive me, but I have some medical training. I am going to see if I can be of some service to the poor man."

"Your honor does you credit, Sir Edmond," she said.

Edmond stood and walked over to the butler, Percy coming up behind him. The butler stepped in front of them.

"Sirs, I can only say I am frightfully sorry about this intrusion," he said.

"Not to worry, my brother has some medical training," Percy replied.

"Perhaps I can help," Edmond offered.

"You are very kind, Sir Edmund, but there is no need." Again, Edmond held in his grimace. Though the pronunciation was very English, and one often used, Edmond still disliked how the British said his French name.

"Mr. Carstairs," the footman shaking the man awake, spoke in a horrified tone. The three men looked down to see the footman staring at his hands, coated red with blood.

"What the devil is going on here, Carstairs?" the Duke of Pembroke walked over. Then, seeing the blood on the man's hands, straightened. "What the devil?"

"We do not want to cause a scene, but I do believe, your grace, that the room should be secured," Percy said.

"Yes, yes of course," the duke said.

"That screen, Carstairs," Edmond spoke to the butler. "Bring it here, we need to cover the body. And someone needs to go get the police."

"The police?" the duke questioned. "No, no, that would be horrific. I cannot have the police treading through here, questioning my guests. Please, Sir Charles, Sir Edmond, I beseech you. I have used your father on more than one occasion and found him to be discrete. I ask you to do the same."

"Your grace, a man is dead," Percy replied.

"Involve the police but only after you have solved this," the duke continued.

Edmond looked at his brother and nodded. "Very well, your grace, but we will need to postpone dinner."

"The final course can be served in the drawing room," Pembroke agreed.

"I will need to speak with Cedric," Edmond said looking at his brother, explaining why with merely a look. Someone had to stay with the prince.

"Let's get everyone out, first," Percy replied. "Knowing Cedric as I do, he'll stay to see what is going on."

It was decided and Pembroke walked over to the prince to inform him of the decision. Percy and Edmond helped move the screen in front of the body. Hearing Pembroke speaking to the guests gave the brothers a chance to write a note in Percy's notebook.

"Have this taken to 221b Baker Street and see it is given to our father," Percy said.

"I will send his grace's man to do it, sir. Beyond trustworthy. I would do it myself, but—"

"Understood, Carstairs," Edmond replied. "Now, I will also need to speak with the servants. Where does that door lead?"

"To a hallway to the backstairs," Carstairs explained.

"What else is down there?"

"There's an unused study, used to belong to his grace's father but is not used now. And a back entrance to the ball room."

"Thank you, please hurry with that note to our father, but keep the hallway clear," Edmond said. The butler dashed off through the main door of the dining room.

"Percy, Edmond, what the devil is going on?" Cedric's voice came from beside the partition.

"Ah, Cedric, thank god," Edmond said standing from where he crouched looking at the body.

"Is he..."

"He's dead," Percy confirmed. Cedric paled.

"His Grace has asked us to investigate. I need you to stay with the prince. Keep an eye on him," Edmond said.

"Of course," Cedric replied.

"Gentlemen, is there anything I can do?" Lady Berkley walked up beside him.

The men bowed but Edmond saw a sort of tension around her lips and eyes as she stared at the body.

"My lady, I would not have you look," Percy stepped in front.

"Please, Sir Charles," Lady Berkley replied. "I am not prone to fainting nor am I afraid of the dead. It is the living who frightens me more."

Edmond watched her as she took in the body of the young

man. "My lady, might I ask, where did you go after our dance?"

Her eyes whipped up to his as the footman turned the body over.

"I beg your pardon? Are you questioning me, Sir Edmond?" She asked.

"I will be asking all guests the same question, my lady," he replied.

"If you must know," she answered. "I was refreshing my toilette. I am the personal friend of the Duchess of Cornwall and York. What would a footman be to me?"

She looked down at the body and Edmond saw the change in her features, subtle but still a change.

"Do you know him?" Edmond asked.

She looked up at his sharply. "No, of course not," she replied. "He's just so young."

Carstairs returned and bowed. "The note has been sent to Baker Street, sirs."

"Excellent, I have some questions for you first, Mr. Carstairs," Edmond started then turned to look at Lady Berkley. "If you could join the others in the drawing room, my lady. My brother and I will be there shortly."

Lady Berkley looked to be in some sort of trance like state as she left the dining room. Edmond nodded to Percy and his brother turned to the butler as Edmond crouched down to inspect the wound.

"What is his name?" Percy asked Carstairs.

"Nicolas... Nicolas Bright. He's only twenty-two, oh goodness," the butler said.

"Any family?" Percy asked.

"No, he always said he grew up in an orphanage," he replied. "He got on well with the staff."

"How long had he been with you?" Edmond asked.

"About a month? Hard working, kept himself to himself."

"Thank you, Mr. Carstairs," Edmond said. "Please tell the staff to remain below stairs and keep everyone together. Let no one leave, understood?"

"Yes, sir," he bowed.

"My father will want to speak with you when he arrives," Percy said.

"I will be sure to allow him in, will it be all right to come back up when the door rings?"

"Yes, indeed, and make sure, if you would, that the valet you sent to get him returns," Edmond stated.

"I will make sure all are accounted for."

With that, Mr. Carstairs left the dining room and Percy crouched down opposite his brother.

"What have you discovered?" He asked.

"It's a knife wound, a rather nasty one at that," Edmond moved the lapel of the livery to show his brother. "He would have bled out instead of immediate death."

"How long ago then?" Percy questioned.

Edmond blew out a breath, "with a wound like that," he went on. "Probably no more than ten minutes?"

"So, what would a footman know that would have gotten him killed?" Percy asked.

"That is the question," Edmond answered. He went quiet for a moment and Percy looked at him.

"I know that look, father has it all the time. What are you questioning?"

"Did it seem odd to you how he entered? I mean, was it my imagination or was he looking for someone?"

"I saw him scan the crowd, but I don't know if he was looking for someone specifically or if he was looking for help."

"But if you're a servant, why would you come upstairs instead of looking for someone in the kitchens? It's clear there would be people all over the kitchens at this time of night so why risk coming all the way up here?"

"Perhaps he was already here? Perhaps he was closer to upstairs than down?"

"True…" Edmond agreed. "Unfortunately, all we have right now are questions." He looked back down at the man, now lying on his back. "Perce, look at this." Moving the man's cuffs to show his wrists, Edmond showed the bruised flesh to his brother.

"Tied up? Held down? What?"

"I'm not sure. It's still too fresh. It may show fingers, or it may show restraints. But either way, this man was murdered while he was tied up or held down no longer than ten minutes ago."

"Do you want to go see if we can find where?" Percy asked.

"I want to wait for dad. He should be here soon," Edmond said.

"What do you think?" Percy questioned.

"I don't know," Edmond answered. "He's only been in the employ of the Duke of Pembroke for a month and was restrained before being killed while the prince is a guest…" he huffed a sigh. "Why, is what I want to know."

"Let's figure it out, son." They looked up to see their father walking into the dining room. Dr. Watson coming in behind him.

"Doctor," Percy greeted his father-in-law with a smile and a handshake.

"Good to see you, Percy," Watson replied. Then turned to look at Edmond. "Good to see you too, Edmond. How was your trip?"

"Eventful, Doctor," Edmond stood and shook his hand. "But we have someone here for you to inspect."

"So I see, what have you discovered so far?" Watson knelt beside the body as Edmond explained what he had observed.

Holmes stood next to Percy listening. "I would agree. No longer than ten minutes with that type of wound," Watson said. "Holmes, do you have your magnifying glass?" Holmes handed it to him. "Yes, hmm," Watson said as he took a closer look at the wound.

"What do you see, Watson?" Holmes asked.

"It was a non-serrated blade, no more than six inches. Went in cleanly, very sharp."

"Any sort of defensive wounds?" Holmes asked.

"None that I can see, apart from the bruising on the wrists but it looks to be made with some sort of rope," Watson replied.

Holmes bent as soon as Watson stood, and checked the body. "What happened, Edmond?"

Edmond explained to his father what he had seen and how the man had staggered in, looking almost drunk.

"Have you investigated this hallway?" Holmes asked.

"I wanted to leave as much of it undisturbed as possible," Edmond said. "We waited for you."

"Good," Holmes said distractedly. He checked the face, hands, and chest of the body. Raising the wrist, Holmes took a sniff. "Hmm."

"What is it?" Edmond asked.

"Smell for yourself," Holmes offered. Edmond took a quick sniff.

"Hemp."

"Indeed. Hemp rope used to secure the wrists. Thick from the looks of it," Holmes said. "Also, check his pockets."

Edmond helped his father check the trouser pockets and the outer coat pocket. When they came up with nothing, Holmes looked down at the man's hand.

"Was his hand clenched when he came into the room?" Holmes asked.

Edmond thought a moment. "Yes," he answered. "Percy?"

"Yes, I believe so," he answered.

"Nothing very strange about that, Holmes. Death grip," Watson offered.

"Watson has all my teaching been for naught?" Holmes questioned.

"You think there's something inside his hand?" Percy offered.

"Something he clenched in his dying moments," Holmes said.

Rigor had not set in yet, so Holmes and Edmond easily unclenched the man's hand and found the scrap of paper he was clutching.

"What does it say?" Percy asked.

Holmes checked it and showed Edmond. "It's a torn piece of paper from a diagram plan."

"There's a bit of a word at the bottom, Dad. Did you see it?" Edmond asked.

"I did."

"Do you know what it is?"

"It looks like something beginning with N-A-S but other than that, I cannot tell," Holmes replied.

"There's also a date," Edmond went on. "Eighteen twenty-six."

Holmes and Edmond looked up to Percy and Watson who shook their heads. It meant nothing to them.

"I want to investigate this corridor. Watson, will you stay with the body?"

"Of course," Watson said.

"Capital, old fellow," Holmes thanked him.

Holmes, Edmond, and Percy opened the door and walked carefully through the long hallway. The almost immediate scent of jasmine and rosemary perfume hit Edmond's nostrils. One thing was certain, Lady Berkley had been in that corridor and recently. It was dimly lit, only a sconce every seven steps set on low gas. Every few steps, Holmes would hold up his hand stopping his sons from stepping closer, his eyes on the ground. Once, he bent to check a substance on the floor, but it was not blood.

"For such a traumatic wound, there's no blood?" Percy asked. "That does not make sense."

"Much of this does not make sense," Edmond replied. "Why a footman? What possible threat could he have been to warrant being killed."

"I would imagine he saw something he wasn't supposed to," Holmes answered. "And whatever it was, was in this room, here."

"Is that a blood smear?" Edmond questioned looking closer at the hand-like print on the door casing.

"Yes," Holmes answered. "Be on your guard."

Both Edmond and Percy nodded and after a beat, Holmes opened the door.

Chapter Twenty-Two

The empty study that greeted them gave the impression of having not been used in a long time, but there were clear signs of someone having been there recently. The dust on the desk had been disturbed, a fire had been banked, books were open on the table by the window that held no dust, and most damning of all, a chair with remnants of rope, was sitting in the middle of the room.

"This is clearly the location where the man was held," Percy said.

"Indeed," Edmond answered.

As expected, Holmes said nothing and hurried to the desk. Looking undoubtedly for the paper from which the scrap was torn, Holmes moved books and other mementos.

"Nothing," he muttered. "It's been cleaned. Clearly the captor, seeing the bird flown cleaned up after himself."

"What does it all mean, Dad?" Percy questioned. "A footman? Of all people, why?"

"That is what we need to discover, Percy," Holmes answered. After a moment, he huffed. "We'll learn no more from here, let us return."

They walked back to the door leading to the dining hall. Watson looked up. "Well?" he questioned.

Holmes said nothing as he crouched down again to observe the body. Percy walked over to Watson and explained what they found.

"I need to speak with his highness," Holmes said without preamble.

"He's in the drawing room," Edmond explained. "Cedric is with him."

"Excellent," Holmes stood and walked quickly to the door. Edmond, Percy, and Watson hurried after him.

Holmes found the butler outside the drawing room. "My name is Sherlock Holmes and I need you to go back into the dining room to guard the young footman's body," Holmes ordered.

"But sir, my station is with his grace," the butler said.

"Now," Holmes stated.

"Eh, yes sir, yes," he hurried off.

"Really, Holmes," Watson rebuffed.

"I have no time to be nice," Holmes replied and opened the door.

The guests looked up and as soon as they saw Holmes, murmurs spread through the room like wildfire. Holmes scanned the room for the prince then hurried toward him. Edmond, his brother, and Watson trailed behind. Lady Berkley sat, rather pale, beside her highness, the Duchess of York and Cornwall.

"Holmes," the prince said. "What the devil happened?"

"Sir, I must speak with you... privately," Holmes said.

"Of course," he replied then turned to their host. "Pembroke, your study?"

"At your disposal, sire," Pembroke said.

Edmond thanked Cedric for his guardianship and followed his father through to the study. Glancing back to see Lady Berkley watching him, he wondered again why her perfume had been in the hallway and where she had gone after their dance. She smiled slightly but something, *something* about her countenance worried him.

The prince turned to them as soon as they were alone and the door to the study was closed.

"What is going on, Holmes?" the prince demanded.

"Sire, does N-A-S and the year eighteen twenty-six mean anything to you?" Holmes asked without preamble.

"N-A-S? Eighteen twenty-six? No, can't say it—" he cut off.

"Your highness?" Holmes questioned.

"Could it have been Nash?" he asked.

"It could have, why?"

"John Nash was the architect who did major extension

work on Buckingham Palace in eighteen twenty-six, my grandmother talked about it," the prince said.

Percy stepped forward. "Buckingham Palace?"

"Yes," the prince replied. "Is it important?"

"Where are you staying, your highness? While you're in London?" Holmes questioned.

"St. James' at Marlborough House," he provided. "Why?"

"No reason," Holmes answered. "Thank you, your highness. I think we are finished with the upper classes. They can go."

"Father?" Percy questioned.

"Indeed, the sooner the better. I assume Pembroke or someone in the household has a list of the attendees?" Holmes asked the prince.

"I... I would assume so."

"Excellent," Holmes said. "Thank you, your highness, please return to Marlborough House."

The prince looked from one to the other then back at Edmond.

"I will see you in two days' time?"

"Indeed, sire," Edmond replied. "Could you wait to leave until I can check with your guards?"

"I will be in the drawing room with her highness."

After the prince left the room, Edmond turned to his father.

"Dad, forgive me for questioning you but what on earth? You sent them home? Why?" Edmond asked.

"Trust me, Edmond," he said. "I have a plan. You and Percy go back to your residences. Watson and I will handle the police. Where is the next ball?"

Edmond breathed deeply knowing he would get no more out of Sherlock Holmes.

"Two days hence," Edmond answered. "At the Earl of Wicklow's."

"Good, then I will see you there."

"You attend a ball, Dad?" Percy questioned.

"Is it such a wonder?" Holmes queried.

Edmond laughed. "See you soon, Dad," and pulled Percy out of the room.

"We will speak soon," Holmes' voice followed them.

"I'm not sure I like it, Edmond," Percy said.

"It's not for us to like, Percy," Edmond replied. "But there's more to this. Dad will keep us updated. He doesn't want me to ruin my reputation. This is more important."

"Clearly," Percy stated.

"Come now, brother mine," Edmond answered. "We have much to sleep on."

Percy and Edmond headed back into the drawing room. Approaching the prince, they waited with the others as the prince told Pembroke and the duke made the announcement. Edmond hurried out of the townhouse as the king's carriage rolled to a stop. The footman who travelled with them a week ago, jumped down and bowed.

"All well, Saunders?" Edmond asked.

"Yes, sir, forgive me, I didn't recognize you," he said.

"A new duty for his majesty," Edmond justified.

"I see. All is well, sir. We never left his highness' carriage out of our sight. Even when his grace's man was insistent we have something to eat. We took turns."

"Excellent, well done."

"You taught us well, sir."

"I am glad to be of service. His highness will be out shortly."

Saunders bowed and stood beside the door. Edmond headed back into the townhouse sneaking back into the drawing room.

"Sir Edmond," Lady Berkley approached him.

"My lady," Edmond bowed, seeing she was still pale but forcing a smile.

"Tell me, what happened to the footman?" she asked.

"Unfortunately, he died, my lady."

She took a deep breath. "Poor man. Is your father taking the case?"

"He is looking into it," Edmond confirmed.

She nodded but looked everywhere else but at him.

"Will I see you at the Wicklow's in two days' time?" Edmond asked.

She forced a smile. "Why, yes," she answered. "I am dear friends with the earl's daughter, Heather."

"Then perhaps you would consider... holding a dance for me?"

"Again?" she questioned. "Do you think it proper? Any

more dances and society may consider us courting."

"And if they did?" Edmond asked.

"Well, what would they say? I, a widow, and you, the most eligible bachelor this season?"

"I care not," he answered.

She smiled and for the first time since the footman stumbled through the door, it was genuine. "Then, Sir Edmond, I would be happy to accept." She offered her hand to him. "Until we meet again."

"Two days' time, my lady," he answered kissing her knuckles. "Or if I am fortunate enough to see you while riding in the park."

"I look forward to it," she said and then swept out of the room after the prince and princess.

"As do I, my lady. We have much to discuss," he whispered to the empty room.

Chapter Twenty-Three

"It truly is a beautiful day," Cedric said again for the fourteenth time since he met Edmond at the stables. He had a grin on his face and a stupid look of *everything is wonderful.* Edmond did not want to know why his brother-in-law looked like that as he was sure it had something to do with his sister.

Going for a ride around Hyde Park was expected from a gentleman of leisure and truth be told, Edmond had missed riding. As a boy, he and Percy would take their horses out for a slow jaunt at the edge of where the Mediterranean Sea met the beach. Their house stood on a plateau overlooking the beautiful waters. But on some occasions, he and Percy would ride together, sometimes speaking, other times not saying anything. Grateful he was able to keep his horse in a London boarding stables, it was a joy to be greeted like an old friend from the sable-colored animal. Although he nearly ripped his trousers when he swung up on the horse's back.

Cedric took a deep breath beside him and let it out in a happy sigh.

"All right, enough, Ced," Edmond chuckled. The baron looked over at him.

"What?"

"With the happiness and sentiment. I'm sure I will regret asking, but why are you so happy this morning?"

Cedric stared at him and eventually shrugged. "It's a beautiful day, I'm doing one of my favorite things with one of my favorite people. I suppose," he grinned and looked away. "My wife—"

"Ah," Edmond cut him off and held up his hand. "Thank you, no, my worst fear coming true. Say no more."

Cedric chuckled. "I was going to say, my wife, the love of my life, carries my child and all is right in the world."

Edmond still shook his head. "How is she?" Edmond asked.

"The doctor says she's doing very well. He says he has not seen a woman in such wonderful shape ready to have a child. It put my heart at ease more than you know."

"I am sure." Edmond thought a moment. "Mama never allowed her to wear a corset, perhaps that is why."

"Very probably. Torture devices for women and damned difficult to get them out of for us men," he teased with a wink.

"Can't say I've ever had to worry about that, Ced," Edmond answered. "My women weren't wearing one to begin with."

"Sir Edmond," a voice spoke behind him.

Instantly, his cheeks flamed. Turning, both he and Cedric bowed to the Duchess and Lady Berkley. Sitting on their horses, their playful eyes showed they had overheard the men's bawdy conversation.

"Your grace, my lady," Edmond greeted. "Forgive our rather lewd conversation.

"What conversation was that?" Lady Berkley's eyes twinkled.

Edmond cleared his throat. "May I introduce my brother-in-law, Baron Hughes."

Cedric bowed and greeted them.

"Lord Hughes," the duchess said. "My husband speaks highly of you."

"That is a very great honor, your grace," he answered.

Edmond never understood why the wife of the prince would be called *your grace* instead of *your highness* but that was the way of things in England.

"Your horse is very fine, Sir Edmond," Lady Berkley said. "A Percheron?"

"Indeed, my lady," he answered. "I have had him since my thirteenth birthday."

"Very fine," she replied. "You stable him with Gregory's, of course."

"Alas, I have utilized Simpson's since my arrival in England and have not had reason to move him."

"Simpsons is a fine boarder," her grace said.

"I have always found Amadeus well taken care of."

"Amadeus?" Lady Berkley questioned.

"Named after my favorite composer, my lady," Edmond stroked the horse's neck.

"I see, I too am partial to Mozart."

"Arabella and I were just about to take tea. Do join us."

"It would be our pleasure, your grace."

They turned their horses around and followed the ladies to the edge of the park. Once they arrived at the tearoom, an attendant bowed to the princess and took their horses.

"Arabella and I come here at least twice a week, do we not, dear?" the duchess said.

"Indeed, their clotted cream is some of the finest in the city."

"Your grace," a young handsome attendant bowed to her as she entered. "Mother will be so happy to see you," he went on. "Your usual table?"

"A four top, please," she smiled sweetly at the young man. "We have friends joining us."

"Of course," he looked to Cedric and Edmond and bowed. "Please follow me."

Before Edmond had a chance, Cedric offered the duchess his arm leaving him with Lady Berkley. Offering his arm to her, he ignored the spark that past between them as she wrapped her arm around his.

"You come here often with her grace?" Edmond asked.

"Indeed, as she said," Arabella answered. "It is a marvelous little place. I have not seen one this quaint since my time in France."

"You were in France?"

"For a time, I went to school on the continent after my parent's died," she revealed.

"I am sorry for your loss," he said.

"Oh, it's been years and I hardly knew them. But thank you, Sir Edmond. Such gallantry is sorely lacking in the gentlemen of today. But tell me, how do you know Lord Hughes?"

"He is my best friend. We met in primary school. He married my sister Rebecca four years ago."

"And they are expecting their first child?"

"They are," he answered.

"I am pleased for them. Lord Berkley and I had no children."

"I am sorry," he answered. "Did you want children?"

"In a manner," she replied. "But we were married for only a short time before he left for war. Perhaps we were not blessed because it was known he would not be coming back. And you, Sir Edmond? Do you have any children?"

Edmond hated how he had to lie about Henri, but as the adoption had not happened as yet, he felt only a twinge of guilt as he responded in the negative. "Not that I do not want them. Children are a blessing."

"They are indeed," Arabella answered as they sat at the table near the window.

"If I may be so bold, your grace," Edmond stopped her. "Might I take the chair with my back to the wall?" Glancing at Cedric, he went on. "I have a minor phobia of having my back to people." In truth, he wanted the vantage point of seeing everyone in the room to not be taken off guard.

"Oh, of course, Sir Edmond. I did not realize."

"I appreciate your understanding, your grace."

Cedric helped her sit and waited until Lady Berkley sat opposite. Once settled, the waiter arrived, bowed to the princess, and asked if she would like her usual. The duchess agreed and after a moment, Edmond ordered a pot of floral black tea he had tried at his uncle's. It was the only British tea he was able to choke down without wincing. Green tea was so much more soothing on his stomach. Even as a boy, he could not enjoy black or brown tea.

When they were alone again, the princess turned to him. "Tell me, Sir Edmond, how is the investigation going? I heard from my husband all about the unpleasantness at Pembroke's."

"Indeed, your grace," Edmond began. "The investigation is firmly in my father's hands. Have no fear."

"If anyone can discover what happened to the poor man, it is Sherlock Holmes," Arabella said. "He is a national treasure."

"Though his manner sometimes leaves things to be desired," the duchess winked. "His results speak for themselves. I know many friends at court who have utilized his skills and discretion many times."

"I can only apologize for my father's manner, your grace," Edmond said. "It is true he claims to have little time for civility. My mother is loath to let him out without her."

Those at the table chuckled and soon their tea was placed before them. A woman, with an air of authority and good grace walked over to their table, Cedric and Edmond stood.

"No please, have no fuss," she said.

"Lady Hendon," the duchess greeted. "It is wonderful to

see you again."

"And you, your grace," she bowed. "I do hope you are enjoying."

"Immensely," she answered. "Forgive me, have you met Lord Hughes and Sir Edmond?"

"Lord Hughes," she bowed. "And, yes, Sir Edmond, it is wonderful to see you again."

Edmond realized with a start she was the countess he sat beside at Sandringham house.

"My lady," he bowed over her hand. "Forgive me, I did not realize."

"Of course," she smiled. "I understand."

"Lady Hendon and I sat together at the dinner party in Sandringham, your grace. It was a wonderful evening. And I owe much to her charming conversation," Edmond explained.

"I was the one charmed. I told him had my Agnes not married a few months ago, I would be ever so happy to introduce them," she replied.

"Thankfully, sweet Agnes is partnered in a love match," Arabella answered. Edmond looked over at her to see an immediate pink tinge her cheek and she glanced away.

"Oh indeed," Lady Hendon stated. "I will not keep you, your grace. I merely wanted to check that everything met our high standards for your visit."

"Indeed, Lady Hendon. My compliments and thanks," the duchess answered.

Lady Hendon curtsied once more and with a final look at Edmond, left their table. Edmond and Cedric sat back.

"A charming lady," Cedric answered. "She has owned this

for how long, your grace?"

"Oh, going on ten years I believe, Lord Hughes," she answered as she poured clotted cream over a scone and prepared her tea.

Edmond poured a cup for himself, grateful for the sweet scent of orange peel and bergamot. Cedric spoke to the duchess, complimenting the tea and scones as Arabella leaned over to him.

"Tell me, Sir Edmond, is your father any closer to discovering what happened to the poor footman?"

Edmond looked at her. "You seem rather fascinated with that man's death, my lady."

"One does not see death very often and to be there when he was alive one moment and gone the next, does rather bring one's own mortality to the forefront of one's mind."

"It does indeed," Edmond took a sip of his tea happy with the taste. "Tell me, my lady, where did you go after our dance?"

"Pardon?"

"You left the ballroom," he went on.

"As I said, I was refreshing my toilette."

"Indeed? In the hallway?"

"I beg your pardon? What are you inferring?"

"Nothing, my lady. Merely wondering why you are lying."

"Sir Edmond, I take offense to that."

"And I take offense to someone lying to me when a man has died. The scent of your perfume was caught in the hallway where the man was stabbed. Now either you were there when you refreshed your toilette, or you had a hand in what happened to him."

"I had nothing of the sort."

"Then tell me, my lady, what were you doing there?"

She stared at him for a long moment and then looked away. "You are dangerously close to impertinence, Sir Edmond."

"And you, my lady, have crossed that line."

"How dare you," she breathed.

"Tell me the truth, my lady."

"There is no truth to tell," she replied. "I had nothing to do with his death."

"Then why lie?"

"I am not lying."

"I smelt your perfume, my lady."

"Then perhaps you need to check your nose, Sir Edmond. For I was nowhere near that study."

"Study? Who said anything about a study?"

She paled and then stood, garnering everyone's attention.

"Forgive me, your grace, I am feeling unwell. I believe I will return to St. James."

"Oh, my dear, you are quite pale. Are you all right? Was something wrong with the tea?"

"Not the tea," she shook her head.

"Very well, then, Sir Edmond would you kindly see our horses are brought?" the duchess asked.

"Of course, your grace," Edmond bowed and headed to the front of the tearoom asking the attendant to call for the horses.

Once all four arrived, Edmond assisted the duchess onto

her white mare as Cedric helped Lady Berkley.

"Thank you for such a wonderful time, gentlemen," the duchess said. "I am only so sorry it was cut short."

"Our pleasure, your grace," Cedric bowed.

"We appreciate the offer to accompany you," Edmond answered.

The duchess smiled and offered her hand to them. After they kissed it, she turned to Arabella.

"Come dear, let us get you home."

The women clicked to their horses and the beasts started at a steady pace. Edmond watched.

"What the hell happened, Ed?" Cedric questioned.

"The lady doth protest too much, methinks," Edmond quoted.

"You must have said something to her. The poor woman can hardly stay atop her mount."

Edmond looked over and, sure enough, Lady Berkley swayed on her horse precariously. Waiting a moment, his eyes roamed the horse from its flank, to the saddle, to the way of its rump. Just as he thought all looked fine, something snapped loudly enough for them to hear. Lady Berkley screeched as she tipped to the side and the horse reared back at the sudden noise and pain as she gripped the mane.

"Arabella!" the duchess screamed, trying to reach for her friend. But the horse took off, racing through the streets.

It only took Edmond a split second. He swung up on his horse with practiced ease, ignoring the sound of ripping cloth. Keeping low on Amadeus, he kicked his horse into a gallop. The black Percheron snorted and raced after the mare.

Though Lady Berkley's horse was a thoroughbred, Amadeus came from good stock and was trained since birth. He jumped over a fruit wagon, Edmond squeezed the horse's sides with his thighs, urging him to go faster. They felt as one. Horse and rider. His father had often commented how fluidly Edmond rode.

One more jump over another cart and Amadeus and Edmond were neck in neck with the mare and Arabella.

"Arabella," Edmond shouted over the noise. "Swing over to me."

He was surprised at how calm she appeared on the back of a runaway horse, but her eyes, when they locked with his, held fear. She nodded once, grabbed his outstretched hand, and jumped. He pulled her behind him and wrapped her arms around his waist.

Amadeus slowed as if he knew what was going on and snorted. The mare took her cue from him and slowed as well. Arabella clutched Edmond's waist, holding on with shaking arms. Once slow enough, Edmond grabbed the mare's reins and pulled them all to a stop.

He felt Arabella panting as she buried her face between his shoulder blades. Unable to comfort her in their current positions, he turned the horses down an alley and out to another main road. Finally arriving back at where Cedric waited with the duchess, Edmond stopped the horses.

"Oh dear lord," the duchess cried. "Arabella, are you all right?"

Arabella took a moment more buried in Edmond's back, before she pulled away and faced the duchess.

"Thanks to Sir Edmond's quick thinking," she answered.

Edmond offered his arm to her and she swung off his horse, landing on shaky legs. Cedric held her arm as she wobbled.

Edmond jumped down and patted Amadeus.

"Good boy," he whispered thanking him. The horse snorted again and nuzzled his shoulder.

"I am so very grateful for your excellent horsemanship, Sir Edmond," Lady Berkley said.

"I am glad I was there, my lady," he replied. "May I ask, what happened?"

"I am uncertain," she answered. "I have ridden her many times, but for some reason this time I could not get my seat. Then something snapped and I felt the saddle drift to one side and the reins loosened."

Edmond stepped over to the mare and inspected the saddle. What he found clenched his stomach. The girth of the saddle had been cut with a short knife and the throat lash of the reins had been sliced just enough that with any pressure the bridle would snap.

"It appears the saddle has been tampered with," Edmond revealed.

"But why?" the duchess asked. "What could come of hurting Arabella?"

Edmond said nothing for a moment as he took in the two horses. They were both white mares just over fourteen hands and they both had slight dappling on the right hind leg.

"I very much doubt it was Lady Berkley they intended to hurt, your grace."

Both Arabella and the duchess gasped as they realized what he meant.

"Cedric, will you escort the ladies back to St. James? I want to speak with the stables that housed our horses while we were at tea."

"Of course," Cedric replied.

"If you would permit me, my lady, I will take your horse with her saddle and the reins with me to speak with them. You are welcome to ride Amadeus. Cedric will stable him for me."

"If you are certain, Sir Edmond," she replied, her voice still wavering.

"I am, my lady. And if I may be so bold as to call upon you to check on you later?"

"Yes, thank you," she answered. "And thank you for saving my life. You are a skilled rider."

"I am glad I was here, my lady." He turned to his horse and scratched his nose. "Take care of Lady Berkley, Amadeus." The black horse bobbed his head and sniffed him. "Apples later," he teased. Turning back to her, he offered his hand and assisted her onto his horse's back.

Once the duchess and Cedric were seated on their horses, Edmond took the reins of the mare and watched them leave. Turning toward the tearoom, he ignored the looks of others, and some applause he received for saving Arabella. As he guided the horse around behind the stables, he paused for a moment and pulled the saddle off, curious about the first part of Lady Berkley's story. His eyes caught something under the saddle and his blood ran cold. A book between the horse's back and the saddle. The title and author clear. *Guy Fawkes* by William Harrison Ainsworth.

Chapter Twenty-Four

Edmond stared at his uncle, father, and brother beyond frustrated. "A man has died," he said again. "Lady Berkley's saddle was tampered with. How do you expect me to go to dinner and flirt when there is so much more I could be doing? And besides the prince isn't even going to be there."

"It is part of the act you must portray, Ed," Percy replied. "And it's one day, a few hours at that. You need to do this."

"This is beyond asinine," Edmond answered. "The duchess was the intended target, that book proves it. There is more to this than any of us realize. We are all needed here to strategize our next move." Looking between them, he knew he would get no sympathy. Huffing a sigh, he sat in the chair that had become his favorite over the past few days in his new set of rooms. "Fine," he continued. "But I have an hour or so before I am needed to leave. What have you discovered?"

"The police arrived after everyone left," Holmes began. "Bradstreet was the one in charge, so thank heavens we have someone with a little brains from Scotland Yard. He took the body and we searched the room. Nothing else apart from what we discovered. Watson and I spoke to the servants. Apparently, Bright was gregarious, and well liked but no one knew he was missing for the apparent hour he was tied up nor why he would be in the former master's study. No one saw him speaking with anyone they did not know. It was rumored he was entertaining and older woman. A titled woman who was close to the prince."

"An affair?" Edmond questioned. A sour feeling churning in his belly. If Lady Berkley and Nicolas Bright the footman were having an affair, it was a perfect reason why she was hesitant to mention it to him.

"Apparently, now, whether there is truth to it, no one knows. But he was seen with furtive notes and had snuck out after hours but could give no good answer as to where he had been. He was also secretive apparently, giving the same answer to questions about his past."

Mycroft said nothing and Edmond watched him. "Uncle? Any information you may have would help. Did he work for the Home Office?"

Mycroft looked over at him, his face a cool mask of indifference. "Poor lad, one is always sorry when one so young dies. But of course, I'll make inquiries. He didn't work for me."

"So, we have no information about the structural plan? No

further information about who killed him?" Percy asked.

"None, yet," Holmes answered. "But we have the where and the how. I am going back to Pembroke to question a few more servants. Bradstreet has asked for my assistance."

"Will you keep me updated?" Edmond asked.

"Of course," Holmes agreed. "Tomorrow night you have another ball?"

"Yes, at the Earl of Wicklow's," Edmond answered. "Then Bolingbrook Wednesday."

"It might be prudent to have you visit the prince for dinner the two days there is not a ball. To keep an eye on him and the duchess. If what you believe is true, she could be used to get to the prince."

"I will, of course," Edmond agreed.

"As far as Bolingbrook, we all will be attending, I think," Holmes said.

"All?" Edmond questioned, looking at his uncle.

"Oh no, not me, my lad," Mycroft chuckled. "You know I have no taste for those things. But it sounds like the king might make an appearance."

"Wonderful," Edmond replied sardonically. "Will he have some royal guards? Does he know not to mention Henri?"

"He will and he does," Mycroft answered.

"If it comes down to it, Edmond," Holmes started. "You are to protect the prince. Your uncle and I will watch the king."

"I will make sure the king has his guards," Mycroft agreed. "And his secretary will be there."

"Oh, that makes me feel so much better," Edmond replied

sarcastically.

"I'm sensing some animosity, brother," Percy answered cheerfully.

"His secretary is half my size, Percy, and scared of anything that moves. The king will not be protected."

"Are you sure that's all?" Percy questioned.

"I see no point in reiterating how I feel. I'm wasting time flirting and going to tea and dinners when I could gather my chosen men, Yancy, Jakob, Kirkpatrick, any of them and we could protect the king and the prince. But I have no time," Edmond replied. Then, taking a deep breath, he closed his eyes for a moment. "Forgive me," he said calmer as he opened his eyes. "I do not know what has happened to me. I am not this emotional nor am I usually this frustrated. I apologize."

"No apology needed. It's good to see you're human. Even I have had the occasionally slip, Edmond," Holmes said. "And I agree, if you trust those men, bring them. Talk to them Sunday."

Edmond looked over at Mycroft who nodded.

"Good, that makes me feel better."

There was a knock at the door, and everyone turned to see Terrey standing there.

"Yes, what is it, Terrey?" Edmond questioned, remembering at the last moment he was in his apartments in Piccadilly and there could be eyes and ears everywhere.

"Forgive me, sirs," he bowed slightly. "But it is time to get Sir Edmond ready for his tea engagement."

His momentary meditation helped prevent the response he wanted to give. But soon, he found himself dressed and bundled into a carriage heading for his tea engagement. From the moment he entered the house of Lady Pike and her daughter,

Edmond wanted to leave. It wasn't that Lady Georgina was uninteresting. She was demure, but the conversation was stilted, and as he had seen her furtive glances to one of the footmen attending the ball the night before. Clearly the bookish lady was hiding a scandalous nature and she was not interested in him. Still, he gave it his best, but he was glad when it was done.

Kissing both ladies' hands, he thanked them for a charming afternoon and let them know of a dinner party he was planning at his townhouse in Piccadilly for the end of the following week, his one day free of obligations. His invitation was readily accepted by Lady Pike and he made a note to himself to tell Terrey. He hadn't the first idea how to plan a dinner party, nor why he had said it, but it was said, and he couldn't back out.

As soon as he returned to his lodgings, Terrey hurried him up the stairs to bathe, change, and prepare for the dinner at Lady Biddlesbe's. Mentioning the idea of a dinner party to him, Edmond watched Terrey's brows shoot up in surprise. But with a promise he would handle most of it, Terrey turned Edmond to the mirror. Once again, everything a whirlwind, Edmond turned when he was told, stayed still when he was asked, and allowed Terrey's critical eye to rove over him. Finally, he was again bundled into a carriage and set off for Arlington Street.

That evening after dinner with Lord and Lady Biddlesbe and their daughter Elizabeth, he dragged himself up the stairs to his bedroom. Terrey was there, up as late as he was, ready to help him undress and get ready for bed.

"I don't know how they do it, Terrey," Edmond said as he let his valet help him out of his dinner coat, waistcoat, tie, and shirt.

"Do what, sir?" Terrey asked.

"I don't know how anyone is able to go to tea and dinner and flirt with young women who want nothing to do with them.

It's difficult enough for me to talk to my own family."

"Well, sir, that sort of talk is different than the mindless chatter at tea and dinner. Your family knows you. Anything you say, they scrutinize to see if there's something deeper there. You can have a look and they know something is wrong. It is a family's prerogative."

"Do you miss your family?" Edmond asked.

"We were never very close, sir," Terrey answered. "But I do miss my father and my mother writes to me. My brothers, well, not so much," he chuckled. "But there are family members who are not blood. And I don't like seeing what this is doing to them."

Edmond looked over at him as he hung up his waistcoat. "What what is doing to whom?"

"What this case is doing to you, Edmond," Terrey replied turning back. "You said you look at me as a brother, the feeling is entirely mutual, though it shouldn't be, considering I am your servant. I see what this is doing to you and I don't like it. You're not yourself. You have changed."

Edmond sighed. His eyes drifting to the drawing Henri had given him. He kept it by his bedside to remind him who he was every night and every morning.

"Have I ever told you why I am the way I am?" Edmond asked.

"Besides your training in China?" he questioned.

"Yes, besides that."

"No," Terrey said.

Edmond nodded slowly. "Pour us a drink, Ter, and come sit with me." Edmond sat in one of the wingback chairs by the fireplace. Terrey did as he asked. "One of the reasons I never sought the limelight is because of my training in the Orient, but the other is… Nothing said here can ever be repeated."

"My word, sir," Terrey replied.

"Thank you," Edmond nodded and took a drink. "Percy, at a young age chose his path. He knew he wanted to dress a certain way, act a certain way. He took the fact our name was hidden to carve out his own. When we lived in France, we were not able to use the name *Holmes*. My grandfather was constantly looking for us and dad decided that we would be hidden. Percy took piano, politics, and fashion as his escape. He knew he wanted to be a concert pianist simply because he could. He had no ambition to actually make a living off it. He used fashion to be noticed. I was in his shadow. Always. And I was fine with that choice. But it also meant I did not know how to express my own individuality. Men have very few ways in which to showcase themselves.

"Percy was always the flagship. He was always the one comfortable in situations that I never understood how to navigate. It was only when father and mother took us to a fairground and I saw how two men, Chinese, fought. It was a demonstration of the martial arts. I was fascinated. My father noticed it and taught me what he knew; bartitsu. Then I asked to go to the Orient. While there I was at home. I felt happy and knew what I wanted. But even there, I was an outsider. I was able to blend in and not be noticed while Percy was out there. He was the face of the new Holmes family. And I was perfectly happy with that. Now, I am still an outsider because I know nothing about this life. This way of being. The warship has now become the flagship and I don't know what to do."

"May I speak out of turn?" Terrey asked.

"Of course, always, you know that."

"That is shite," Terrey replied. Edmond looked at him surprised. "Edmond, you have just as much to offer, to showcase, and to be proud of as any Holmes family member. In fact, more.

You have a soul within you that understands all people. Understands how they think, act, their desires, their subconscious. You do not exploit it for your own gain. You abide by the law. You uphold the law. And you are never recognized by society because you don't want it or need it. You are affirmed in your life, by you yourself. You don't need anyone's permission, anyone's appreciation. You know who you are beyond a shadow of a doubt. And that is something not everyone can say they know. You are a warship, but you have every right to be seen, heard, and honestly, feared. No one fears Sir Charles. No one thinks more of him than he thinks of himself. But Edmond, I have seen how people look at you.

"All over the world, they see you, whether you know it or not. You have been the name and face of the Holmes' family because you are just like your father. Honorable, intelligent, trustworthy, loyal, and honestly, the best damn friend I have ever had. So, your idea of not being seen? Of hiding? It's bollocks. Now, you have a chance to not only show the world with it is to be a Holmes, but what it is to be *Edmond* Holmes. And no one can change who and what you are. You know why the warship hides behind the flagship? It's so the other ships don't see the most valuable player in the fight. But make no mistake, when they see it, the flagship? Means nothing. You are the queen on the chess board, you are the trump card, you are the one everyone needs and is damn glad to have."

Edmond was silent for a long moment and Terrey finished his drink.

"Now, you are exhausted, and have a very long day tomorrow," he stood and gathered Edmond's soiled clothing. "Sleep well, Sir Edmond."

With that, Terrey left the room leaving Edmond to mull over his words.

Chapter Twenty-Five

That next morning, Edmond woke with sunlight streaming across his face. Taking a deep breath, the smells of lavender surrounded him from the oil lamp he used the night before. After their conversation, Edmond needed a little help dulling his mind and lavender was a godsend for him. A sharp knock on a door stirred him even more.

"*Entre,*" he called. Terrey opened the dressing room door and bowed.

"Sir, I have your clothing ready. Would you like a bath and

a shave?" Terrey asked.

"A shave, but I will hold the bath until before the ball tonight," Edmond replied removing the sheets and standing. He had pulled on his *changshan* after Terrey had left the night before. Peeling it off, he pulled on his trousers Terrey had brought with him and sat in the shaving chair without shirt. It was freeing to be in nothing but his skin from waist up. The idea of having to wear tight clothing again... well, he mentally shook his head, he understood why women disliked corsets so much.

Terrey went about lathering up the shaving cream as Edmond let the warm towel around his face lull him into a sense of serenity. Once Terrey began brushing the cream on his face, Edmond looked up at him.

"Thank you," Edmond said.

"For what, sir?"

"For your words last night," Edmond explained. "They meant far more than you know."

"I meant every single one," he stated. Terrey paused a moment and smiled down at him. "Besides, the image of you as a mermaid figurehead on a warship was very disturbing."

Edmond laughed harder than he for the past few months. "Oh, Terrey there are times I wonder about you."

"I am nothing if not unpredictable, sir," he threw his own words back at him with a grin.

Edmond chuckled but the smile that grew was one of affection. "I am glad you are here, Terrey. I haven't thanked you for all you do."

"I would say it was my job, sir, but that would imply I don't like it," Terrey winked.

"Still," Edmond said. "Thank you."

"You're welcome," he answered. "Now stop talking so I don't cut you."

Again, Edmond chuckled, feeling lighter than he had in a long time. After the shave, Terrey helped him into his waistcoat and morning coat and pronounced him ready. A quick breakfast and he was out the door to meet his uncle, father, brother, and his chosen men at the Diogenes Club for a quick meeting about the needed security for Bolingbrook's ball in a few days. Terrey promised to lay out his clothes and Mr. Yardley would assist him in dressing as Terrey was needed at the Earl's house to help prepare for the ball. The letter of engagement he had written worked and Terrey was lined up for the next few balls as footman.

He let Edmond know Cook had been informed of the upcoming dinner party and Mr. Yardley would need to speak with him about hiring temporary staff for that evening. There were some decisions Edmond would need to make and Terrey promised to be there when Rachel asked him about colors and place setting. He would guide him as best he could without compromising his image. With that, Edmond sat in the hired cab, heading to his uncle's club.

Reaching the Diogenes, Edmond signed in and headed to the Stranger's Room where his party waited. Opening the door, he quickly scanned the room seeing his father, uncle, brother, Yancy and Jakob along with Fitzpatrick, a great beast of a Scotsman who was a master boxer and Edmond's favorite sparring partner as they were well matched in strength. Greeting the men with a firm handshake, he thanked them for coming.

"We have very little time to go over everything," Holmes said greeting his son with a nod.

"But I must say, you look very sharp, Ed," Percy stated.

"Thank you, Perce," he answered.

"You look like a toff," Fitzpatrick stated good naturedly, his strong Scottish brogue coming through.

Edmond chuckled. "Then thank the good lord it was me chosen for this instead of you, Fitz."

"Och aye, they'd never get me into that," he grinned. Yancy and Jakob nodded in agreement.

"You speak too soon. You will be wearing something very similar on the night in question," Edmond replied.

"Oh no, I don't think so," Fitzpatrick answered.

"Yes, actually. Here's the plan," Edmond sat and leaned forward.

Chapter Twenty-Six

Edmond returned to his townhouse after the Earl of Wicklow's dinner party. Fortunately, the entire evening went off without incident. Being the talk of the town and the party, Edmond fended off as many ladies as he could. Apparently, word had gotten around of his daring adventures and heroic actions saving Lady Berkley from the wild horse. Happy to conveniently ignore most of the praise, Edmond was toasted as the guest of honor and seated beside the prince across from the earl. Once the dinner was finished, and the women excused themselves for sherry and gossip in the drawing room, the men were alone to enjoy brandy and cigars. Edmond was grateful none of the men mentioned the issue. Saying goodbye to the prince as he gathered the duchess and Lady Berkley, Edmond helped them into the carriage.

"Thank you, Sir Edmond," Lady Berkley squeezed his hand and locked eyes with him.

"You are more than welcome, my lady," he answered. For assisting her into the carriage or saving her from the horse, he wasn't sure, but he knew he would always be happy to receive her appreciation.

As he trotted down the stairs of his rooms at Piccadilly that next morning, he entered the breakfast room and greeted Yardley who stood ready to assist him. Pouring some tea and adding food to his plate, he sat and opened the newspaper placed at his setting.

"How are plans for the dinner coming, Yardley?" he asked absently.

"Very well, sir," he answered. "Cook would like your approval on the menu and I have several footmen hired for the evening."

"Thank you for putting this together so quickly. I know I sprung it on you all."

"Our pleasure, sir," he answered. "I know my wife is anxious for your approval on the place settings."

"I would be happy to take a look. Shall we say in ten minutes?"

"Indeed, sir," he replied. "I shall let her know to procure samples. If you would excuse me, Sir Edmond."

Edmond waved for him to do as he needed and sat reading the paper. When he turned the page, his face surprised him. A story of his daring rescue had made the morning paper. He skimmed the story, glad to see they did not inflate the truth. He had finished his breakfast and first cup of tea when a knock came from the door.

"Come," he called.

Terrey entered with a bow. "Excuse me, sir, but Mr. Yardley said you would be available to speak with Mrs. Yardley regarding the place settings."

"Indeed, is she ready?"

"Yes, sir," he answered and stepped aside. Edmond's stomach twisted; he did not know anything about place settings.

Rachel walked in with a quick curtsey and set the basket down. She pulled out two napkins and two settings of plates and utensils. Edmond stood when she finished and walked over to her.

"These are the options available here, Sir Edmond," she explained. "The napkins are eggshell and ivory. The plates are Limoge Rose or Limoge Haviland. The utensils are silver or gold."

Edmond looked at the place setting. The napkins looked exactly the same shade to him. The plates were different, but he did not like either. He keenly felt Terrey's eyes on him and was grateful.

"I prefer the Haviland and the gold utensils would look well."

"Indeed, sir, an excellent choice," Terrey praised. Edmond breathed easier.

"And for the napkins, Sir?" Rachel asked.

"The... ivory?"

"A bold choice, sir," Terrey replied. "It is nice to see though most would have chosen eggshell, it is refreshing." Terrey stressed.

"Well," Edmond paused understanding. "Now that I look at it more, I do like the eggshell better."

"That is an excellent choice, sir," Terrey said.

"Then eggshell it shall be," Edmond replied. "Any other choices, Mrs. Yardley?"

"No, sir, I will be sure to have the plates and utensils polished and the napkins pressed." She bowed and left the room.

Edmond turned to his valet. "Eggshell or ivory? Come now, Ter, there's no difference in shade."

"There is a difference to those who care, sir," he teased. "And ivory is a *faux pas.*"

"I am glad you were here to help me. Did I do well with the others?"

"Indeed, a good choice."

"I have an engagement with Lady Penelope to walk along the promenade. Am I dressed appropriately?"

"You are indeed, sir," Terrey's eye passed over him and he nodded. "Do not forget the invitations will need to be sent today."

"Have them ready for me."

With that, Edmond left the townhouse and hurried to make his appointment with one of the debutants.

The rest of the week flew by as Edmond went dinner after dinner. Fortunately, by the end of the week, his townhouse at Piccadilly had been transformed, ready for the dinner he was hosting. All but three families had indicated they would attend.

As Edmond stood in his rooms, watching as Terrey brushed his coat to relieve the wrinkles, he took a deep breath. He wasn't sure why he was nervous but part of him wanted to run away.

Terrey went to his oriental box and retrieved his cufflinks. The diamond surrounded by sapphires were his least favorite as they were the most expensive and gauche but for the dinner party he was hosting, it was needed. He also noted how his signet ring glistened in the lights. Terrey had scrubbed it to gleam.

"Ready, sir?" Terrey questioned.

"Do I look it?"

"Indeed, if I do say so myself," he smiled. "All will be well. I will be below stairs directing."

"You do not serve above stairs?"

"No, sir, I am a valet, not a footman. It is not done."

"I would have you dine with us if I could."

"I know, sir, and I appreciate it," Terrey took one last look at him and nodded.

Edmond headed down the stairs and out to the main foyer. Mr. Yardley stood ready to open the door and announce the guests. Taking a glass of champagne from the passing staff member, he thanked him and drank it down. His nerves eased as his family was announced.

Greeting his mother, sister, brother-in-law, brother, sister-in-law, and father as they came in, he felt at home.

"My goodness, *mon cher,* this is beautiful," his mother said.

"I am glad it passes muster, mama," he replied. "Can I get you something to drink?"

"A champagne, I think," she answered. "Thank you, love."

More guests began arriving and soon his townhouse was filled with music from the string quartet he had hired. As he watched the guests revel in the passed food and drinks as they waited for dinner, a sort of peace filled him.

The prince walked up to him and slapped him on the back. "For someone not born into this life, Holmes, this is extraordinary."

"My thanks, sire," he answered.

"I also want to thank you for saving my wife's life."

The sudden change of subject surprised him. "Anyone would do the same, sire."

"Still, my thanks. Lady Berkley sung your praises."

"Will she be here?"

"Alas no, the duchess begs you to forgive her, she had a headache and Lady Berkley was loath to leave her."

Disappointment swirled in his belly, but he merely nodded and thanked the prince as other guests drew his attention. The evening continued without incident and for a moment, Edmond allowed the peace to lull him into a false sense of security. All too soon, the fallacy was broken.

Chapter Twenty-Seven

Percy and Edmond stood together in the ballroom of the Earl of Bolingbroke's home, a glass of wine in their hand. The ballroom swarming with people. The doors open allowing a breeze. His brother spoke low but loudly enough for Edmond to hear.

"You are doing fantastic, Edmond," Percy said. "I wanted you to know that."

"Thank you, Percy, I appreciate that," he answered.

"The dinner was exquisite. And how you were able to

speak with everyone is fascinating. There's a weight lifted from you. I don't know what it is," Percy stated. "But I am happy to see it."

"There is," Edmond agreed. "And I thank you. This may have started out as something I did not wish to do, but I will say, I enjoy it."

"That is something I never thought I'd hear you say," Percy teased. "Can one ask if this newfound optimism is in relation to anyone in particular?"

"Terrey helped me see somethings. He has great insight."

"Terrey?" Percy questioned. "Well, not exactly the person, nor gender I was expecting."

Edmond chuckled. "In truth, my head has been turned by someone."

"Oh indeed? Do tell."

"Not yet," Edmond answered. "Soon, I promise you."

"Sir Charles, Sir Edmond," a man's voice came from behind them. When Percy's acquaintance, Lord Beaumont, brother to Lady Grace walked over to them. They bowed.

"Lord Beaumont," they said.

"Dash good to see you," he replied. "My sister sung your praises the other night, Sir Edmond. Said you were quite the gentleman. I thank you."

"Lady Grace lives up well to her name, my lord. She excels in grace and beauty."

"Yes, demme that is why I am so surprised she has not caught anyone's eye. I am eager to have her married. Since my father died, it has been dashed awkward caring for her."

"I am sure her ladyship will soon turn heads. She has much

231

to offer. From my brief visit with her, she is an accomplished young lady," Edmond replied.

"Yes, and her dowry of twenty thousand should be enough to turn any head, if not for her beauty but for her money. I don't intend for her to become an old maid."

"She has far yet to go before she could be considered that, my lord," Percy said.

"To tell the truth, I believe she was enamored with an old school chum of mine but since his father lost all his money, I've seen neither head nor hide of him. Grace doesn't seem to understand, we cannot mix with that sort," Lord Beaumont said.

"And what sort would that be?" Edmond questioned.

"The disgraced." The way his lordship said the word made it sound more like the *filthy unwashed.* But before he could speak more, the lady in question arrived at her brother's side.

"Lady Grace," Edmond bowed. "A pleasure to see you again, I am only so sorry our dinner was cut short the other night. But I was pleased you and your aunt accepted my dinner invitation."

"Sir Edmond, thank you. And your dinner party was magnificent. I was quite impressed. Your heroism in helping that poor man is commendable. What did happen to him?" she asked.

"He died unfortunately, my lady," Edmond replied.

"Oh, dear," Lady Grace flushed with mortification. "I am sure you did all you could to help him."

"I tried my best, my lady," Edmond stated.

"Yes indeed, of course it is terrible when anyone passes but to be there and see it," she shook her head. "I shall pray for him."

"I hope you were not sorely disturbed my lady."

"No, no, indeed. I thank you, Sir Edmond. I—" she cut off, her eyes growing wide as she had glanced to her left.

"Lady Grace?" Edmond questioned. She snapped her eyes back to him.

"Forgive me," she said, glancing back to what had held her attention. Edmond casually looked around but the only thing he saw was Terrey standing stoically to one side. "I thought I saw someone I knew."

Her blush increased and flushed her chest and cheeks.

"Would you perhaps do me the honor of a dance, my lady?" Edmond asked. "I am particularly fond of this orchestral arrangement."

"I would be honored, thank you," she replied. Lord Beaumont looked pleased with himself but, as Edmond led her to the dance floor, he could sense the hesitation in her body.

They danced once together until the herald drew everyone's attention. "His Royal Highness, Prince George and Her Royal Highness, the Duchess of Cornwall and York."

The music stopped as everyone turned and bowed as the prince and duchess entered the room. Lady Grace curtsied prettily beside him, but her eyes kept drifting over to the same location that had held her rapt attention.

Curious, Edmond looked over again, but that time he caught Terrey looking at him a stunned look on his face. Then, Edmond realized, Terrey wasn't looking at *him* at all. In fact, his eyes were solely focused on Lady Grace as Lady Grace's were fixed on Terrey's.

Before he could think any more on it, Edmond heard the herald proclaim, "the Marchioness of Berkley."

Edmond watched as she glided into the room and took her place in line to greet the hosts. Her unadorned red gown was exquisite, and her chocolate-colored hair was piled on her head in a manner that was both practical and elegant. Her gaze landed on Edmond and she bowed her head in acknowledgement, but her eyes held a different sort of amusement and it caused a shiver to race down Edmond's spine. He remembered their heated banter at the tearoom followed by her flirtation at dinner. She heated his blood while simultaneously drawing his ire. But the very male part of him wanted to kiss that smirk and make her groan his name. He shook his head. That was very unlike him.

"Sir Edmond, would you find it an imposition to take me back to the side? I find I am… overheated and in need of something to drink," Lady Grace asked, but her eyes were filling quickly with tears.

"Of course, my dear lady. I would be happy to fetch you something to drink. Are you well? Should I call for your brother?"

"No!" She cried then looked away. "No, I thank you. Just a drink."

Edmond agreed and walked her over to a seat by one of the open doorways leading outside, with some fresh air flowing.

"Stay here a moment, I will return." Edmond hurried through the throngs of people to the refreshments. Percy caught up with him.

"Dear lord, she is beautiful, Ed," Percy breathed. Edmond turned to see his brother watching Lady Berkley. "I didn't get a good look at her the other night."

"She's… intriguing me," Edmond admitted.

"Indeed, fascinating woman," Percy replied. "But how was your dance with Lady Grace? She seems a remarkable woman as well. This being the, what? Fourth time you've stood up with her?

Chins will start to wag."

"She is lovely, but it is clear her eye will not be turned by anyone as her heart is already someone else's," Edmond said.

"Indeed?" Percy questioned. Then looked around the room. "Whose?"

Edmond looked at him, then walked over to Terrey still standing at the same place by the wall, a tray of champagne in his hand.

"You there," he called to him. Terrey looked up and immediately bowed. "There is a young woman by the door over there who is overheated. Take this to her, would you?"

Terrey looked at him a moment, confused but when Edmond changed his expression to one of urging, Terrey took the glass of punch and headed to the door. Edmond watched him go, desperate to see if they were looking at each other from across the room for a reason. His view was obstructed, and his attention went back to the prince.

Soon, the herald announced another important guest. "Your Grace, my lords, ladies, and gentlemen, their majesties; King Edward the seventh and Queen Alexandra."

Everything stopped as everyone turned and bowed low when the king and queen entered the room. It had been only two weeks or so since Edmond had seen the king and yet it seemed like just yesterday. Yancy and Jakob stood as silent sentries on opposite sides of the room and Fitzpatrick stood at the entrance to the garden, opposite the main door. Glad to see them at attention watching the king with a following eye, Edmond relaxed just slightly. His mission was the prince. The others would watch the king.

In order to maintain his identity, Edmond danced with three more ladies and accepted an invitation to dinner from another two. Keeping his eyes on the prince when he could, he caught movement out of the corner of his eye. Lady Berkley walked over to him and he bowed low.

"My lady," he said.

"Sir Edmond," she replied. "I was hoping you would make good on your promise of another dance this evening."

"But of course," he answered. "It would be my pleasure."

"Mine as well," she smiled and offered her hand. He took it and they headed to the dance floor.

They danced in silence for a moment before Lady Berkley began. "Sir Edmond, I wanted to apologize for my uncharacteristic display the other evening. I was merely wanting to assist you and did not realize the young man was dead."

"There is nothing to apologize for."

"There is, it made you suspicious of me and that simply will not do," she answered. "The truth is... I was merely wanting to see you and your brother solving a crime. I am a true fan of your father's work and thought it would be fascinating to watch you both use his methods."

"I understand, my lady and I hope my question did not embarrass you. We were merely trying to establish where everyone was."

"Of course, and no it did not embarrass me. But I thank you for your candor."

"Then perhaps you would grant me another impertinent question."

"Indeed?"

"Were you and Nicolas Bright lovers?"

She stared at him, then her tinkling laugh reached his ears.

"Is that what you truly think?"

"Not me, my lady," he said. "It was a rumor."

"A rumor? No, Sir Edmond, the young footman and I were not lovers."

"What was the nature of your relationship?"

"There was no relationship." Then she changed the subject. "Perhaps, Sir Edmond, you would escort me into dinner?"

"I... ehm," Edmond started.

"For I found watching you sitting with Lady Grace to be very distracting. I am not a jealous woman, Sir Edmond but I could not bear seeing you flirt with her, not when I wanted you to flirt with me."

Edmond swallowed audibly. "My lady," he began. "You have nothing to worry about. For sitting with Lady Grace was a task done to be kind. She is a sweet young lady, but I had little in common with her and the conversation was stilted. My one saving grace was to have you sitting across from me."

"You hardly looked at me."

"One cannot look into the sun often and not be blinded, my lady."

She stared at him for a long moment then smiled. Waiting until they were finished with the dance, she did not drop his hand when he escorted her back to stand at the side of the room. Instead, she kept his hand in hers, pulled him toward a doorway, down a long dimly lit corridor, and into another room. A fire roared in the fireplace. She locked the door and, in an instant, cupped his face, pulled him to her, and pressed her lips to his.

Chapter Twenty-Eight

Edmond's shock wore off quickly as he felt her melt into him. Pushing her gently to lean against the doorway, he slanted his lips over hers. The soft sound she made, spurred him on. Their bodies were pressed tightly together as she thrust her fingers through his hair, holding his mouth in place. Holding her to him, one hand on her waist, another behind her neck, Edmond let the passion that had built inside him since he first saw her, loose. Never had a kiss tasted so sweet. Never had he not wanted to break apart even for air. It could have gone on for hours and he wouldn't have known. Just the feel of her lips on his, her soft body pressed against his, was nearly too much.

Finally, his mind cleared enough, and he pulled back just a hairsbreadth away from her. Her glassy eyes opened and gazed up at him. Their labored breathing mixed with each other's. The pink tinge to her cheeks and how her lips were swollen red from the brute strength of his kisses, made something inherently male puff out its chest within him.

"I knew," she said breathlessly. "I knew your kiss would be the best I ever had. I was not proven wrong."

"My lady," he breathed.

"Arabella," she replied. "Call me Arabella."

"Arabella," he answered. She grinned and kissed him lightly once more. A gentle push on his chest had him pulling back.

She unlocked the door and left without another word. Edmond stood there, the heat of the fire on his back, and the lessening heat of her body at his front. Taking a deep breath, he closed his eyes. Never had he experienced anything as all-consuming as her kiss. Even the other times he had kissed or been kissed paled in comparison to what she was like. One more deep breath and he walked out of the room to find his way back to the ball room.

Before he found the main door, something sounded to his right. Looking into the shadows of another corridor, he could see little but then, he heard it again. Someone's cough.

"Hello?" he questioned.

"Help, me," someone whispered. Edmond walked down the unlit hallway, the light from the flickering gas lamps in the main corridor, the only light.

"Where are you?" he called into the darkness.

"Please."

Then, he felt someone reach out and grab hold of his ankle. Bending, his eyes adjusted to the dimness to see the man on the floor, pale and sweating. But he recognized him.

"Brown?" he questioned the king's secretary. "Dear god, what happened to you?"

"I didn't think you knew my name," he panted.

"Are you injured?"

"Someone..." he tried to get out, then coughed again. "Someone stabbed me."

"Where? Where are you injured?"

"My side," he answered.

"Edmond?" he heard Percy call from the door of the main corridor.

"Percy!" he shouted. "Bring a light!"

His brother rushed down the hall and Edmond saw the torch he had taken from the wall.

"Edmond?" he raced to him. "What happened?"

"I'm not sure. This is Brown, he's his majesty's secretary and valet," Edmond explained. "He's been injured."

"Someone, in the darkness. I heard them in the study," he weakly moved his hand to the door behind Edmond. "I went in, but they doused the light and then I felt a sort of pain in my side. Oh, god, I'm going to die."

"Don't be so dramatic," Edmond told the mousey man as he examined his bleeding side. "Looks to have missed anything vital but we need to stop the bleeding. Percy, find Terrey, he'll know what to do."

"Of course," Percy stood and started back down the

corridor.

"And Percy," Edmond shouted. Percy turned. "Protect the prince. Tell Yancy and Jakob to watch the king."

"I will." Then, he was gone, swallowed up by the darkness.

"I knew you were still working for the king. I'm glad he has someone like you watching him," Brown stated.

Edmond said nothing in response to that, instead he tried to keep him alert.

"You didn't see anything, Brown?" Edmond asked as he untied the man's neckcloth and pulled out his handkerchief. Pressing both to the wound, he kept pressure on it. Brown buckled in pain.

"Nothing," he said through clenched teeth. "All I heard was rustling and then a shadow."

"What sort of build? Man or woman? A scent?"

Brown shook his head, and his eyes began to close. "No, stay awake. Eyes open."

Brown tried but Edmond did not like how the blood coated his hands.

"Are you a bleeder? Brown, keep your eyes open. Are you a bleeder?"

"Don't know. Never cut myself before."

"Sir?" he heard Terrey's voice from the door.

"Down here, Terrey. Hurry," Edmond called.

Terrey's hurried footsteps echoed. "Are you all right, sir? Oh, dear god, Brown."

"We need to stop the bleeding," Edmond said.

"Of course," Terrey replied and took over for Edmond. "Lie back, Brown. Let's get you straight." Seeing Terrey had everything well in hand, Edmond took in the area around him. They were in a one of the oldest parts of the house. Stone lined the walls a nod to the medieval origins. Brown lay at the base of circular stone stair leading up but not further down. Edmond found the door Brown had indicated and tried the handle. It was unlocked. Stepping into the room, Edmond took a deep breath but could smell nothing. Brown was right, whoever was in the room and attacked him, hadn't worn any cologne or perfume. Edmond walked over to the desk and looked at the papers on top. The contents seemed undisturbed except for one piece of parchment, old as the edges appeared worn and the ink faded. There was little he could read but what he could make out turned his blood cold.

"*Anno Domini nostri Jesu Christi, one thousand six hundred five, my lord, out of the love I have for some of your friends, I want to make sure you are safe... do not attend this sitting of Parliament...*" Edmond stopped reading to glance at the signature line. *Francis Tresham.* "Oh, *mon dieu,*" Edmond breathed.

"Edmond?" Holmes' voice came from the hallway.

"In here," he answered. Holmes appeared in the doorway.

"Terrey has been successful in stopping the bleeding. I brought a couple of the footmen with me. They're getting him to a room where he can lie down. Brown will be all right."

"Thank god," Edmond replied but noticed his hand was shaking.

"What is it?" Holmes questioned. "You look pale."

"Look," he offered the letter to his father. "Brown said he heard someone in this room and when he went to look, the person extinguished the lamp and attacked him. But look what was the only piece that was disturbed on this desk.

Holmes read over the letter and when he saw the name, he looked over at his son. "Francis Tresham."

"Partner to Guy Fawkes. Part of the Gunpowder Plot to assassinate King James the First."

"That's who I thought it was," Holmes answered.

"Why would Bolingbroke have a letter from an executed traitor?" Edmond questioned.

"I am not certain," Holmes admitted. "But it obviously has something to do with the notes found, the sliced saddle, and the book."

"Are they trying to assassinate the king?"

"It's possible," Holmes said. "Put it back where you found it, and let's go speak with him. Dinner has begun."

Edmond nodded, his mind too distracted to remember his promise to escort Lady Berkley. When they reached the dining hall, Holmes leaned over to the butler and asked him to tell the king they needed to speak with him urgently. As impolite as it was to request the king to leave during dinner, it was also a matter of life and death. The butler whispered in Bolingbrook's ear who leaned over to the king. Edward turned to look at them. Seeing their stoic faces, he nodded. When he stood, everyone at the table scurried to stand in respect.

"No no, please, I won't be a moment, as you were," the king motioned for them to sit. Edmond's eyes caught Lady Berkley's and the slight concerned frown that pressed between her eyebrows made him nod to her.

Suddenly realizing he was supposed to escort her, he was grateful to see Cedric seated beside her. Remembering their kiss and how she smelled sweetly of jasmine and rosemary, two of his favorite scents, put his mind at ease that she could possibly be the one to attack Brown. The room and Brown would have reeked of her perfume much like the hallway did after Nicolas Bright was killed. He still did not get a satisfactory answer from her on that score.

Pushing the thoughts aside, he followed his father and the king to the small study and shut the door. Yancy and Jakob took their places in front of the door.

"What the devil is going on, Holmes?" the king demanded.

"Forgive me, sire," Edmond said. "But there has been a development. Your secretary Mr. Brown has been attacked."

The king looked from Holmes to Edmond, concern on his face but no more.

"He is alive," Edmond provided. "But it appears to be the same weapon used in a previous death."

"A week ago, at the Duke of Pembroke's," Holmes began. "There was a young footman who was tied up and killed. In that young man's hand there was a scrap of paper with the letters N-A-S and the year eighteen twenty-six. Your son has provided us with the name Nash who expanded Buckingham Palace for your mother in that year. Tonight, we found a letter written by Francis Tresham in sixteen-oh-five. As you know, your majesty, he was involved in the gunpowder plot."

The king's face went pale. "You mean... the note I found in my study?"

"The same, your majesty," Edmond replied. "It is my belief someone is trying to wind you up and perhaps try and repeat history."

"The gunpowder plot was unsuccessful," the king reminded him.

"Quite so, but that does not mean the person or persons responsible for this, will fail, sire," Holmes stated. "I believe it would be best if you retired to Marlborough House for the time. It is much smaller and the ability to protect you is greater without over seven hundred rooms."

"I cannot," he answered.

"Sire, this is a matter or your life."

"I appreciate that, Holmes," the king said. "It is not because I don't want to. But rather, we're hosting a ball in ten days' time to celebrate my mother's first birthday after her death. It is a time of remembrance of course but also a celebration of her life. I cannot miss it."

Holmes and Edmond exchanged a look. "Then, your majesty," Edmond began. "I must request a room within Buckingham near to yours, in order to watch over you. And I also highly recommend his highness and her grace be brought from St. James' Palace and into the living quarters in Buckingham. With you both under one roof, I will be better adept at protecting you."

"Done, of course," he answered. "And we will provide room for your man and the guards who protect me even today. They shall also all be knighted when this is over. And your temporary knighthood, Edmond? Consider it no longer temporary. I would be dead many times over if it weren't for you." He walked over to him. "Thank you, my friend."

"The honor was and is mine, your majesty," Edmond bowed surprised he felt at ease with the knighthood. "I shall have my man finalize the information and will move in tomorrow."

"Excellent, yes," the king said. "Find whoever is threatening me but protect my son. No matter what. I cannot lose another child."

"His highness will be protected, I swear it to you, sire," Edmond agreed.

"Yes, good, capital," the king said distractedly. "Now, let us finish dinner and be on our way."

Though Edmond had no stomach for food, he followed the king into the dining room and found an empty seat. His father sat beside him. No words were spoken between them, none were needed. The safety of the empire was paramount and that meant protecting the king and all within.

Chapter Twenty-Nine

The next morning, Edmond dressed without complaint and again went out with Cedric for a ride in the Park. That evening he went to luncheon with one of the new debutant's family who asked him to join them. But his thoughts kept returning to Lady Berkley and their kiss. As soon as he returned to Piccadilly, Terrey met him in the lobby and cut his eyes to the study. Following him, they were alone.

"The king's man has been in touch, sir," Terrey said.

"And?"

"I didn't think you would mind if I responded on your behalf. He says to bring your cases in today at teatime. I agreed. If all right with you, I will oversee your move while you take tea with his majesty."

"Of course, did he ask for me to join him for tea?"

"Yes," he said. "And a certain lady will be in attendance." Terrey winked.

Edmond felt his cheeks redden. "How did you..."

"The scent of Jasmine was on your neck collar, sir," he replied.

"Well... I... ehm," Edmond tried.

"Whatever you get up to in the privacy of your own time, sir, is not for me to know. But I am happy for you," Terrey stated.

"It's nothing... just a moment's indiscretion," Edmond said.

"A moment could turn into more if you let it," Terrey replied. "But let's prepare you for tea. The *lavender* waistcoat, sir?"

"Oh stop," Edmond grinned. "But yes. Apparently, it brings out the lavender in my grey eyes."

Terrey laughed but headed up the stairs and brought out the waistcoat helping him dress.

"Tell me, Terrey," Edmond began. "What happened with Lady Grace last evening?"

Terrey dropped the waistcoat, cursed, and snatched it back up. "Lady Grace, sir?"

"Oh, come now, I saw how you both looked at each other. Is there history there?"

Terrey's shoulders fell. "Yes, sir. She was my intended."

"Your... what?" Edmond gasped.

"My intended. Her brother, the current Lord Beaumont was my dearest friend since boyhood. Their property abuts my family's. Lady Grace was always the innocent little girl who would follow her brother around and concurrently, me. When Hugh and I went to Oxford together, we returned for the ball they held hosting the prince, our now king. I went at his request to see Lady Grace. She was... is... beautiful. It was her first season. I was smitten and begged my father to make an offer for her hand to his friend the late lord. Out of friendship, it was accepted though I had no prospects and little to offer. But they thought with her dowry I could set up as a gentleman and help Hugh run the estate. Our marriage was to take place in December. That June my father died, and we lost everything." Terrey looked down. "I had not seen her since. Three years ago. When I saw her standing there... dear god, she..."

"Did you love her?"

"In my way, I did," Terrey replied. "But Hugh forbade the match due to my impoverished circumstances. I beseeched him to take me in. I offered to work for him, but he refused. Treated me like trash. Grace was taken away to live with an aunt abroad until the scandal died. Since we were engaged, she was considered used even though we never did more than a brief kiss."

Edmond let him think for a long moment. "I am sorry, my friend. If it helps you at all, she could not stop looking at you. I believe there is still something there. Did you speak with her?"

"Her brother found me and intercepted. Ordering me away. I could not make a scene."

"I know that must have hurt to see your dearest friend treat you in such a poor manner."

"It hurt more than you know, sir," he replied. "It was a reminder my life is not what I expected, nor is it what I would have chosen for myself. Please don't take it wrongly, I am honored and glad to be working for you, but it is not what I saw myself doing five years ago. Even three... And seeing Lady Grace? It brought it all back."

"I am sorry, my friend. But maybe you will be able to speak with her more at a later time."

"I doubt it, sir," Terrey said. "Hugh, Lord Beaumont keeps a close eye on her. No doubt keeping her from another scandal."

"I can speak with Lord Beaumont, if you would like?"

"No, thank you, sir," Terrey stated. "That part of my life is over. I must turn from that door as it is firmly shut." Terrey took a deep breath. "Now, then, shall we prepare you for your tea at Buckingham?"

Terrey's sudden change of subject showed Edmond he was done speaking of it, but his heart was heavy. One problem at a time, but if he was able to help his friend, then he would do anything he could.

Chapter Thirty

Edmond was announced at Buckingham Palace around five o'clock for tea. He entered the room and kept his awe in check. The palace was beautiful, and he was honored to be able to call it home for as long as he would.

The queen, Duchess, and Marchioness of Berkley greeted him. His eyes found Lady Berkley and would not leave. The woman stood beautiful in her yellow gown and playful eyes.

"His majesty begs your forgiveness, Sir Edmond," the queen said after greeting him. "But he and our son had business to attend to and will join us later."

"Of course, your majesty, I am grateful for the opportunity to meet with you and the other ladies for tea."

"But of course, Sir Edmond, it is not what you were hoping for," Lady Berkley said.

"I find I am an easy man to please, my lady," Edmond replied. "Whenever there is good conversation and beautiful things to look at, I am in good spirits."

Lady Berkley grinned at him as he was offered a seat opposite her, but Edmond remained standing.

"Allow me the pleasure of serving you some tea, Sir Edmond," Lady Berkley said. "How do you like it?"

"Tangy, and yet sweet, my lady," he answered and was pleased to see her cheeks brighten with color. After blushing so often in her presence, it was refreshing to have the tables turned.

"I hear from the Countess of Selbourne your mother is very excited for your sister's confinement," the duchess said.

"Indeed, we are all anxious for her, your grace," Edmond replied. "It is her first."

"But not your first nephew or niece?"

"No indeed, my brother Sir Charles and his wife Lady Alexandra have given me one of each."

"Do you enjoy being an uncle?" Lady Berkley asked handing him his tea. Their fingers brushed and tingles shot up his arm.

"I find fewer pleasures in life, my lady," he stated and sat after all the ladies were seated.

"But of course, when you settle down and have children of your own, Sir Edmond, you will find even more pleasures trust me," the queen said.

"I can only hope for such a future, your majesty." Edmond noticed Lady Berkley and continued. "But I would be happy with no children if I have a wife I adore."

The women oohed at his words and Lady Berkley smiled at him.

"Has any young lady caught your eye?" The duchess asked.

Lady Berkley locked eyes with him as she offered a tea biscuit from the platter before them.

"One," he answered still staring at her as he took a biscuit with jam in the middle. Then, turning he plastered a smile. "But I cannot give any more information until I know the lady's feelings."

"Do give us a hint, Sir Edmond," the queen asked.

"I am sorry, your majesty," he shook his head. "I am as silent as the grave. But infinitely more animated," he winked.

The queen and duchess laughed prettily, and Lady Berkley caught his eye with a smirk.

"Tell us, Sir Edmond," Lady Berkley began. "You are to stay here in Buckingham?"

"I have that honor, my lady," he answered.

"And you stay in one of the personal apartments?" she questioned.

"I do, my lady. Near the king and prince, I believe."

"Is there a particular reason you stay here and not at your lodgings in Piccadilly?" she asked.

Edmond glanced at the queen who shook her head slightly. The duchess and Lady Berkley did not know his true purpose, but the queen clearly did.

"Being a close friend of the prince, I do believe his highness has asked me to stay to help prepare for the ball. My man Terrey is a wonder and though I am new to this life, I apparently have a critical eye for all things beautiful."

"That is a wonderful sentiment," the queen said.

"Indeed, his highness has told me more than once how fortunate he is to have you as a friend, Sir Edmond. I hope you will have a wonderful stay here with us. I look forward to speaking with you further," the duchess stated.

"And I with you, your grace." Edmond caught Lady Berkley's eyes. She was studying him with such a look he shifted uncomfortably in his seat.

"Tell me, your majesty," Edmond began, trying to remove the attention from him. "Is this the first ball held here at Buckingham?"

"Not ever of course, but it is *our* first one," the queen said. "It is in honor of the birthday of my late mother-in-law."

"An honorable occasion," Edmond replied.

"Indeed," she answered. "It will be the first birthday since she passed, and my husband wanted to hold a remembrance. But of course, he may act like he is the stoic Englishman, but she was his mother and as such he will be melancholy."

"As any man would," Edmond stated. "I could not imagine my mother passing. She is a wonderful woman and I love her deeply."

"That is such a wonderful thing to say, Sir Edmond," the duchess said. "I am pleased you feel confident in your manhood to express such emotions."

"Oh, your grace, have no fear. I am very confident in my manhood," he said, and the ladies giggled. "Forgive me, I should not have spoken so vulgarly."

"Oh, please, Sir Edmond," the queen waved him off. "We are all married ladies."

"Some of us, your majesty," Lady Berkley corrected with a twinkle in her eye.

"You have many wonderful years left, Arabella," Duchess of Cornwall and York said. "With the right man," she looked over at Edmond and smiled.

"Come now, Mary," Lady Berkley stated. "Sir Edmond would much rather have an innocent blushing debutant than a widow."

"I have never been one to be turned by an innocent debutant, my lady," Edmond said.

Her eyes lit with a fire that stoked Edmond's blood.

"Dear me, did it get warm in here, mama?" the duchess teased looking at the queen.

"It did indeed," the queen giggled.

A knock at the door drew their attention and when the queen ordered the person to enter, Edmond was surprised to see Terrey lingering behind the royal servant.

"Forgive me, your majesty," the servant bowed. "Your grace, my lady, but Sir Edmond's man has received a word from Sir Charles." Edmond instantly grew concerned.

"Of course, come forward," the queen waved Terrey in. Terrey bowed to both the queen and the duchess then turned his eyes on Edmond.

"Forgive me, Sir Edmond," he began. "But your brother has sent word. Lady Alexandra's pains have begun. He asks for you to join him at Cavendish."

"Oh, how exciting," the duchess clapped her hands.

Edmond stood, the subtle tension in his shoulders at the fear he knew Percy must be feeling tightened his shoulders. He bowed to the queen and duchess, his eyes lingering a little longer on Lady Berkley.

"Forgive me, your majesty, your grace, my lady," he said. "But I should be with my brother."

"Of course, of course," the queen stood and offered her hand, which Edmond took and kissed. "Do let us know when your sister-in-law delivers and if you have a new niece or nephew. Our good wishes go with you."

"Thank you, your majesty," Edmond bowed once more and hurried to the door.

"Until later, Sir Edmond," Lady Berkley called. He turned back and bowed to her then followed Terrey down the hall. She beguiled him and made him cautious at the same time.

"How long ago?"

"She has been laboring since luncheon," Terrey replied. "I only just received word from Sir Charles and came to fetch you."

"And is Dr. Watson there?"

"At her side," Terrey replied. "Things are progressing well, apparently."

"Good," Edmond shrugged into his coat as Terrey held it for him. He headed to the door to see Percy's carriage waiting for him. Turning, he noticed Terrey standing at the door. "Are you not coming?"

"No, sir, I am needed here," he replied. "As you have requested."

Edmond then remembered he had asked Terrey to watch

the prince if he was unable and he thanked him. Bustling up into the carriage, he knocked on the top, telling the driver to whip up. The carriage jolted forward and soon travelled through London's streets toward Percy's residence.

"Alexandra, she is beautiful," Edmond said has he delicately held his new niece in his arms.

"You look so handsome with a babe in your arms, Edmond," she said. She looked tired but no less beautiful as she joined the family for a late breakfast the next morning. Percy hovered around her. Alexandra's pains continued well into the night and the sounds of the squalling babe eased everyone's mind at three in the morning. And after several hours, Alexandra came down to see everyone.

"We are so happy you are doing well, my dear," Marguerite walked over to her and took her hand.

"Thank you, mama, and thank you so much for taking care of Philippe and Eleanor," Alexandra replied.

"It was a pleasure, my dear," she answered. "I am only so glad we were able to return from the country with such haste." She looked at her daughter who stood beside her husband. Henri had joined them but was currently still asleep in one of the rooms upstairs.

"I could not have done this without you," Alexandra stated. "Though I will say all of our children, Lillian's birth was the easiest."

"You should not tire yourself, my love," Percy said.

"I am quite well and want to hear all about what Edmond has been going through. I have heard some interesting tales from you," she beamed up at her husband. "But it is nothing compared to the splendid suitor I see before me."

All eyes turned to Edmond. He smiled and passed his niece to Dr. Watson and sat.

"I will start by saying it is not as difficult as I thought it would be," he said, accepting tea from the maid. "I merely emulate my brother and I am well on my way."

"I know I make a wonderful teacher," Percy winked.

Edmond chuckled. "But the balls and parties have been a fascinating study in human nature."

"Yes, yes, but tell us about the important things," Alexandra said.

"And what would that be?"

"The murder," she began. "What have you discovered? Is it true you found the king's valet stabbed in a secret passage?"

Edmond looked over at Percy then at Dr. Watson who chuckled. "Leave it to my daughter, Holmes to think of murder among the important things."

"She is a brilliant woman," Holmes teased.

Edmond chuckled and began to explain what he had seen and what his theories were. His family listened with rapt attention, tossing thoughts around as they enjoyed their tea and breakfast.

Chapter Thirty-One

Edmond walked through Buckingham Palace with Terrey to freshen up. He has spent the morning and through luncheon with his family. He did not realize how much energy his family gave him until he was ready to depart. He felt rested, even though he had not slept and energized, though he was exhausted. Looking forward to a long hot bath and a chance to sleep for a few hours, he was chatting with Terrey when he saw Lady Berkley step out of her room and stop when she saw him.

"Sir Edmond," she smiled.

"Lady Berkley," he and Terrey bowed.

"How is your sister-in-law?"

"She is doing very well," he answered. "Thank you."

"I am very glad to hear it," she replied. "And do you have a niece or nephew?"

"A beautiful niece."

"Oh, how splendid. Children are a blessing."

"They are, indeed," Edmond said. "Though I can claim none I look forward to the time I may." Lady Berkley still knew him as the gentleman seeking a wife. He needed to play the part. Though they had shared a kiss the other day, he could not break character.

They stared at each other a long moment. Terrey had taken a few steps back and kept his head bowed.

Not wanting to end their conversation, Edmond continued. "How has the planning come along? I confess I feel a fraud as I have not assisted."

"Planning?" She questioned.

"For the party?"

"Oh, very well indeed," Lady Berkley said.

"I am pleased," Edmond answered. He glanced down the corridor then looked back at her. "Perhaps... Lady Berkley, the trip to my family and a new child has made me think."

"Think of what, Sir Edmond?"

"Of what I may want."

"Want?"

"Desire," he clarified.

"And what is that?"

He stared into her deep chocolate eyes. "May I be so bold as to invite you to dinner this evening?"

"Dinner? This evening?" Lady Berkley questioned.

"Indeed, there is a wonderful place I know just off Cavendish Square."

"Surely if we are seen together having dinner, there will be talk."

"I do not mind if you do not, Arabella," his voice was low. Her eyes turned soft and a seductive smile lifted her lips.

"Of course, I do not mind, Edmond," she answered. "But perhaps it is not time yet to let others know of our... attachment?"

He pulled himself up, prepared to be rebuffed. "Well of course, If you do not desire it."

"There is much I desire," she stepped closer to him. "And I was only thinking of you. You have many young hearts in your hands."

"There is only one I have set my eyes on."

"Oh? And who is that?"

"I think you know."

"Then perhaps, Sir Edmond I will accept your offer. Dinner would be lovely, but not tonight."

He stepped even closer. "I would be happy to do anything you desire."

Her smile lifted even more. "I will keep that in mind."

With that, she swept down the hallway, leaving Edmond staring after her. Terrey cleared his throat and Edmond backed away from Lady Berkley's doorway.

"This way, sir," Terrey said with a smile.

Edmond lay awake in his bed, reading the latest from Charles-Louis Philippe by the light of the dim candle. Not one of his favorite authors he still enjoyed the story. Just as he was about to extinguish the light, a soft knock on his door drew his attention. Standing, he wrapped his housecoat around him. Opening the door, Lady Berkley stood, wrapped in a housecoat, her hair unbound.

"Arabella?" he questioned.

She smiled at him, but then furtively glanced down the hallway.

"Come in," he said.

She hurried in and shut the door behind her.

"What are you doing here?" he asked.

She turned to look at him and took the lapels of his housecoat. Pulling him into her, she pressed her lips to his. He melted into her embrace, enjoying the feel of her in his arms. She still tasted so very sweet and her body, without the corset between them was lithe and graceful. He held her to him as their lips devoured each other's and their tongues dueled. When her hands went to the rope that tied his housecoat together, he pulled back.

"Your reputation," he panted.

"Be damned," she answered taking hold of the tie again. "I am a woman and I know what I want, Edmond. And that is you."

"The scandal would be..."

"Immaterial," she answered taking his lips again.

"Arabella," he breathed. She froze in his arms for a moment, then pulled back. Looking up at him, her dark eyes assessed.

"I see. You do not want me."

The look in her eyes, unsure, insecure, made him step closer to her. "I do. But I..." he tried. The words died on his lips as the look in her eyes changed. Those innocent eyes promised wickedness and heaven help him, he did not want to stop. She reached up and caressed the back of his head.

"Arabella," he began. "I do not take this sort of thing lightly."

"Neither do I, Edmond," she replied. "I am here of my own accord. My own desires have spurred my action."

"And mine," Edmond agreed. "I never want to cause scandal to touch you."

"It will not," she answered. "I want you. Do you want me?"

"Yes, undoubtedly," he replied.

"Then no words are needed, Edmond," she said leaning up and pulling his head down to brush her lips against his.

"Only a few," he answered. "I have wanted you since the first moment I saw you, but I feel I should tell you... It has been a while and I may be..."

She breathed a laugh but nodded. "As am I. We can help each other. I am no innocent, Edmond. I know what goes on between a man and a woman, but never have I desired someone the way I desire you. Since I met you, only you have occupied my thoughts. I want to know where you are, what you are thinking, and if you might feel the same. I was jealous when I saw you standing up with other ladies. When I saw you smile at them, I wanted you for myself. Is that selfish?"

"If it is, I am guilty of it too," Edmond replied. "For I find I want to be the sole object of your attention. I want to know you as a lover, a friend. You intrigue me, Arabella. I have never met a woman like you, and I doubt I ever will again."

"One request?"

"Name it," he answered running his fingers through her silky hair.

"Kiss me? And don't stop."

"That I can grant, *mon Coeur,*" he answered and lowered his mouth to hers. Before long, they fell into his bed and spent the rest of the night in each other's arms.

Chapter Thirty-Two

Edmond had a secret, one he could tell no one but when he thought of her while walking down the corridor to the ballroom, he grinned. Five days had passed since he and Arabella had first made love and each night they spent entwined in each other's arms.

The ball was that night, and he had a very special request to ask her when they were alone. He was falling in love with her. They had already shared so many confidences while holding each other. She told him of a lover she had as a young woman before she married, a scandal but it told him what he already knew, she was a passionate woman. He told her of Lei, his guilt, and her death.

Though they had spent every night with each other, that night they would not be able to. The ball, the party, Edmond needed to stay focused. He was glad to have his brother, uncle, father, and Cedric attending that night. Terrey, Yancy, Jakob, and Fitzpatrick would be on duty as well. It had been quiet, and Edmond wanted to take it as a sign the worst was over. But he knew better.

Edmond found his way to the ball room. It was empty apart from servants rushing back and forth making sure the refreshment tables had enough glasses. Lady Berkley stood by the doorway leading to the garden. Edmond made his way over to her. Standing close, he took in her sweet scent of jasmine.

"You look beautiful," he whispered. She smiled slightly and leaned back into his chest. She said nothing but he felt the tension in her shoulders. "What is wrong?"

She took a deep breath. "Nothing."

"Ara," he breathed. "I know something is troubling you. Tell me?"

She turned to look up into his eyes. "You know... you know I care for you, Edmond?"

"Yes," he answered without hesitation. Words had not been spoken between them regarding their feelings, but he felt it every time she came apart in his arms.

"There is," she began, then hesitated as a servant rushed past them.

"What?"

She cupped his cheek, but her eyes looked oddly heavy. "Just know that there is nothing I wouldn't do to protect those I love."

"Me too," he answered.

"I know," her voice cracked. Again, she stared into his eyes and then moved quickly away, leaving him staring out the glass door leading to the patio and gardens.

Arabella was distant, so unlike the fiery woman he had in his bed every night. Something was clearly on her mind. Unable to think more on it, he found Yancy, Jakob, Fitzpatrick, and Terrey and a quiet place. Talking over the plan, Edmond relaxed slightly. This party would be fine. He was sure of it. But why he couldn't shake the feeling that something was going to happen that night, he wasn't certain.

Heading back up the stairs, he met Terrey in his room, ready to prepare for the ball. It was going to take everything within him to keep a steady eye on the king and the prince. Nervous energy bubbled in his belly and all too soon he found himself standing with the prince as the doors opened and the hundreds of people began to be announced.

Edmond greeted his family as they came down the line, his mother looked radiant in her ivory gold gown and his father, brother, and brother-in-law were dressed in their finery. After everyone was announced, Edmond was expected to mingle. A discrete word to the prince, he made his way to his family who stood by the unlit fireplace drinking a glass of champagne.

"You look quite fine, *mon cher*," his mother said when she saw him approaching.

"Not as fine as you, mama," he answered. "You look beautiful."

"I couldn't agree more," Holmes smiled. But then his and Percy's eyes locked for a brief moment and a sly smirk appeared on both their face.

"What?" Edmond asked.

"Nothing," Percy replied. "You just seem... different, brother."

"Different?"

"More... relaxed," Cedric answered.

"I give a good impression. One that is false. I am more on edge than ever. The plans were for Buckingham. I will need all eyes for anything out of the ordinary."

"They'll hardly do something with so many people about," Marguerite offered.

"I doubt it, mama, but I am ready for it," Edmond stated.

"Of course you are," Holmes answered. "But we will keep a close eye for anything unusual."

"Speaking of unusual," Percy said taking a step forward and moving Edmond's collar down to reveal the fading bruise on his neck from Arabella's amorous attentions the night before.

Edmond moved away from Percy's hand, and glanced at his mother. Marguerite looked down, fighting a smirk, a soft color staining her cheeks.

"Margot," Holmes offered his hand. "Dance with me? Let's let our boys talk."

Marguerite glanced up at Edmond, his cheeks on fire knowing his mother knew of his activities, and more importantly how she knew of them was because she had done them herself. He wasn't sure which part scandalized him more. Once their parents were on the dance floor, Percy, Edmond, and Cedric stood closer.

"Did you have to bring that up with mama here?" Edmond questioned.

"Oh, come now, Ed, she's done worse herself with our

father," Percy answered.

"Please," Edmond shook his head. "I do not need to think about that." Cedric chuckled and Edmond turned to him. "No, *you* say nothing. I don't want to know or think about you and my sister."

Cedric pressed his lips together, as his eyes lit with a playful sort of fire. Edmond suppressed his shudder the best he could.

"But still, Edmond," Percy went on. "I am pleased. You seem to be living a little. You are being careful, I'm sure."

"I am not discussing this with you, Percy," Edmond stated.

"Just tell me one thing," Percy said. "Who is it? Is it the lovely Lady Berkley? Or are you hiding another from me?"

"Percy," Edmond raised is chin to him. "I am not talking to you about this."

"Besides, it is not the right time," Cedric replied. Then, looking around the room, he asked, "where is the prince?"

Edmond whirled around, frantically scanning the room. His eyes darted from the refreshments table to where the duchess was standing with the queen, to the opened doors out to the private lawn leading to the pond behind the palace. The prince was nowhere to be found.

Without another word to his brother or Cedric, he hurried through the throngs of ball attendees heading toward the duchess. Some people stopped to watch as Edmond barreled forward but others ignored him.

"Ah, Sir Edmond," someone called.

"Forgive me, I am needed quickly," Edmond said to the person without a glance to see who it was. He approached the duchess who looked over at him, surprise in her eyes. He bowed and schooled his features. "Your grace, forgive me," he began. "But I have a rather important... wager with my brother that only his highness can assist with. Do you happen to know where he is?"

"Oh," the duchess replied. "I, well, no. I was here." She turned to the queen and another lady-in-waiting. "Have you seen him?"

"Not since earlier, your grace," the other lady said.

"Did he say anything to you, mama?" the duchess asked her mother-in-law.

"No, my dear. I am sorry, Sir Edmond," the queen answered.

Edmond's heart hammered in his chest.

"Have you checked his highness' personal study, Sir Edmond?" A voice behind him asked. He looked back to see Lady Berkley standing there.

"His study?" Edmond questioned.

"I saw him sneak out but a few moments ago." She looked at him intently as if he was supposed to understand something she was saying.

"Thank you, my lady," he bowed to her. "Forgive me for causing you distress, your grace," he turned back to the duchess. Once they bowed to each other and he was able to leave, he glanced at Arabella who again watched him intently.

He nodded to his brother and Cedric hoping they would understand to follow him. Thankfully, they did. With another quick glance at Arabella, hoping she would understand him running out on her, he hurried to the main door and down the grand staircase intent on running through the Green Drawing Room to the corridor and into the private apartments. His clothing unfortunately, would not let him do more than walk briskly.

Finally, he reached the prince's study. Holding up his hand to Percy and Cedric, he told them to stay and knocked on the door.

When he didn't hear anything on the other side, he opened the door quietly. Relief rushed over him to such an extent it nearly made him lightheaded. The prince sat hunched over his desk, looking intently at his stamp collection, seemingly not having heard his knock. Edmond entered the room fully and shut the door behind him.

"Sire, you cannot stay in here." The prince jumped then looked a little sheepish. "I was sent to protect you, and I cannot do that if you are out of my sight," Edmond said.

"I am sorry, Holmes," he replied. "I didn't think about it. But I do not want to stay there."

"I understand but you cannot leave the ballroom without letting me know," Edmond's voice was kind, but he hoped the prince heard the urgency.

"Yes, I am sorry for that."

Edmond walked further into the room standing just before the desk. "What is troubling you, your highness?"

The prince huffed, leaned back, and gestured for him to sit. "Have you heard of my father's plans to name me Prince of Wales?"

"He told me he was thinking of it, sire," Edmond said.

"Well, he's decided it will happen," he answered.

"And you do not desire it? It is your rightful title. You are to be king."

"Is it wrong of me not to want to be king? I was never supposed to be. My elder brother was trained since birth. I could not imagine."

"I do not believe it is wrong of you," Edmond began. "You have every right to worry or be concerned, sire. Being a king is not easy, nor is being a prince. But, sire, you have the opportunity to do good for your people. You have the chance to make the world better. Not many men have the chance nor the power to make it so. Just think of all the good you could do."

"I only wish Albert was here. He would know what to do." The prince's face fell even more at the mention of his late brother. Edmond said the one thing he knew the prince could not argue.

"If he was here, you would not be married to her grace and you would not have your children."

A soft smile lifted prince's lips. "That is true. I cannot fault your logic."

"There is so many things a king is able to do. He can change the world. Tell me, sire, what is the one thing you want to do to make the world a better place?"

The prince thought a moment. "I would end wars. Too many of our men have died. I would not want it on my conscience."

"Then work toward that, sire. You have the chance to end conflict. Yes, you may not have been born knowing you would be king, but you have been given a gift. Do not waste it."

"You are a wise man, Holmes."

"I do try, sire." Edmond smiled.

"I only hope my sons never have to worry. George, my second born should never have to have the burden of the throne on his shoulders. Edward will make a wonderful king. I am sure of it. And I hope he has someone like you at his side to help encourage him."

"I am honored to have your trust, sire. But now, come with me. Put your collection away for the time being and come with me back to the party. It is a celebration."

"It is," the prince agreed and stood from his desk. He walked over to Edmond and offered his hand. Edmond took it in a firm shake. "Thank you for your watchfulness. My father has let me know about the note he found on his desk. I have to say, I am concerned. You do not think they want to destroy Parliament like Guy Fawkes tried to do, do you?"

"I believe the note was to instill a sort of fear, your highness. But make no mistake, this person, or people are cunning and they have already killed. Be on your guard, sire. If something like this happens again, I just may need to tie a rope around our wrists, so I know where you are at all times."

The prince chuckled. "That would look dashed awkward."

"It would indeed," Edmond grinned.

They opened the door and walked back toward the ball room where his guests mingled, danced, drank, and enjoyed themselves. Edmond was glad to see Percy and Cedric had left the area when they were assured of the prince's safety.

"Tell me something, Holmes," the prince began.

"Anything, sire," Edmond replied.

"What are your plans after this?"

"Plans, sir?"

"Well, do you want to settle down? Stop being given dangerous missions? Find someone to marry? Raise a family?"

"My first loyalty is to my family, sire," he said. "But I am needed. I am here."

"I know this has taken a lot out of you," the prince replied. "I have seen the way you are around the debutants. Especially a certain lady of our mutual acquaintance? You could easily decide a life out of the rigors of security is much more your style. I only ask you to think on it. You have served my father and myself proudly. I would do anything to assist you."

"And I am ever grateful, sire," he answered. "I will think on it. At the moment, I am more interested in finding who is threatening you and bringing them to justice."

"Well," the prince continued. "Anything I can do to help; know I am at your disposal."

"My thanks, highness," he answered as they reached the door of the ballroom. Stepping through, his eyes were drawn immediately to his family then to Lady Berkley who stood with the duchess. Her eyes found his and she nodded slightly, almost in relief.

"She is a beautiful woman, and quite the catch, Holmes," the prince whispered in his ear. "You'd be a fool not to pursue it."

"I am no fool, highness," he replied with a subtle smirk and a quick wink.

The prince chuckled but slapped him on the back. "I'll be with my wife."

"No more sneaking off," Edmond all but ordered.

"I have learnt my lesson, Holmes," the prince said. "I will stay here."

Edmond watched him go. His eyes scanned the room once more. Terrey walked through the crowd with a tray of champagne. Edmond caught Lady Grace staring at him more than once. It was clear she still cared deeply for the man who was once her fiancé. Seeing his uncle standing by the doorway near Fitzpatrick, Yancy, and Jakob. Edmond headed back over to his family for a long overdue discussion.

"Edmond, there you are," Holmes began. "All well?" his

father's eyes questioning more than his words.

"Yes," he answered.

"We just had a delightful conversation with Lady Berkley, brother," Percy stated. Edmond's eyes snapped over to his.

"You... what?"

"Yes, indeed, she is a charming young woman," his mother said.

"Why?" Edmond questioned.

"Why what?" Holmes asked.

"Why did you talk to her?"

"She came over, *mon cher,* began speaking to your brother and Percy introduced us," Marguerite said. "Why?" she looked between Edmond and Percy then, her eyes grew wide with understanding. "Oh, I see."

Edmond wasn't sure how he was ever going to look his mother in the eye again. "Mama," he began. "I am sorry. This was not how I was hoping to..." he glanced at his brother and Cedric. "That is... I never expected you to learn... ehm."

"Edmond," Marguerite stopped him and placed a loving hand on his forearm. "You are a grown man. Nothing you do or say can shock me, my love. I am pleased you have found someone you care for. She is a lovely woman."

"I merely," Edmond began again, then cleared his throat. "I am sorry you learnt about it this way, mama. I wanted to introduce you properly."

"But you wouldn't have," Marguerite said. "So I am glad she came over and did it for you."

"We're just so damned happy for you, Edmond," Percy replied.

"Percy, language," Marguerite scolded softly.

"Apologies, mama," Percy bowed shallowly. "But it is how I feel. I am so very happy for him."

"We all are," Cedric answered.

Edmond looked at his father. Holmes produced a forced smile and nodded to him. Curious what that meant, Edmond was about to ask when Percy's voice again cut in.

"Speaking of the beauty," he said. "Where is your lady? I would enjoy seeing you two dance."

Edmond looked toward the prince and the duchess but did not see Lady Berkley. "I am not sure."

"Find her, love," Marguerite said.

"Keep an eye on the prince?"

"Between the four of us," Holmes began. "We have enough eyes to keep watch."

Edmond nodded and headed toward the place he saw her last. Terrey walked by and offered him a glass of champagne.

"All well?" he asked Edmond.

"Yes," Edmond answered. "The prince was in his study."

"I am glad his highness was well, but that is not what I meant."

"What did you mean?"

"I meant between you and Lady Berkley. I saw her walk outside just a moment ago. She didn't look pleased," Terrey said.

The hair on the back of Edmond's neck stood on end. "Outside?"

"The terrace," Terrey replied.

Edmond looked over Terrey's shoulder and nodded. "Thank you."

Making his way over to the doorway, he was waylaid by Lord Beaumont, Lady Grace's brother.

"I say, Holmes," he greeted, and Edmond immediately froze. Lord Beaumont hadn't called him by anything other than *Sir Edmond* in all of their short acquaintanceship. He turned and bowed to the earl.

"Lord Beaumont," he said. "I know we are only acquaintances, but for the good of polite society, I would prefer you address me properly."

"But I am, aren't I?" Lord Beaumont questioned.

"What do you mean?"

"I heard a rumor your knighthood never actually took place."

"I don't know what you are talking about," Edmond stood to his full height and looked down at the rat-like man.

"I have been making inquiries," Beaumont said. "And it appears no one of my acquaintance knows when or why you were knighted. And no one, it appears, was there."

"I was there, Beaumont," the prince's voice came from behind him. "Does my testimony count?" Edmond looked over his shoulder and bowed slightly when the prince stood beside him. His piercing light eyes boring into Lord Beaumont's.

"Your highness," Beaumont had the grace to bow and look sheepish. "I was merely questioning."

"In future, I would appreciate it if you have a concern as to mine or my father's credibility or a question as to why we did what we did, bring it to us instead of questioning our subjects and making an ass of yourself," the prince stated.

"Sire, I had no intention of questioning you or his majesty. I merely... Sir Edmond has been courting my sister, Lady Grace and her feelings have grown. I merely wished to check Sir Edmond's credibility."

"This man is a close personal friend of mine," the prince said. "That should be credibility enough."

"Indeed, please forgive a brother's overprotective nature toward his sister. We are all we have, you understand, and her welfare is in my hands."

"I appreciate your concern, but again in future, perhaps it would be best to hold your tongue, and your liquor, better," the prince looked deliberately down at his champagne glass.

"Forgive me, sire," Lord Beaumont bowed low, then bowed shallowly to Edmond. "I ask your pardon, Sir Edmond."

Edmond nodded crisply once and watched the man walk away. "Thank you, sire."

"I've had my eye on Beaumont for years ever since he swindled his neighbor out of hundreds of thousands of pounds," the prince said. "He ruined a good family."

Pausing a moment, Edmond looked at the prince. "His neighbor?"

"Yes," he answered. "A noble family, untitled, but still good friends. There is little evidence, or the man would be behind bars."

"Who was this family?" a sinking feeling churning acid in his stomach.

"Terrey was their name," he said. "Lawrence Terrey was a friend of my grandmother's chaplain who was my tutor as a boy, Canon Dalton. He had three sons I believe. My brother Albert was friends with the middle son, he went into the clergy I believe. Albert begged Canon Dalton to help him succeed. I'm not sure what happened to the younger son, but he was engaged to Beaumont's sister Lady Grace. He's not been seen for a long time."

Edmond's eyes found Terrey passing champagne glasses to his family and his chest ached.

"What do you mean about Beaumont swindling your tutor's friend out of money?" Edmond asked.

"Mr. Terrey's eldest son went to his solicitor after he discovered several large payments to an H.M. Notes in the memorandum stated, they were payments for an investment in a new Catholic Cathedral in Africa. There was no plan for one. Beaumont used the money for restoration of Beaumont Estate and kept promising Mr. Terrey would receive letters of thanks from those poor souls in Africa. It was all discovered just after Mr. Terrey died, but without evidence, Terrey's son was not able to do anything against him."

Edmond was going to be sick as he caught Terrey's eye. His friend, valet, and confidant was the victim of a jealous and contemptable man. One he had called best friend.

"Thank you for telling me, sire," Edmond said. The walls seemed to close in around him. He needed to get out of there. "A damnable story, indeed. Forgive me, I must get some air." He needed to think on what to do and how he could help Terrey's family. The prince nodded and Edmond hurried to the door.

Once outside, he took a deep breath of the fresh, cooler air. There were a couple people outside taking in the evening, getting away from the heat of the ball room. According to the king, the fireworks would begin shortly. That was the time of the evening Edmond worried about most. Fireworks could so easily mask the sound of a gun.

All thought of Lady Berkley was forgotten as he contemplated what the prince told him. Closing his eyes to meditate his mind, he was surprised when he heard a familiar voice speaking in hushed but harsh tones in the shadows to his left. Walking over, Edmond saw two figures standing on the pathway hidden by the balustrade of the terrace. He recognized Arabella's voice and figure almost immediately. Pausing, he listened to her words.

"You don't understand," she was saying. "I cannot keep this from him any longer. He deserves the truth."

Edmond's brow furrowed as he stuck to the shadows and listened.

"If he finds out he will think I betrayed him. I cannot let that happen," another voice said. Pitched low it wasn't easy to place the voice.

"I don't want to hurt him."

"If he finds out, Arabella, he will think you betrayed him. You cannot tell him anything." Edmond's stomach dropped when he finally recognized the voice. "You should never have let it get this personal. That was not the plan."

"It was not the plan to keep him in the dark. Why haven't you told him?"

"Because he doesn't need to know and if you hadn't led with your heart instead of your head, you would still understand this. I told you the things I told you about him to help you get closer to him. Win his trust. Not to become intimate and play happy lovers."

There was the slap of flesh against flesh. "How dare you. You trained me on the things I needed to know. You were the one who wanted this. You said win his trust first."

"I said, make him believe you."

"I should never have allowed you to convince me this was a good idea. There's not much I have asked for the past five years, but I beg of you, let me go. Let me tell him the truth."

"The truth? All of it? The fact that everything he thinks he knows about you is a lie? I never told you to lie to him. The fact you took everything I told you and used it to seduce him? That was never the plan. You were only to work with him to stop this. You came to us, don't forget."

"And it is fast becoming the worst decision I ever made."

Edmond could not stop himself. The words he was hearing, the two people he cared for more than anything else… no, it was too much. Putting on a mask of indifference, he stuffed his rage away and stepped over to the balustrade, above where they spoke.

"Well, well, well, I never thought I would see this," he said. The figures' gazes snapped up to his. "My lover, and my uncle," he said coldly. "What a surprise."

Chapter Thirty-Three

"Edmond," Arabella breathed. Then, her face relaxed into a forced innocence. "Your charming Uncle was just helping me back inside. I grew overheated and needed some fresh air. I got lost."

"Did you, madam?" he questioned. "That's interesting for I could have sworn you were speaking of something else."

"Something... else?" her voice rose higher.

He lifted his head and looked down his nose at her. "Indeed but considering the stench of betrayal lingers in the air, I am surprised others have not been able to sniff you out."

"What do you mean?" she questioned.

"Isn't it obvious, Arabella?" Mycroft offered. "He heard us."

Even in the dim light, he saw her eyes grow wide as she looked up at him.

"Edmond, it's not what it seems."

"Much apparently is not as it seems," Edmond stated. "You lied to me. You used me. I invited you to my bed. I made love to you. I fell in love with you. And in none of those times you thought about telling me the truth? Not when you were lying in my arms? Not when I told you about Lei?" he paused and remembered their conversation. He breathed a laugh. "Dear god," he looked at his uncle. "You told her already." He looked back at Arabella. "You already knew. The other night when I told you about my past, about the woman I loved and about my duties here, you already knew?" he was close to yelling, something he hadn't done his entire life.

When neither replied, he thought he might vomit up his meal.

He stared at her. "Was any of it real?"

"Yes!" Arabella sounded on the verge of tears. "I wanted to tell you. I knew we were both getting in over our heads, and I needed to tell you. When I saw Mycroft, I begged an audience. I had to tell you."

"And yet, you wouldn't have."

"I would! I was going to tell you no matter what he said."

"And why wouldn't you have allowed her to tell me, Uncle? What is the story there?"

"There is much more going on here than you know,

Edmond. I told you at Sandringham not to get involved. I told you she was trustworthy, but I never once thought you would allow a woman to distract you. I thought you were better than that."

"A family trait, I see. You told her my most intimate confidences. Let me guess, the fact you wear jasmine and rosemary perfume isn't a coincidence, is it, madam?"

Arabella said nothing. Edmond breathed out, shock giving way to betrayal and animosity.

"Dear god, is anything about you real?" then a horrible thought occurred. "Please for the love of god, tell me Terrey knew nothing about this."

"No, of course not," Mycroft replied as if the very idea repulsed him. "I would never betray such a confidence."

Animosity gave way to sheer and burning rage. "You already did!" Edmond shouted so loudly people came running.

"It's all right," Mycroft defused the situation. "We're play acting something we wrote for the prince."

The bystanders seemed happy with that and went on about their business. But Edmond never looked away from Arabella's eyes. People began pouring out of the ballroom all around them. Edmond wasn't sure how long he stood there staring at her but once the first firework burst in the sky, it illuminated her face. A face he had stared at every night, a face he was starting to love. The face of the woman who betrayed him in such a horrible way. Tears streaked down her cheeks as she closed her eyes. Mycroft looked up at Edmond and tried to speak but Edmond held up a hand. Whatever he had to say, he did not want to hear. Finally, he looked back at Arabella and waited until she opened her eyes again.

"I never want to see you again, madam," he said. Her tears broke and she covered her mouth as she sobbed. The apathy and emptiness were new feelings, but he held on to it as he looked at his uncle, the man he looked up to like a father. "I will be moving back into my father's house as soon as possible, sir. I will not continue to live under your roof. You have betrayed me in the worst possible way. Not just by keeping this from me, but by using my confidence for your own gains. Goodbye to both of you. I do not intend on speaking to you again."

With that and a particularly loud boom of the fireworks, he turned on his heels and strode back into the ballroom.

Chapter Thirty-Four

Edmond knew the gravity of the situation would crash over him soon, but until then, he needed to maintain his composure. He crossed the ballroom and headed for the door.

"Edmond?" His father's voice stopped him. Turning, he locked eyes with him. Holmes took a deep breath and walked over to him.

"Please tell me you didn't know. Please, tell me he didn't tell you."

"No one told me anything," Holmes said and placed a hand

on his son's shoulder. "I... figured she wasn't all she claimed to be. Actually, that she was *more* than she claimed to be. But I knew nothing of your uncle's betrayal until I overheard just now."

"Why? Why would he do this to me? Have I not done everything he asked? Have I not put my all into everything he wanted? Why? Why did he have to take this away from me?"

"I don't know, son," Holmes said.

He couldn't breathe, his lungs seized. "Get this off me!" he wanted to yell as he nearly ripped his coat open and tried to shove it down his arms, but it stuck at his elbows. Holmes moved closer and helped pull the coat off. Edmond undid his tie and started unbuttoning his shirt. "I can't breathe." Knowing he was hyperventilating and stopping it were two separate things.

Holmes turned him to the door and pushed him out of the room. They walked together down the corridor and into the yellow drawing room. No one was around and Edmond gasped for breath.

"I can't... I... can't..." he tried to say.

Holmes grabbed his shoulders and forced him to look at him. "Looking at me, son. Breathe. Look at me, Edmond." When he did, Holmes nodded. "Good, yes, good, that's it, breathe. Calm." It took valiant effort, removing his vest and unbuttoning his shirt, but Edmond was able to get his breath back.

"I have never, in all my life before, been so humiliated, hurt, and angry."

"And you have every right to be all those things, Edmond," Holmes said. "Your uncle crossed a line."

Edmond looked up at his father, his face swam before him as he realized with disgust, he had tears in his eyes.

"I was in love with her," Edmond admitted. "And yet all she

was doing was playing me. I even told her everything, dad. I told her I was there to protect the prince not as a friend. I told her the truth. I wanted her to know I cared enough about her to tell her everything so she wouldn't feel betrayed and yet... she keeps this from me? Why?"

"You told Lady Berkley everything?"

"Yes, like a damn fool," Edmond sat on one of the settees. "She even told me she forgave me for lying to her. Do you know how much of a fool that makes me feel? She actually claimed to forgive me of an imagined slight when she knew all along!"

Holmes said nothing for a moment, then walked over to the sideboard and found a decanter. Opening the stopper, he sniffed and then poured two large glasses. Handing one to his son, Edmond took a gulp and shuddered when the strong whiskey slid down his throat.

"I was falling in love with her, dad," he hated the whine in his voice. "I thought maybe, just maybe I could actually have what you and Percy have with mama and Alexandra. I could have a companion, a confidant, a lover, someone to spend my days with. But no. My uncle used my deepest secrets, the things I told him in the absolute assuredness he would keep my trust. He tells someone and they use it against me in the most horrific way possible, all for a case?" he looked at his father. "Please tell me that is madness."

"It is madness," Holmes answered. "I have no answer as to why. I can think of only one explanation. It is obvious there is more at risk here than the king and prince. I can only imagine England is at stake."

"And how does the life, secrets, and betrayal of one man have any effect on it?" Edmond questioned.

"Because of what I was to do," her voice behind them made Edmond jump up from the settee. He turned scathing eyes on her.

288

"Get out," he ordered buttoning up his shirt. She stood her ground but pressed her lips together as if to prevent a sob. Her eyes shone brightly with unshed tears. "I said get out!"

"Edmond," Holmes soothed.

"I never want to see you again."

"At least listen to what we have to say," Mycroft's voice came from behind her and he entered the room fully.

"No, no. Nothing you have to say could possibly be worth what you did," Edmond said.

"You have some explaining to do, Mycroft," Holmes' voice was sharp.

"If we can all calm down, I will explain," Mycroft said.

"I don't want to hear this," Edmond turned to go.

"Moriarty is alive," Arabella stated as he walked to the door.

Everyone in the room froze. Edmond slowly turned back to look at her. "What did you say?"

"Moriarty is alive," she said again.

"How do you know this?" Holmes questioned.

"Because, I was like a daughter to him," she announced.

"You... what?" Edmond challenged.

"Ten years ago, Professor Moriarty found me on the streets. Do you remember the lover I told you about?" Edmond refused to answer. "Because of our indiscretions, my grandfather, the Duke of Pendleton with whom I lived after my parents died, tossed me out onto the streets. I was damaged goods to him," she began. "Moriarty was one of my grandfather's friends and when he found out, he searched for me. He found me, took me in, gave me a job, treated me as a daughter. He always said I had a calculating mind and was eager to teach me. He involved me in some of his plans and after a while I realized the whole picture. He was evil. I didn't know what to do, but knew he had to be stopped. Five years ago, when he was reading the *Times*, he grew into such a fury. Said he would get his revenge. When I asked him on whom, he looked at me and said a name. It was a name he had called me by many times."

"What was the name?" Holmes asked.

"Marguerite," she answered.

Holmes' jaw set and Edmond glanced up at Mycroft.

"He left for a fortnight and I took that opportunity to search for evidence in his private study. I came across a ledger, coded of course, but for one who knew his code, it was easy to read. It showed names, dates, payments, it was a list of every transaction he did. I had my evidence, but I had no one to take it to. Then, I remembered reading about a great detective, Sherlock Holmes. But I knew it was more important to take it to the government. I made discrete inquiries, but one night while Moriarty was gone, I sat up reading Dr. Watson's account of the *Greek Interpreter*. I saw the name Mycroft Holmes and a description of what he did for the British government. I saw the address at the Diogenes Club. I travelled to London and waited outside the club asking anyone who passed where Mr. Holmes was. He had been in Yorkshire or, so I was told. I hurried home sure I was going to be found out.

"Moriarty was home, injured by buckshot. I took out the pellets myself. While under my care, he told me everything. I needed to see justice done. He was a monster. But I wasn't sure what to do."

"She wrote me a note and came to London to meet with me," Mycroft explained. "I immediately saw the importance of the ledger and we discussed it with my superiors. Once it was proven that this ledger was Moriarty's we involved Sir Henry Lyons, Commissioner of Scotland Yard. The only problem was by that time Moriarty had discovered the missing ledger and had flown. Seeing Arabella's talents, I recruited her for the Home Office. She is highly skilled in the art of deduction and with the revolver. She would help us track down Moriarty. Knowing all of his hiding places."

"But you clearly didn't find him," Holmes said.

Edmond tried but failed to move his gaze from Arabella. Seeing her beside his uncle, head bowed was nothing like the temptress he had gotten to know over the last few weeks. Though his heart and soul were shattered by their betrayal, his mind was clearer than it had been in a long time. Arabella had always challenged him, stoked his curiosity, and kept him on his guard. To know it was all his uncle's doing was a bitter pill to swallow.

"No," Mycroft answered, and it took Edmond a moment to remember his father's statement. "We did not. But we knew enough about him to know he would not rest. I have had Baker Street watched these many years to be sure all was well."

"Yes, so I observed," Holmes replied. "But all of this does not answer the question as to why you used my son." His voice was bitter and held an even darker meaning behind it. Holmes was not going to forgive his brother easily.

"Arabella was adept at playing the role she had been trained to do since birth. I got her an audience with the duchess and things progressed. She was to be an inside observer. Protect the future queen. That was what was important."

"And me?" Edmond asked.

"You were never to know. The entirety of your relationship was supposed to end long before intimacy was established," Mycroft explained. "I needed her to get close to you.

So you both could watch the royal couple. Make no mistake, I never encouraged intimacy. She was to distract you if you thought of Moriarty. I couldn't have either you or Sherlock know of our plans. You would want to go off on your own and we would never catch him."

"And your husband, madam?" Edmond questioned. "The war hero?"

She looked up at him, then down again. "Lord Berkley's son works for Mycroft and his lordship married me in name only," Arabella said.

Edmond let out a self-deprecating laugh.

"And what was your connection with the footman who died? Nicolas Bright. You clearly were upset by his death," Edmond went on. "Not to mention I could smell your perfume in the corridor. Was he your lover?"

"No, he was my informant. I had heard Moriarty was getting chummy with a peer and I needed to know who. Bright worked for the Home Office. It was his first mission. His death will always weigh heavily on my mind," Arabella said.

"So, if I may summarize," Edmond began. "You worked with my grandfather, learned of his evil ways, wanted to bring him to justice, got caught, turned your loyalty to the Home Office where you were briefed about me, seduced me, used me, tried to learn more about Moriarty and failed, got a man killed, another wounded, and we still are no closer to discovering who is using the Guy Fawkes chronicle for their own personal gains. Did I miss anything?"

Arabella took a step closer to him. "That is not all true."

"No? Then enlighten me, madam, what part was false?" Edmond questioned.

She looked down. "All I know is, there is a greater issue at stake here. The life of the king and prince. This reeks of Moriarty, I know it."

"And yet you are unable to assist us further," Holmes stated. "I do believe it is time for cooler heads to prevail. In fact, I do believe this woman could be tried and sentenced for her part in Moriarty's crimes. And you had her with the duchess... How are we to know she had nothing to do with all of this? If she seduced one man, she could have seduced multiple."

Arabella gasped in indignation.

"No," Edmond spoke up. "She didn't. She had nothing to do with the current plot."

"And you know this? How?" Holmes questioned.

"I—" Edmond started.

"She used you, Edmond," Holmes said.

"I know," he replied. "But her love of the duchess and England is genuine."

"Bright was trying to give me a message before he died. His mission was to find who was working for Moriarty among the peerage and when he entered the dining hall, his eyes fell on someone, I know it," Arabella said.

"And who would that be?" Holmes demanded.

"I don't know," she admitted. "It was too difficult to see. But I know the initials are L.B., Moriarty has a fascination with initials matching. There are L.B.s being used. I believe he knows I am working for the government and it was me who stole the ledger. He is using my initials, my title's initials as a warning. As far as the others, I don't know."

"L.B.?" Edmond questioned.

"He always did love initials," Holmes stated.

"But what does this have to do with you breaking my trust, Uncle?" Edmond spat.

"There is only one answer I can give," Mycroft stated.

"And that is?"

"I needed to protect you."

"Protect me?"

"Live again. I knew Arabella was special from the moment I met her. She reminds me much of Margot," Mycroft looked at Holmes. "I hoped to introduce you both and see what happened but keep a close eye on you. I know you and Sherlock would go after Moriarty on your own and I could not have history repeat and you be injured like your father was."

"You played with my emotions. You could have easily introduced us at a party and be done with it," Edmond said.

"I could have, but would you have thought much about her? No, it needed to be something interesting. Intriguing to you. My methods may have misfired, but my instincts were correct. But I never encouraged her to become intimate with you."

Edmond stared at him then his gaze slid over to Arabella. Her eyes locked with his and shared all the pain she was feeling at his coldness. But he still could not remove the feeling of betrayal. It wasn't some schoolboy crush, he had given himself, heart, mind, body, and soul to her and she had manipulated everything about their relationship. He didn't even know who she was.

"The only thing your instincts were correct about, Uncle," Edmond said haughtily. "If Moriarty is behind this. There is more to his plan than even we know. Someone killed Nicolas Bright and stabbed Mr. Brown. Someone left those notes for you and the king to find. My father and I will continue that investigation while you continue what you are looking into. If and when our paths cross, my father will discuss this with you. What I said in the garden still holds. You both betrayed my confidence in the most cruel and effective way. I hold you no ill will, but I refuse to see either of you again. Father, if you would. I cannot stay any longer in the presence of the two people who mean nothing to me any longer."

Holmes nodded once, but he saw the troubled look in his eye. Sherlock would do as his son asked but held his opinions.

"Thank you," Edmond breathed. Then, with a final turn to Mycroft and Arabella, he continued. "I thank you for giving me a clearer picture of what my purpose was. I bid you both farewell. Please do not attempt to speak to me or call upon me at any time. My man will gather my remaining things from Pall Mall, and I will find more suitable lodgings. Madam, I wish you well in your chosen field. You may rest assured you played your part to perfection, I even thought for a moment you cared about me."

"I do, Edmond," she cried.

"The game is over," he replied. "Good evening." He bowed stiffly, turned his back on them, locked eyes with his father and stalked out of the room. Making his way up to his empty room, he lit the fire and found a decanter of whiskey.

Terrey met him in his room a couple hours later, but Edmond didn't remember what he said to his valet as his words were slurred and mind foggy. Terrey said nothing as he took the glass in Edmond's hand, the decanter from the nightstand, and helped him change into his nightshirt. Edmond fell onto the mattress and pillow still smelling her jasmine perfume. Blindly groping the nightstand, he grabbed whatever bottle of oil he got his hand on and dumped the entire contents onto the pillow and sheets beside him. As the scent of lemongrass suffocatingly filled the room, Edmond closed his eyes and willed his stomachache, heartache, and headache to go away. Things would look better in the morning.

Chapter Thirty-Five

Things did not look better in the morning.

Edmond woke to a pounding in his head as someone shook him awake. His stomach roiled and he knew he was going to be sick. Heaving himself over the edge of the mattress, he was grateful to whoever had slid the chamber pot over. He ejected all the contents of his stomach in three body wracking, bone straining, expulsions. A cool cloth fell over his neck as he spit the bile into the pot. His throat felt as if he swallowed shards of glass. His body shivered with the pain and disgust. The smell in his nose was rancid as his body kept spasming. Finally, someone pressed a cloth under his nose, the smell of ginger eased his body and stomach.

"Thank you," he groaned.

"You're welcome," Arabella's voice said.

He cracked his eyelid to see her standing beside the bed. "Dear god, am I never to have a rest from you? What do you want, woman?"

"Edmond, I—"

"You came here for a reason and it was not to apologize again, madam," Edmond said. "Where is Terrey?"

"With your father," she answered. "He was loathe to leave you in your state but he was the last to see his highness."

Edmond's foggy brain could not understand what she was saying so he merely grunted.

"Here," she offered water, or what smelled like water mixed with some spearmint. He gingerly drank and swished his mouth. Spitting it out into the chamber pot, he drank some more and pressed the handkerchief against his nose.

Then, as if he had been tossed into an icy lake in winter, his senses returned, and he gasped. Looking up at her, he searched her face. *Small lines on her forehead, lips pursed, eyes shining, overall demeanor of suppressed urgency.*

"What do you mean Terrey was the last to see his highness?" he demanded.

Arabella looked away. "Apparently, after the fireworks show last night, the prince left with someone and has not been seen since."

"Left? Left with whom?"

"We do not know," she admitted. "Terrey only saw a top

hat and coat; it was too dark to see anything else. Your father, uncle, brother, and valet are in the same room we were in last night."

Edmond threw the sheets off him and stood, his head and body protested, and he wobbled on his feet. Arabella caught him and held his arms as he got his legs back under him. As soon as he was settled, he ripped his arms out of her grasp as if her hands were fire.

"I need to dress," he stated.

"I can help you," she offered.

"I do not need your help, madam. Please leave."

A look crossed her face, but it was gone before he could figure out what it was. With a huff, she crossed her arms over her chest, stalked to one of the chairs, and sat with a flourish.

"No," she stated.

"Excuse me?" he questioned.

"I am not leaving. You can be angry with me all you want but there is no reason for you to try to kick me out of your life. I love you and that is not an act."

Edmond froze. His head was still spinning and his mind warred with knowing there was no time to deal with her but...

"You love me?" he asked.

"Yes," she answered. "And I know you have every right to be angry, hurt, and upset but there is no need to be downright malicious and vindictive."

"You have no idea what I'm feeling right now," Edmond stated.

"Yes, I do. I know you."

"And how is it you do know me?" Edmond's bitter question made her look away. "We have no time to discuss this. The prince is missing, and it was my duty to keep him safe. I must find him. If I had not been so distracted by a bit of fun this would not have happened." Her soft gasp was loud to his ringing ears. "Now, if you please, I must dress and go down to meet with my father."

Without another word, Arabella stood and swept elegantly out of the room. Only then did Edmond allow himself to fall back on the bed, his hands covering his face. His stomach still rolled, and his head pounded, but he put aside the ill feelings and stood once more. Crossing to the wardrobe, he thanked his lucky stars Terrey had thought to pack some of his old clothes. Pulling out the loose-fitting shirt and an old vest and coat, he shrugged into the clothes, splashed water on his face and stared at his reflection in the mirror with bloodshot eyes. He looked like death warmed over. Not only the alcohol and the revelation the night before, but the fact that the prince was missing. He would never forgive himself if something happened to him.

By the time Edmond entered the Yellow Drawing Room, the king, queen, and duchess had joined everyone. The king paced like a lion in his cage. When he saw Edmond, he turned menacing eyes on him.

"You said you would protect him," he bellowed. "You promised everything would be well. Well, does it bloody look like it's all well?"

Edmond bowed, "Your majesty," he began. "I cannot apologize enough and can only say, I will find him."

"Find him? How do we know he's not dead yet?" the king shouted.

The queen sniffled and the duchess sobbed a moment then regained her composure. As much as he hated it, his eyes were drawn to Arabella who took the duchess' hand in hers and held it in comfort.

"I can assure you, your majesty, the prince is still alive," Mycroft stated.

The king whirled around to look at him. "And what were you doing last night? You should have been keeping an eye on the room!"

"There was something that needed my attention, sire," Mycroft stated. "It was unavoidable."

"Unavoidable?" the king bellowed. "My son is missing!"

"And we will do everything in our power to find him," Sherlock said. "Sire, please show Edmond the note found in his room."

The king seemed to calm under Holmes' gaze and with a nod, he pulled out a folded piece of paper. Edmond stepped forward and accepted it.

May 25th, 1901

Your esteemed majesty,

By now you have received warnings from my colleagues and myself regarding our views on your chosen course of action. We are deeply saddened by the unnecessary death of the young footman – was he a footman? – at the Duke of Pembroke's dinner party. It was unnecessary. Had he stayed immobilized, steps would not have been taken to incapacitate him. Alas, in all war there is collateral damage, and make no mistake, your majesty, we are in a war. You simply do not understand it. But we can help you see. We regret the course of action we have taken may cause great personal grievance to you, but when the law and parliament failed us, we had no choice but to act. We have a list of demands.

Firstly, you will issue a public statement, I will leave the newspaper up to you, stating you are opposed to the proposed bill before the houses that would give the working classes a tax credit if they set up in business. This nullifies the god given right of the upper classes and prevents us from fulfilling our duty of providing our tenants a place to live and retaining the right to keep a portion of their profits.

Secondly, you will strongly and without question release any Jew working for you, in the government, and make it clear you will not support any and all fraternization between the English people and those of Israeli descent. They are a stigma to our nation. You will also no longer conference with Cassel, de Hirsch, and the Rothschilds on financial matters.

Thirdly, and most importantly, you will utterly condemn, without question the Irish Independence bill, the Indian Independence bill, and the Reformation Act.

Once these have been done, you will attend tomorrow evening's performance of Stanford's Much Ado About Nothing *at The Royal Opera House in Covent Garden. You will arrive precisely five minutes before curtain, take your seat exactly two minutes before, and are not permitted to leave your seat. At the end of the third act of the opera, and only at the end, you will get up and meet your son in the lobby.*

If any of these instructions are ignored you will find your son's body floating down the Thames, his throat slit from Ear to Ear.

With deference,

L.B.

Chapter Thirty-Six

Edmond looked over at his father, his body still fighting the effects of the excess alcohol, but his brain was suddenly clear. This was the plan all along. If Moriarty was involved, then he would have a contingency plan. His eyes went to Arabella.

"Where is it?" he demanded. She looked up at him.

"What?" she questioned.

"Where is his message to you?"

She stared at him for a long moment. Then, with a shallow

breath, she pulled out a piece of paper from between her dress and chest. Edmond closed his eyes wishing he was wrong. He looked away from her and was glad to see his father walked over to take the message.

"Does he know you're working for Mycroft?" Dr. Watson asked.

She looked up at him but shook her head.

"Of course he does, Watson," Holmes corrected. "He knows everything about those he wants to keep tabs on. He probably even knows of your..." he looked at Edmond. "Indiscretions."

Edmond looked away. This was not how he had planned everything to go. He remembered his golden rule. Never plan anything, it is a sure way to know it will never happen. He should have taken his own advice. A beautiful woman can manipulate for her own gain and Edmond needed only those who understood that to be around the king at such a vulnerable time. He was a fool.

Holmes showed Edmond the note. It was simple with a date, a time, and a location. The next day's opera at the Royal Opera House.

"What do you know?" Edmond demanded from her. Arabella looked up, fear and hurt in her eyes. "What else do you know? What else has he done?"

"Nothing, I give you my word," she replied.

"Forgive me, madam if I do not trust your word. You have proven not to be very adept at keeping it."

Holmes held up a hand stopping his son and turned to look at Arabella. "If I were to say to you the footman had a scrap of paper in his hand referencing Nash's eighteen twenty-six building plan of Buckingham Palace, or a letter found, written by a known conspirator of Guy Fawkes, and the book *Guy Fawkes* by Ainsworth, would it mean anything to you?"

Arabella's face drained of color. She swallowed audibly.

"Yes, Mr. Holmes," she replied. "It does mean something." Glancing back at Mycroft, she continued. "Before I left to accept the position with her grace," she looked over at the duchess. "I overheard Moriarty speaking with two men. I could not open the door to see who, but I could hear."

"And what were they saying?" Holmes questioned.

Arabella took a deep breath. "They were saying they wanted to make an example of how the king is making a mockery of the monarchy. They wanted to restore the ruling classes and create a deeper divide between nobility and the lower classes. One man said it was like they were the modern-day Guy Fawkes and how he would be revered today if people hadn't been influenced by a king who socializes with..." her cheeks pinked, and she looked down. "They used some derogatory terms, Mr. Holmes."

"You do not have to repeat them, I am sure we could infer," Sherlock replied.

"Ask her what the plans for Buckingham Palace have to do with it?" Edmond demanded.

Holmes turned to look at Arabella, not wanting to waste time in repeating a question she clearly heard simply because Edmond did not want to speak directly to her.

"They knew their majesties were planning a ball in the late queen's honor, and they wanted to use it as a distraction."

"A distraction for what?" Holmes asked.

"I don't know," she shook her head. "When I listened, I heard someone in the hallway behind me and rushed away."

"Did you recognize any of the voices?" Mycroft questioned.

"Not besides Moriarty's. But I did hear a name."

"Don't make us ask," Edmond stated.

She looked over at him. "Brown."

"Brown?" Holmes asked.

Edmond muttered a curse. Holmes turned to him. "Lewis Brown," he looked up at the king. "Your valet, majesty."

"Damnation," King Edward stated. "But the man was stabbed."

"A clever ploy to throw us off the scent," Holmes replied. "A device that has been used as a diversion many times before. In fact, as soon as Edmond told me about it, I was suspicious of the man."

"He would have access to everything," the king went on.

"I believe that was the plan, sire," Holmes said. "Anything else you wish to add, Lady Berkley?"

Arabella looked down but shook her head.

"What was your part to play in all of this with Moriarty?" Edmond questioned.

She looked up at him, her eyes begged him for something, but he ignored it.

"I had nothing to do with the plot," she announced. "I told him I was staying with friends because the season never agreed with me."

"Clearly he knows who those *friends* are if he is sending you notes here."

"Yes, that is my fear," she answered.

"Fear?" Dr. Watson asked.

"It means he knows everything," Arabella said. "If I go to that meeting on tomorrow." She glanced up at Edmond then away.

"It will be my death."

The duchess and queen gasped.

"We will not let that happen, Arabella," the duchess squeezed her hand.

She said nothing as she looked up at Edmond again. His heart screamed with pain and hurt, but his love could not be denied either. With that, he turned away and ignored the pull he felt.

"The question now is," Holmes began. "What to do about the demands?"

"I would not have anyone manipulate royal decisions but for the safety of my son..." the king sighed. "Mr. Holmes, I appeal to you. What do you think I should do?"

Mycroft harrumphed and stuffed his hands into his pockets. "If we give in to his demands and do as he says that does not guarantee the prince's safety. However, it is the best course of action. Once we are assured of the prince's safety and we have these blackguards in custody we can appeal to public sentiment and explain your decisions and why you were forced to condemn the bills. The public's sentiment can change with the correct motivation. So, in my opinion, sire, we give in to the demands."

"And may God forgive me," King Edward stated. "Very well, I will leave the arrangements up to you, Holmes."

"Sire," Mycroft bowed.

"And as for you, Lady Berkley, you will remain here with my wife. Ignore the message. I will not have your life in the balance too."

"Sire, I—" she began to protest but King Edward held up his hand.

"It is decided."

"Sire," she agreed and bowed her head.

"Now, if you would excuse us, gentlemen, I wish to comfort my wife and daughter-in-law in peace."

"Of course," Mycroft bowed once more and headed to the door.

Edmond did not look at his uncle as he passed, nor Arabella when she followed. He, Sherlock, Dr. Watson, and Terrey left the room together.

"Sherlock," Mycroft started. Holmes stopped. "This whole business is abominable. But we must put inconsequential things aside and work together."

"Inconsequential?" Holmes questioned. "And what would that be, Mycroft?"

"You know damned well what I mean, dammit," he answered.

"Those inconsequential things you so hastily want to overlook, have caused more than one person pain and a sense of betrayal. It questions your loyalty, brother. So as much as I agree we could work together on this, those inconsequential matters of which you speak so dismissively, will continue to affect all of us."

"Mr. Holmes," Arabella began. Holmes turned sharp eyes on her.

"I do not believe you are needed, my lady," he stated. "My wife welcomed you into our embrace. My son fell in love with you. And you betrayed my family and our hospitality. You expect me to listen to a word you say? No, madam. As the king ordered, you are to stay here and once we have caught those who plan to do us harm, then perhaps we will discuss proper sentencing for your crimes. Make no mistake, you are far from innocent in all of this. Now kindly leave us alone in order to fix the mess that you had a hand in creating. You are dismissed, madam. And pray I do not ever get the chance to impart my justice on your slight to my son." Holmes turned away from her and Edmond had to force himself not to be swayed by her tears. When she glanced at Edmond, he turned his back on her and closed his eyes when he heard her sob and run down the hall.

"I say, that was uncalled for, Sherlock," Mycroft said.

"Be grateful I need your connections, brother mine or you would be joining her. Me you can manipulate, always have, Mycroft. But the second you play with my family? That is it."

"You have no idea why."

"Don't I?" Holmes demanded. "I have not forgotten our father, and it seems the reason I cannot forget him, is he is standing before me once more but this time in the form of my brother."

Mycroft's jaw ticked as he clenched his teeth.

"Now, I would like to head back to Baker Street since there is nothing more that can be done. Edmond, do you and Terrey want to join us?"

"Yes, please, father," Edmond said. "I can stay here no longer."

"Then come now, son," Holmes replied. "Watson."

"Yes, yes, of course," Watson stated and followed Holmes out the door.

Edmond turned once more to his uncle.

"My methods may have lacked, Edmond," Mycroft began. "But my intension was never to harm you."

"I wish that were the truth. But the part I cannot forgive is when you told her of my past. I told you that in confidence."

"I know I hurt you, my boy, but—"

"But nothing, sir," he answered. "Do not confuse betrayal with hurt. Good day."

Edmond strode out of the hall, following his father to their waiting carriage, Terrey by his side.

"I'm sorry for all this, Edmond," Terrey whispered. "Damn sorry. If I had known her true nature and intention, I would never have encouraged your infatuation."

"If you had known Terrey, I would have lost the only true friend I have."

"My loyalty is to you. I swear to you on my father's grave, I knew nothing about this."

"And I believe you, my friend," Edmond stated. "But there is more going on here than I know. I will need you."

"I am at your disposal."

"We need to find Brown. And we need to find out who is the peer associated with them."

"I have some contacts I can reach out to," Terrey replied.

"Do that and make some inquiries below stairs. See if anyone remembers seeing Brown with anyone other than his majesty. Then, meet me at Baker Street."

"Sir," Terrey bowed and opened the door of the cab for him, once shut, he bowed as the cab lurched forward.

"Terrey reaching out to his contacts?" Holmes questioned.

"He is indeed," Edmond answered. "If Brown is known, he will be found."

"Then let us go back to Baker Street. Everyone will be there."

"Percy too?" Edmond questioned.

Holmes looked at him with an understanding look. "Yes."

"Wonderful. Does he know?"

"He has an idea. I was not going to tell him or anyone. Your mother doesn't know either."

"Thank you for keeping that to yourself," Edmond said. "But I will have to tell them."

"Only if you desire it."

"I do, otherwise Percy will constantly ask, and I do not want to answer."

"I am sorry for you, Edmond," Watson stated. "It's damned messy when it's an affair of the heart."

"Thank you, Doctor. But if I had kept my wits, this wouldn't have happened. You are right, dad, women are not to be trusted even the best of them."

"I only said that in Watson's stories," Holmes answered. "And only for the sake of those reading. Some women, like your mother, sister, and Alexandra are worth trusting."

"But others are not. I have learned my lesson."

"I know it's not my place," Watson began. "But that girl seemed horribly upset. In my experience, women are only like that if there is love."

"Or they are caught in a scheme and have been found out. Facing their own possible demise," Edmond stated and then looked out the window effectively ending the conversation. He could not admit that he felt Watson's words within his soul. The thought of Arabella dying, ached in more places than his head.

Closing his eyes, he willfully stopped his thoughts from wandering to their evenings wrapped in each other's arms. He loved her. God help him, but it was true. Nothing could stop it.

The question was, could he forgive her?

Chapter Thirty-Seven

Henri had never been happier to see anyone before. He had missed *Monsieur* very much since he had left. But the moment Henri saw him, his brow furrowed. *Monsieur* was upset about something.

"*Monsieur?*" Henri questioned.

"Henri," *Monsieur* breathed out when he saw him, a smile cracking his lips. "It is good to see you, son." He opened his arms and Henri hurried to embrace him.

"Are you all right, *Monsieur?*" Henri asked. "You seem...

something."

"I am all right now," he answered. "I have missed you. Thank you for that wonderful drawing. I kept it with me always. It helped me through some of the darkest times."

"I am glad you liked it," Henri puffed out his chest at the compliment. "I have drawn many others. Milady even let me draw the new baby."

"Indeed? I am pleased. You will have to show me all of your drawings soon. But at the moment," *Monsieur* squeezed his shoulder affectionately. "I must speak with everyone about an urgent matter. Then we will have dinner together."

Henri beamed and nodded enthusiastically. *Monsieur* cupped his face and smiled almost sadly. Henri promised right then, he would find out what happened and help if he could. *Monsieur* deserved to be happy.

Monsieur walked further into the room and embraced his mother who brushed her thumb against his forehead as if straightening the wrinkle that formed.

"*Ça va?*" *Madame* Holmes asked him. *Monsieur* nodded, then seemed to think about it. He shook his head.

"Ed?" Sir Charles, who asked Henri to call him *Oncle,* walked over cautiously. "What's going on?"

Monsieur took a deep, almost mournful breath then closed his eyes. "She works for Mycroft and Moriarty."

"What?" everyone in the room, apart from Henri, Mr. Holmes, and Dr. Watson gasped. Henri looked from one to the other of them. He did not know who the second person he mentioned was.

"What are you talking about, Ed?" *Oncle* asked.

"Sit down, *mon cher*," *Madame* Holmes ushered him

further into the room and sat him in one of the two armchairs beside the fire. She poured cognac and handed it to him. "Tell us what happened."

Edmond had never wanted to run away more than he did at that moment. Not run from anyone in the room, or what he was telling his family, but actually run. Find a wide-open space, like he used to in France and China and just run at full speed. He needed the freedom, the welcome ache in his lungs would be a reprieve from the ache in his chest. He remembered when he had lain in his bed, Arabella's head on his chest and he told her all about Henri. He nearly wept when he walked into 221b Baker Street and saw his adopted son. Henri was so fresh, so innocent, so happy. Selfishly, Edmond had hoped some of that happiness, innocence, and freshness would rub off on him, but it didn't. Couldn't.

He told his family everything quickly and made sure to spare his mother the details of their relationship. But when he mentioned Arabella's connection with Moriarty, he saw her flinch and take his father's hand. There was no love lost between her and her father, James Moriarty, as the man had dogged their every move and made life hell for them. But Edmond knew how painful it must have been for his mother to hear Edmond's infatuation with a woman so closely associated with Moriarty and how she had welcomed Arabella into her embrace.

"I am sorry, mama," he finally ended. "Had I known her true relationship, I would never have…"

"There is nothing to apologize for, *mon cher,*" she said. "I am only so sorry you were affected by him yet again."

"That damn woman," Percy muttered. "How dare she use you like she did."

"It was a mutual infatuation, Percy," Edmond said. "She didn't *use* me."

"And for what it's worth," Watson spoke up. "She seemed extremely remorseful. Now, I know I'm not a woman, but in my experiences, women seldom love hard enough to weep. But she seemed genuinely upset by her betrayal."

"She used my brother. Used her knowledge gained from Mycroft to become irresistible to him, and yes, I will not call him uncle at the moment, I don't care how disrespectful it is. Think no more on her, Edmond," Percy ordered. "She isn't worth it."

"All I am saying is, don't lock the door until it is assured everything is on the other side. Air it out. She cares deeply. I saw it in her eyes," Watson said.

"I agree with you, papa," Alexandra answered. "I love you, Edmond and I never want to see you hurt but if there is a chance that you were truly happy with her and she with you, don't you owe it to yourself to see where it goes?"

"As much as I appreciate all of your advice, and I do not dismiss any of it," Edmond began. "We have more pressing business. The prince has been kidnapped and the king has a list of demands these anarchists are wanting. Let us turn our attention to that."

Edmond could not admit even to himself how much Watson's words gave him hope. He had to lock it away. He could not care for her. He could not open that door again. But as he lay on the chaise in his parent's living room that evening, as he could not evict Henri from his room, his mind strayed. They had spent many hours speaking of what they could do to find the prince, but knowing who was behind it, there would be no evidence. They had come to the conclusion Brown would be of no use to them. A valet would not have a hidden place to keep the prince, and without the name of the peer working with them, there was no way they could even compile a list of possible locations to investigate.

Holmes, Percy, Watson, and Edmond had agreed to go to the Royal Theater in the morning and speak to the owner who apparently owed Sherlock a favor. Cedric and Rebecca – who had come over from Hughes Hall in Somerset – retired to their townhouse. Rebecca looked tired and as Cedric shuffled her out of the room and into their waiting carriage, she threw a kiss to her family and leaned back. Edmond was certain she was asleep within moments.

Seeing his sister's stomach round with child, and the loving looks she surreptitiously sent her husband, made Edmond's heart swell with happiness. He quelled the irrational jealousy that quickly followed. Suddenly, he remembered Arabella looking at him one evening as he ordered a bottle of champagne from the passing scullery maid. Terrey brought it up with two glasses and some cheese, dried fruits, and chocolate truffles. Edmond did not question how Terrey knew and only thanked him for the assortment. Shaking his head, Edmond tried to shake the memory. Then, an entirely new thought occurred, what if he hadn't been careful enough? What if Arabella carried his child? That thought made him bolt upright and look around the room panting.

"Dear god," he breathed. The image of her round with his child was the most beautiful thing he never thought he would ever see. He closed his eyes as the life he had hoped for flashed before him. A cottage in the country with space for him to run and perform his routines, Henri racing out every morning to sketch the views, and a wife by his side... not just any woman, Arabella. The last few weeks had been such a whirlwind in his life. Fatherhood, romance, society, they all changed him. As much as he felt at home in his own clothes, like embracing an old friend there was an awkwardness. He was glad to be back in his own clothes, but he no longer felt fulfilled. When he was Sir Edmond, he changed, and he no longer felt the distaste or dissatisfaction of being someone he wasn't. Somehow, over the last few weeks, he embraced his new identity and without it, without her, he was rudderless, floating on an open sea aimlessly.

How could he still love someone who had betrayed him?

"Edmond?" his mother's voice came from the doorway to his parent's room. "Are you awake, *mon cher?*"

"*Oui*, mama," he answered sitting up again and looking over at her. "Are you all right?"

Marguerite walked fully into the room, dressed in her housecoat, her hair was braided in a long braid over her shoulder. She sat in the chair opposite him. Edmond swung his legs over the side of the settee and sat up, the blanket pooling around his waist. His silken *changshan* glided over his skin as he moved.

"Is something wrong?" he asked.

"Oh, no, darling," she answered. "I just wanted to talk to you."

"All right," he replied. "What is it?"

"Did I ever tell you the story about how I found your father and uncle stealing a ledger from your grandfather?"

Edmond's brows furrowed. "Yes, you have. Several times," he smiled.

"Good, then that makes this easier," she said.

"Makes what easier?" his head still ached slightly, and he wasn't following his mother's words.

"Your father betrayed my trust. I was the one who told him about the secret hiding place and the lever in the chimney. When I caught him, I realized what he had done, and I wanted nothing to do with him. He had used me, my knowledge of my father's activities to his advantage. It was later that night as I lay awake in bed, I realized that I loved him more than anything else. I didn't care what he had done, even though his methods were wrong, he proved he loved me over and over again and I could not give him up. I wanted to be with him more than anything. I loved him. That next evening, he came back. Snuck in and sent a servant to get me.

"I hurried to him, my heart aching with the dichotomy of my feelings. He had hurt me, betrayed my trust, and yet I still loved him. When I saw him and saw how he hated himself for what he had done, I could do nothing but love him more. He held me and told me how sorry he was. He swore his feelings for me were genuine and it was only his hatred of crime that drove him to use what I had told him. He said he knew he did not deserve my forgiveness but cried to me telling me how he loved me and couldn't see me living in a world where such evil existed. He begged me to marry him. When I agreed, knowing my love for him outweighed the illusion of betrayal, I never felt such happiness. I want that happiness for you, my love."

Distractedly, Edmond replied. "But Moriarty shot father right after."

"He did," she agreed. "And the hopelessness, fear, and anger that washed over me was worse than I can possibly relate. But he was fine, and that scar reminds me every time of what I nearly gave up. Yes, he hurt me, he betrayed my confidence, but he did it to rid the world of the man who haunted us. It did not change his love for me. Nor, if I am honest, my love for him. We are soulmates, and I have never thought differently. The love we share gave us you and your brother and sister. And now has given us Philippe, Eleanor, Lillian, and Henri. I want you to know what that is like. Perhaps the young lady in China was your true love, and no, your father did not tell me anything, I knew. But if she wasn't, then perhaps Arabella is? You won't know unless you speak with her. What does your heart tell you?"

Edmond looked at his mother and fought the feeling of

tears. "I've loved Ara since I first spoke with her. But how do I know I love her and not the person she was created to be?"

"Because if she didn't care about you and was someone different, she wouldn't be trying to see you."

"What do you mean?" Edmond asked.

Marguerite sighed softly. "Sherlock," she called much louder than she had been all evening.

The door opened and his father walked in, dressed in a smoking jacket, but it was Arabella's tear-streaked face that caught his attention behind his father. Edmond stood with a start when he saw her.

"Arabella?" he questioned.

"I hoped you would be here," her voice pattern was stuttered as if she was hiding the fact she was trying not to cry. "Please, can I speak with you?"

Edmond couldn't take his eyes off her. She was so beautiful and yet, his mind told him he should say no.

"Yes," he finally said.

She took that as a small victory. He saw her eyes change from fear to hope in an instant. Marguerite stood from her seat and walked over to Sherlock. Without another word, she took his arm, and they left the room.

Edmond and Arabella stood staring at each other for a long moment until she spoke softly. "I have decided to keep the appointment in the note."

Edmond's eyes widened and his heart raced. "You cannot do that."

"I can, and I will," she answered gently. "I have to see this through. If there is a way I can end this, end *him* without any fuss,

I will do it. I wanted to tell you so if anything does happen to me, we can part as... friends?"

Edmond's breathing grew heavy and he finally threw the wall around his heart away. "Enough of this," he said and opened his arms. She cried and rushed to him. He tightened his arms around her and finally felt whole again. "This is where you belong, Ara. Here in my arms, just like I belong in yours."

"Yes, yes," she sobbed, her arms tightening around his back. "I wanted to tell you. I wanted to tell you everything. But I wasn't allowed. I needed the Home Office's protection. I couldn't... I had to play by their rules." She looked up at him, the love and tears in her eyes filled him with such longing. "Please forgive me. I love you, Edmond. I don't know how or why or when. I was in love with you before I even knew it. Everything we shared, everything that happened between us, was real. I swear it to you."

"I know," he whispered and pressed her head against his shoulder. "I am sorry I spoke to you the way I did. I was angry and hurt. I wanted you to be mine and only mine. I didn't want to share you. When I heard you and my uncle speaking after what you told me earlier that day, I lost my head. The ugly truth fell over me and I didn't have a chance to catch my breath. I believed the worst and my mind shut to protect itself."

"You had every right to be angry with me and your uncle. We lied to you on some things, but I speak the truth when I say I love you. I have never met anyone like you and any time I'm away from you, I cannot breathe. Please forgive me, my love. I never want to ever hurt you like that or in any way again."

"Ara," Edmond breathed and pulled away just enough to look down at her. "I love you too. It happened quickly, I'll grant, but from the moment we matched wits, I knew I had found the woman I was to be with for the rest of my life."

"You forgive me?"

"I do," he answered.

She smiled and took a deep relieved breath. "Then I can go to this meeting with a full heart."

"You aren't going anywhere. I am not losing you again."

"I must," she answered. "I know him. I know what he'll do. He won't lift a finger. There will be no evidence."

"We will find some."

"There will be no evidence," she stated again.

"Ara," he began.

"No," she leaned up and wrapped one hand around the back of his neck. "All will be well. I promise you. He may try but he cannot hurt me."

"I have a bullet wound in my side from five years ago that disproves that."

"I know." She coyly looked at him while her fingers ghosted over the location of the scar. "I've seen it, remember?"

Edmond breathed a chuckle and grinned. Arabella's face grew serious.

"I have to do this."

"Then I go with you."

"No, he won't show himself if I'm not alone."

"Dammit, Ara," he cursed.

"I'll be all right. I have you to live for." She leaned in and kissed him. Though they had kissed many times since the first time, that kiss felt more intimate as they explored each other, seeking totality, love, forgiveness. Edmond broke the kiss and rested his forehead on hers.

"Stay with me?" he asked. "Always?"

"Always," she agreed. "But now, I want to meet your son."

Edmond smiled. "Henri is upstairs. Let me go get him."

And with that, he pulled out of her embrace and headed up the stairs with a light heart. His mother's words ringing in his ears but love surrounding him.

Chapter Thirty-Eight

The news shocked the nation when the morning papers announced the king's sudden change of position. Gossip ran rampant everything from the king's newest mistress was a Bolshevik spy and poisoned his ear, to an extraterrestrial had taken over the king's form, Edmond chalked it up to one of the newest H.G. Wells books. But as Edmond finished his morning tea, the knock on the study door drew his attention. Holmes folded the newspaper and called for them to come in.

Terrey opened the door, looking rather worse for wear, but eyes bright and smile broad as he bowed.

"Sir," he said addressing Edmond. "I found him."

"Oh, good man, Terrey," Edmond stood and ushered him into the room. "Sit down, have some breakfast, you look in need of it."

"Thank you, sir," Terrey bowed to Marguerite who sat opposite him. "Forgive my appearance, Mrs. Holmes. It was a long evening."

"Do not worry, Terrey," Marguerite replied. "I am used to such appearance when Mr. Holmes is on a case. Do tell us, what did you find out?"

"Is that Terrey I heard?" Arabella questioned walking in, dressed in one of Marguerite's morning dresses, Henri by her side.

Terrey stood quickly and, eyes wide, bowed to her.

"Oh, please, do sit back down, Terrey," she said coming in and sitting on the settee, patting a spot for Henri beside her. "What have you found out?"

Terrey didn't speak as he turned bewildered eyes to Edmond.

"Later," Edmond promised. "But all that is needed to know right now is what did you discover?"

"Ehm, sir, is it wise?" he asked glancing at Arabella.

"Yes, all is well," Edmond answered.

"Oh," he sighed and grinned. "Then, I am pleased," he said. Though he turned stern eyes on Arabella as if his opinion of her was still slightly tainted and her presence worrisome. "I contacted several of my acquaintances in the more underground areas of town and after a laborious search, I found someone who knew where he was. Heading to the..." he side glanced at Marguerite and Arabella, "pub, I was able to find him. He was otherwise engaged if you follow me, sir, but I was able to wait and speak with some of the other patrons as well as... employees. I found out Brown frequented the location but never stayed very long as he always had bad luck with the cards. But apparently last night, he had come into some money and had first decided to... engage in *other* delights besides drink and cards." Terrey was trying for delicacy, but it was taking too long. Edmond noted his father's disapproval of the delay.

"He was visiting a brothel," Holmes finally said. "And he was busy upstairs, time is of the essence, Terrey."

Terrey's face turned bright red as he looked away from the women present.

"Have no fear," Marguerite stated. "I am sure Arabella and I have heard much worse."

"Yes, ma'am," Terrey answered. "When he came to the card tables, I bribed one of the men I was talking to, to buy him a bottle of whiskey and get him just drunk enough he wouldn't recognize me."

"Very sound," Holmes replied. "What happened?"

"After he was a little, shall we say, loosened, I joined in a game of cards opposite him. There was a moment I thought he might have recognized me, but fortunately he was too far gone to think. We played a couple rounds. He was indeed tossing coin around liberally. After a few winning hands, he started talking. Some of his words were nonsensical as it is to be expected, but he spoke of a glorious future one where those who played their cards right would hold more power and have great wealth. He also mentioned something I found highly interesting."

"Go on, Terrey," Edmond prompted.

"His exact words were; *and like Cymbeline, his son is taken by a traitor. Let's see him fall. We can manipulate the son.*"

"Cymbeline?" Henri questioned.

"One of Shakespeare's plays, dear," Arabella explained. "And rather dark."

"Indeed," Marguerite replied.

"Remind, my dear?" Holmes asked.

"Cymbeline, the Vassal King of Britain by the Roman Empire had two sons and a daughter. His sons were kidnapped as infants and his daughter once grown married her love in secret but being Cymbeline's only heir, she needed to marry royalty. Cymbeline's second wife was married previously and had a son whom she wanted married to the princess while she plots to murder both Cymbeline and his daughter."

"How does she plan it?"

"She purchases poison, but the court doctor becomes suspicious and switches it at the last minute giving her merely a sedative."

"There must be something," Holmes stood and paced before the fire. "What happens then?"

"Well," Marguerite thought a long moment. "It's been a little while since I've read it, Sherlock."

"If I may?" Arabella offered.

Marguerite turned to her. "Please."

"The queen gives the potion that she believes is harmful to a servant of the king and princess. But the servant gives the vial to the princess and tells her it is magical. There is a rumored plot to kill her by her husband. He thinks she was unfaithful to him with another. She was not but the servant tells her she must go, and she disguises herself as a boy. As she journeys, her health declines and she is found by a man and his two sons, who also, it is revealed are her brothers."

"Do they know who they are?"

"No," Arabella explained. "They are unaware they are anything more than the sons of a hunter. The queen's son has followed her and after insulting the two sons, he is killed. With her health declining, the princess takes the potion, thinking it will save her. She is still dressed as a boy. The men find her and, thinking she is dead hurry away to prepare the now two bodies, one of the princess and one of the queen's son, for burial. In the meantime, she wakes up and is discovered by the envoy from the Roman Emperor. He takes her as his own servant. Then the hunter, the two sons, and the lover of the princess all join forces to help Cymbeline against the Roman invasion intent on taking his throne. Everything turns out well, though, the sons are restored to the king and the princess is allowed to remain married her love. It's a quick synopsis and not well detailed, Mr. Holmes. I am sorry."

"And what happened to the queen?"

"She dies," Arabella stated, then her eyes grew wide. "Oh, dear god, no."

"Terrey, call for a cab. Ara, get back to Buckingham and protect the queen and duchess, call for my brother. He will help," Edmond ordered. Terrey hurried to the door and raced down the stairs. Arabella hurried to grab her cloak and hat.

"Will you—"

"I'll be fine," Edmond promised going over to her. "I'll send word once we captured them."

"Be careful."

"I will. You be careful, too. I can't be there to protect you."

Her smile turned proud. "I don't need you to protect me. I'm a crack shot and have studied how to defend myself."

She leaned up and pressed a quick kiss to his lips.

"Love you," she whispered and rushed out of the room as

Terrey came back up to say the cab has been summoned.

Terrey, Edmond, and Marguerite turned to look at Holmes.

"This isn't just about the queen," Holmes was still pacing. "Something about that story…"

"And if it was, then why kidnap the prince, sir?" Terrey asked.

"That is the crux of the matter, Terrey," Holmes answered. "I need to think."

"And that means silence, come Henri, let us go back upstairs. I want you to continue reading," Marguerite stated. "If you would like, Terrey, there is still the bath set up in Mr. Holmes's room. I will ask for hot water to be brought for you."

"I would be grateful, ma'am," Terrey replied.

"Go," Edmond offered. "I will stay with my father."

"Yes, sir," Terrey bowed and headed into the other room as Marguerite and Henri, after calling down to Mrs. Hudson, went upstairs to Henri's room where Marguerite was continuing his reading lessons.

Edmond watched his father continue to pace, then sit in his armchair. Holmes' eyes glazed as if he wasn't seeing anything before him and he leaned back, fingertips pressed together in his usual contemplative pose. Edmond remained silent as his father thought, only lighting a cigarette for him, and offering it before lighting another and sitting opposite him.

The story of Cymbeline was not one of the Bard's works Edmond was familiar with, but as he turned to look at his father's bookshelves, the complete works of William Shakespeare stared at him. Grabbing it, he flipped it open to the table of contents to find it. Once he located the page number, he began reading the Forward of the play.

Though attributed to Shakespeare, the reader may notice subtle changes in the tone of some scenes. It is questioned if there was a collaborator on the work as the play has similarities to Philaster, or Love Lies a-Bleeding by Beaumont and Fletcher.

Edmond bolted upright. "Dad," his voice urgent. Holmes shook out of his thoughts and looked at him. "I know who the peer it."

"Tell me," Holmes said.

"Hugh Manson, Lord Beaumont," Edmond handed the book over and showed him.

"Oh excellent, Edmond," Holmes stated. "Where is Lord Beaumont's residence?"

"I don't know. But I know someone who would." His eyes drifted to the closed door where Terrey bathed.

Chapter Thirty-Nine

Standing outside Beaumont's townhouse, Edmond, Holmes, and Terrey waited for the door to open. When an elderly butler greeted them, the man's eyes turned to Terrey.

"Mr. Terrey, sir," he smiled. "It has been a long time, sir. How are you?"

"I am doing well, Pots," he answered. "It's good to see you. Is Lady Grace in?"

"She is indeed, please come in, sir, come in."

"And his lordship?" Terrey questioned as they crossed the threshold.

"Spent the night at his club, sir," Pots replied. "But I know her ladyship will be pleased to see you. Where have you been, sir? It has been so long since you last called upon us. You always were our favorite caller."

"And I always dearly loved to see all of you," Terrey answered, though Edmond heard the strain in his voice. "Things had changed for me, unfortunately, but I am here now."

"We are glad, sir," Pots said. "Please wait here and let me announce you."

They waited in the entryway after removing their hats and coats as Pots announced them to Lady Grace. A clang came from the breakfast room and soon the flushed face of Lady Grace appeared, hurrying toward them.

"Palmerston?" she questioned and all but ran into his arms. Terrey embraced her, holding tightly. "I hoped you would call."

"Your brother wouldn't let me," he answered. "Seeing you at the ball, I—"

"I didn't want to go," she replied hurriedly, pulling out of his embrace, and looking up at him. "Hugh forced me. I never wanted to meet anyone else. You were the only one. But I saw you were a footman?"

"I was assisting a friend. I am actually a… valet."

"A valet?" she asked.

"I had to have income and there is little I could do with my economic studies without a sponsor."

"But surely Hugh? Or my uncle?"

"Alas, they would not help me."

"You never told me what happened. All I knew was Hugh told me the engagement was broken."

"I am sorry... I wrote to you. Did you not get it?" he questioned.

"No, when?"

"Right after," he replied. "I wanted you to know it wasn't of my doing. I did not wish to end our engagement."

"Nor I," she breathed. Then realization dawned in her eyes. "Damn him. Damn my brother for keeping us apart. He must have stolen your letter. Oh, Palmerston, I am so sorry. What happened?"

"As much as I need to tell you, my dear, we need some important information," Terrey said and then looked back at Holmes and Edmond standing behind him.

As if seeing them for the first time, Lady Grace blushed and looked down, then parted from Terrey but stayed near enough as if worried walking away from him would cause him to disappear.

"Sir Edmond," she curtsied.

"Forgive us for interrupting you, my lady," Edmond replied. "May I introduce my father Sherlock Holmes."

"Mr. Holmes, of course," she curtsied to him. "It is an honor."

"Thank you for seeing us, my lady," Holmes answered.

"Please do come in," she offered.

"Thank you, but we must decline," Edmond replied. "We are unfortunately in a hurry."

She took a step closer to Terrey. "What can I help you with?"

"Your brother, my lady," Edmond began. "Where is he?"

"I believe he spent the night at his club. The Carlton."

"Grace," Terrey said, pulling her attention. "If he was going to try and... not be found, is there a place he would go?"

Her brows furrowed slightly but Edmond was glad she didn't waste time asking questions.

"The only place I can think of would be Papa's old office. We still hold the deed, and it is quite remote."

"The address please, my lady."

"Thirteen Wiltshire Lane," she answered.

"Thank you," Edmond bowed. "My apologies this cannot be a longer visit. Terrey, take a moment, but we must hurry."

Terrey nodded as Edmond and Holmes left the house and climbed into the cab. Terrey took no longer than two minutes and as soon as he bounded down the steps and into the cab, they were off.

Thirteen Wiltshire Lane was indeed remote, but also clearly near to a less than savory area of town. The office building was rundown and looked abandoned. Terrey shook his head.

"I don't think he's here, sir," he said. "Hugh would not be caught dead in a place like this."

"Which may make it the best place to be," Edmond offered. "Let's go and check."

"No, Edmond," Holmes caught his arm. "You stay with the cab. One look at you in those clothes, and any thief or murderous ruffian will think you're easy pickings."

"That would go very badly in their favor," Edmond stated.

"And we cannot let that part of your background be known, yet. Terrey and I will go and look around. Trust me, son."

Edmond looked between his father and Terrey but nodded once. As much as he hated being excluded, he knew his father was correct. He still needed to be Sir Edmond for now, at least while wearing his fancier clothes. He also needed to tell Terrey about what the prince had told him. Hugh was the cause of his family's problems. Edmond had yet to understand why he would ruin Terrey's family.

Ten minutes later, movement to his left caught his eye. Holmes and Terrey hurried to the cab, gave the address for Baker Street, and leaned back as the cab jolted forward.

"Anything?" Edmond asked.

"Hugh wasn't there, but we were able to learn that he was there this morning and just left an hour or so ago," Terrey explained.

"Apparently he was only there for enough time as to pick something up. Nearly ran the squatters off," Holmes went on.

"What did he pick up?" Edmond asked.

"A book or ledger, they weren't certain," Holmes answered.

"Why are we going back to Baker Street?" Edmond questioned.

"Because the next part of our journey will need to be in much more inferior clothing," Holmes said cryptically.

"We're going to the theater early," Edmond surmised.

"Quite so." Holmes leaned back, closed his eyes, and said no more.

Chapter Forty

Their time at Baker Street was quick. A smile and embrace to both Marguerite and Henri, and a change into more appropriate attire, makeup, and a fake nose, and they were off again. Terrey staying to prepare Edmond's theater attire. Curtain was set for eight o'clock that evening which gave Edmond and Holmes four hours to scope out the opera house and see if they could find the prince or Beaumont and Brown.

Theater folk were tightlipped and loyal to each other. Holmes and Edmond needed to disguise themselves as two of the travelling stagehands. Once they spoke with the manager, they were put to work. Edmond, being seen as strong enough to manage the flies, worked in the wings of the stage. Holmes was utilized below in the actor's dressing rooms helping the costumer run costumes to the racks above. It was the perfect cover for them both. While Holmes was working, Edmond wasn't needed and could wander around, unquestioned.

He had just found a locked door below in the waiting area commonly referred to as the Green Room, when the Chief of the Flies yelled; "'Ere, what you doin' down 'ere?"

"I ain't doin' nuttin', guvna," Edmond replied, knowing his usually polished voice would not work in that situation. "Jus' thought I'd get a look see."

"You leave em women alone," the chief stated. "I'll repor' you to the manager."

"Aw, come off it," Edmond said. "Jus' a wee peek. I won't tell."

"Tell wha'?"

"Tha' you know where them women are. Been sneaking 'round youself?"

The man's face went bright red and Edmond knew the man before him wasn't accustomed to his sins being found out.

"What's all this then?" Holmes' voice, heavily accented in the Yorkshire accent came from another room.

"Nuttin'," Edmond answered, his eyes still on the Chief of the Flies. "I weren't sneakin' 'round."

He looked at the door deliberately for his father to know what he was thinking.

"I'm gettin' outa 'ere," Edmond said. "No need to stay where I ain't wanted. Or where I'm surrounded by the likes of you."

Edmond walked past the Chief of the Flies and banged his shoulder as he left. He needed to get back to Baker Street and change into his theater attire. But he also needed to tell Terrey something before he left. And it was likely his friend would need a comforting hand.

"Terrey," Edmond spoke as he stood before the full mirror Terrey had brought from Piccadilly along with the clothes they needed that evening. "I need to speak with you."

Terrey paused by the wardrobe where he was pulling out the white waistcoat. "Is everything all right, sir?"

Edmond took a deep breath, turned, and sat in one of the armchairs. "Come, sit for a moment."

Terrey eyed him concerned but did as he asked. "Is there something wrong?"

"No," Edmond answered. "I... found out something and it's only right you learn the truth."

"The truth?"

"About what happened to your family. Your father."

Terrey's brow furrowed even deeper. "What do you mean?"

"What I need to tell you will be hard to hear. I only just found out myself at the ball at Buckingham. Terrey... Palmerston, do you know why your father rendered your family destitute?"

"No, my brother never told me. He just said it wasn't something I needed to know."

"And there's a reason for that."

"What reason?" Terrey questioned.

"Your father was giving money to a certain individual who lied to him about using the money to build a church in Africa. In fact, this person was using the money for their own gains."

"What? Who? Why?"

Edmond looked down, knowing what he had to say, was only going to hurt him. "I'm sorry, but it was found out that the person who cheated, lied, and stole from your father was... is Lord Beaumont."

Terrey stared at him for a long moment. "What?" he breathed. "Hugh?"

Edmond nodded. "Apparently there were several large withdrawals found in your father's ledger and all of them were to an H.M. Correct me if I am wrong, but Lord Beaumont's surname is Manson, correct?"

Terrey said nothing, but the color had drained from his face and his body had gone rigid.

"Terrey?"

He snapped his gaze over to Edmond and took ragged breaths.

"What? Oh, ehm, yes. Manson. But... why? Why would Hugh, my dearest friend, do this to us? What possible motive could..."

"My thoughts are, he didn't want his sister to marry..."

"Beneath them?" Terrey provided. "He stole hundreds of thousands of pounds from my family simply because he wanted Grace to marry someone else?" His eyes filled with horror. "Dear god, please tell me she didn't know."

"I am almost absolutely positive she did not. She loves you

Terrey."

"And I her, but because of her brother's villainy, I can never be with her."

"That is not true. He will be brought up on charges of treason and Grace will need someone she can trust to take care of her. And I know you still love her."

Terrey said nothing for a long moment. "I just don't understand. How could he have done this to us? We were best friends. It was a respectable match and a love match. I just... how could he?"

"We will find out as soon as we catch him. But Terrey, I need you focused tonight. I need your eyes and your ears. Are you with me?"

Terrey let out a breath as he nodded. "Always."

"Good man," Edmond smiled and slapped him on the back. "Now, can you assist me with this evening's attire?"

"Of course," Terrey still held a faraway look as he dressed him.

"While I'm with the king, I need you to get down to the Green Room of the theater and help my father. There's a locked door down there and I have a feeling there's more behind it than fancy costumes."

"Understood, sir," he answered.

"And if you see Brown or Beaumont, do not engage without someone with you. They are formidable and could be armed."

Terrey's jaw clenched, but he agreed. Soon, Edmond was dressed and ready to attend the opera with the king. Terrey hailed a cab while Edmond spoke to his mother. Marguerite told him to be careful and Henri offered to help. Edmond crouched down to look at the boy in the eye.

"Henri, I need you to stay here for me. Will you do that?"

"But I can help, *Monsieur,*" he said.

"I know and you would be a marvelous help, but I need you to stay here, all right?"

Henri huffed but agreed. Edmond embraced him and then his mother. Finally, he stepped onto Baker Street and into the cab waiting to take him to Piccadilly where the king's carriage escorted him to Buckingham.

Arabella met him just inside. "The queen is safe," she stated.

"Good," he replied. "Any news?"

She shook her head. "But I did receive another message from..." she glanced around and lowered her voice. "You know who."

Edmond swallowed down the flare of anger and betrayal. "And?"

"It's more specific instruction. He wants me to meet him above the stage on the catwalk."

Edmond's hair on the back of his neck prickled. "No, Arabella," he stated. "It is a trap."

"I know, but if there is a chance I can capture him, is it not worth exploring?"

"No," Edmond's tone was final. "It's not worth your life, Ara."

"It's wonderful to hear you say that, Edmond," she began. "But I think it would be worth anything to take him down."

"I cannot have you there, Arabella. If you are there, then

my mind will not be on the more important things. I have to focus on his majesty and finding the prince. I cannot have you there."

Her face morphed to understanding. "I understand. I will stay here."

"Thank you," he said.

"Edmond," Percy's voice called from down the hallway. Turning to see his brother dressed in his finery, he looked at the king who stood beside him. "His majesty asked if I would join since the ladies are in for the evening."

"Excellent, it will give me a chance to look for his highness. I believe I know where he is."

"You do not believe they will give him back to me, do you, Holmes?" The king questioned.

"I do not believe they will, sire, no," Edmond stated. "But my father is there now and Terrey, my man has joined him. They are searching for him. I am certain we will find him unharmed, sire."

"Then let's get this over with."

Turning with the king, Edmond glanced back to Arabella who smiled encouragingly at him as they left the palace. "We will be early, sire, so I ask that you follow the instructions in the letter. I will go in early and see if I can discover anything. I also want to check your theater box."

"I can do that, Edmond," Percy replied. "You go see if you can help Father."

"Good, excellent," Edmond thanked him. "Have no fear, sire, with us there tonight, we will keep you safe and find your son."

"I do hope so, Holmes. I need him safe."

"I understand. And he will be," Edmond stated.

The carriage rattled through the streets of London to Covent Garden and to the opera house. Those inside said no more, as they waited for the carriage to come to a stop. Once it did, Edmond left and hurried into the building, along with many other patrons. But instead of going straight into the hall, Edmond turned right and headed down the steps beneath the stage.

"Edmond," he heard his father whisper. He peered into the darkness but did not hesitate to move toward the voice. "I tried to get in, but it is locked from the inside with a bolt that cannot be taken care of here. We need to wait and see who comes out."

"Any sighting of Brown or Beaumont?" Edmond asked.

"None yet, but I have a feeling Brown at least out lived his usefulness. Beaumont might be inside there with the prince."

"Terrey?"

"He arrived about an hour ago," Holmes went on. "I asked him to try and blend in above and to occasionally check out in the alley. It would be an easy way for our prey to escape."

Edmond could not answer as there was a commotion above stairs, just as the fanfare erupted, signaling the king had entered. They hurried up the steps and down the corridor to see what happened. The stage manager was in a panic, someone had rushed past him and the costumer, causing the costumer to drop the most extravagant dress for the Prima Dona. Holmes and Edmond took in the scene, then peered past the curtain to see the king accept his subjects' adoration. Suddenly, Edmond and his father exchanged a look.

"The door," he said. They raced down the stairs and cursed. The door was open. Hurrying in to see, there was a chair with ropes and a handkerchief tied as if a gag.

But there was no prince.

Chapter Forty-One

Henri dropped from under the carriage as soon as it began to pull away from the opera house. Ducking into the shadows, he hurried to the alleyway, freezing for a brief moment when he saw an all-black carriage waiting just outside the door. When the door opened and a bag of trash was tossed out, Henri rushed forward and got inside. Seeing people bustling around carrying props and costumes, he saw a stairwell to his left and hurried down it. Recognizing *Monsieur's* voice, Henri waited.

"Any sighting of Brown or Beaumont?" *Monsieur* asked from under the stairs.

"None yet, but I have a feeling Brown at least out lived his usefulness. Beaumont might be inside there with the prince," Mr. Holmes whispered.

"Terrey?"

"He arrived about an hour ago," Mr. Holmes went on. "I asked him to try and blend in above backstage and to occasionally check out in the alley. It would be an easy way for our prey to escape."

There was a loud crash up the stairs making Henri jump. He ducked into the shadows as Mr. Holmes and *Monsieur* race up the steps. He saw the door they were looking at, open and a mousey looking man peeked out.

"Stay here," he threw over his shoulder, then chuckled as if he made a joke. He hurried out of the room and up the opposite stairs Mr. Holmes and *Monsieur* used.

Once Henri was sure he had time, he hurried to the door. It was locked but it didn't take Henri long to pick the lock and open the door, grateful the bolt was not engaged. A man sat, bound, and gagged in a wooden chair. He was dressed in a uniform, but it looked dingy and the seam was ripped near the shoulder. He looked up, his intense light eyes assessed Henri. One of his eyes was rimmed with a bruise and the handkerchief had a few drops of blood. From the dried blood on his nose, it was clear he had seen the wrong side of a man's fist.

Henri hurried over to the man. Somehow, though he had never met him, he knew he was the prince. The man looked like the king but younger and leaner.

Taking out the gag, Henri questioned, "You are the prince?"

"I am," he answered. "Who are you?"

"I am Henri Holmes. I found you, sir!" He beamed. "Let me

344

help."

"Quickly my bonds," the prince said. "We must stop my father. They are going to blow up the king's box after the third act."

Henri's eyes grew large, but he cut the bonds and helped the prince stand.

"Can you walk?" Henri asked.

"I can," he answered.

"Good. My father is looking for you. He'll be able to help."

They hurried out of the room but stopped when a man stood in the main Green Room. His eyes grew wide.

"Your highness?" the man exclaimed.

"Beaumont!" the prince exhaled. "Oh, thank god. It's good to see you."

"I am so pleased to see you, sire. Half of London is out looking for you," he answered.

"Beaumont?" Henri questioned. The man looked down his nose at Henri.

"And who might this urchin be?" the man named Beaumont queried.

"I am Henri Holmes, son of Edmond," he said.

The man's eyes grew wide. "Edmond? Sir Edmond has a son? That jackanapes bastard. He tried to woo my sister and all the while he lied?"

"Don't listen to him, your highness. He's the one behind this. I heard my father and grandfather talking about him. He and a man named Brown. They are working for another. He's behind this."

The prince's eyes whipped over to Beaumont. "Is this true?

Are you the one who kidnapped me?"

"No, your highness," the man gave a convincing scandalized response. The prince's eyes twitched but then he looked down at Henri unconvinced by Beaumont's performance. "Your highness, you know me. Let me take you to safety. You will see I mean you no harm."

"It's not me I worry about, Beaumont. It's my father. Do you mean him no harm?" the prince questioned.

"Henri?" *Monsieur's* voice came from the stairs as he hurried down. "What are you doing here?"

"You have some explaining to do, Sir Edmond," Beaumont stated. "You lie as you woo my sister."

"I am not wooing Lady Grace, she is still in love with her fiancé. My valet."

"Valet?" Beaumont looked aghast. "Dear god."

"He's only a valet because of you," *Monsieur* answered. "You swindled his father out of his money. I need to know why."

"I would like to know why too," Terrey stated slowly coming down the steps.

Beaumont's face screwed up as he looked at Terrey. "I owe this man nothing. He is nothing to me. A mere valet."

Terrey raced across the room and his fist flew, connecting with Beaumont's jaw before *Monsieur* could stop him. Beaumont fell onto his back with a screech.

"He attacked me! I will have him hanged!" Beaumont screamed.

"I didn't see any one attack you," the prince said. "In fact, I think you merely tripped. You owe Mr. Terrey an answer. You ruined his family."

"I owe him nothing!" He shouted.

"Just tell me one thing, Hugh," Terrey began.

"It's Lord Beaumont to you, you filth."

"Why? Tell me why."

"You don't deserve anything from me."

"And there it is," Mr. Holmes answered. Then, turning to Terrey, he answered for him. "Your engagement to Lady Grace. You are untitled and everything Beaumont does is to further his name. He wanted to marry his sister to some titled lord. It didn't matter your match was one of love. It meant nothing to him. He wanted a union that would further his agenda."

Terrey closed his eyes and looked away. "So, he ruined my entire family, my life, simply because he wanted to sell his sister to the highest bidder?"

"Yes," *Monsieur* stated. "But unfortunately, that can't matter now." He looked over at the prince. "Sire, it is good to see you. This man and Brown were behind your kidnapping. They are working for a man named Moriarty."

"The professor?" the prince asked. "And your grandfather?"

"The same, sire," *Monsieur* answered.

"And where is he?"

"In the carriage, out in the alley," Henri explained. "I saw him when I came in."

"Not only that, they are planning on blowing up the opera house after the third act. We need to find the bomb and throw it into the Thames," the prince said.

"Do you know where it is?" Mr. Holmes questioned.

"In my father's box."

"All will be well, sire, stay with Edmond," Mr. Holmes ordered and hurried up the stairs calling for *Oncle* Percy.

Monsieur stood near the prince. "Terrey, watch over Beaumont." Terrey nodded. "Are you well, sire?"

"I have been better. Brown approached me at the ball just before the fireworks, saying I was needed, and I went with him. I thought I could trust him."

"He was your father's valet, sire, of course you did," *Monsieur* said.

"No!" Henri yelled and rammed into the prince just as a loud gunshot rang out.

Chapter Forty-Two

Edmond spun around to see Brown standing on the other stairs, smoking gun in his hand. He aimed it at Edmond next, but Edmond was too fast. He raced to the king's secretary, knocked the gun out of his hand and spun around kicking Brown across the face. The secretary went down hard, and Edmond landed in his ready position. The position he had shown Henri. His blood went cold.

"Henri!" the prince shouted.

Edmond turned from the unconscious man. Henri was still

over the prince, but blood poured from Henri's shoulder and he was whimpering holding his arm.

"Henri!" Edmond screamed and raced to his son. "Henri, Henri!" He pulled him off the prince and into his arms. "Get a doctor!" Terrey ran to the stairs and took them two at a time.

"*Monsieur?*" Henri's voice was small and filled with pain.

"Stay with me son, stay with me," Edmond begged.

"I saw the gun," he said. "I saw he was pointing it at the prince. I had to protect him. Like you would."

"You did, you did protect him, son," Edmond replied. The prince knelt beside him and placed a hand on Edmond's shoulder.

"I did the Holmes name proud?" he asked.

"Yes, Henri, you did the Holmes name proud."

"I'm glad. I wanted to make you proud."

"You did, Henri, you did," Edmond rocked him back and forth. "You're going to be all right."

Terrey ran back down the stairs with another man in tow. The man hurried to Henri and examined the wound. "It's a flesh wound. He'll be fine. Let me help."

Edmond nodded and though he didn't want to, he handed his son over to the doctor.

"You see? That's what he gets! He doesn't deserve to live. He's not wanted, nor needed, the little cretin," Beaumont said. "We are the chosen people. The king wants to socialize with paupers and Jews, but we are the ones who should rule. We are the masters of others not just ourselves."

Edmond seethed. He stood, Henri's blood on his white waistcoat. He stood over Beaumont and didn't hesitate as he kicked the man's head, knocking out two teeth, but preventing him from saying anything more as he lost consciousness.

Turning back, he saw the prince helping the doctor and murmuring to Henri. "Thank you, my boy. Without you, I would surely be dead."

Terrey looked over at Edmond and nodded.

"Stay here?" Edmond asked. "I need to help Father."

"Of course," Terrey said.

Edmond walked back to Henri. "Go," Henri said. "I'll be all right, *mon pere*."

Letting out a breath, he stroked his son's hair. "I'll be right back, *mon fils*."

Henri nodded and Edmond stood. Looking at the doctor, Edmond said, "take good care of my son, doctor."

"I will, sir."

With that promise, Edmond hurried up the back stair and tried to find his father in the darkness.

Arabella wore trousers and a shirt she found in Henri's closet. They were dirty but it was perfect for the character she embodied. Hurrying to the opera house, she snuck down the alley seeing the black carriage. She paused. She would know that carriage anywhere. Still, she tried to move past it, but the door opened, and a cool voice spoke from inside.

"Arabella, my dear," Moriarty said. "I hardly recognized you in those clothes. Not something a *lady* should wear, now is it?"

A shiver ran down Arabella's back as she turned to look at him. Unable to make out more than his shadow, she was drawn in like a moth to a flame.

"Come in, come in," his smooth voice said, and Arabella was powerless to refuse. More than once, she wondered if he had hypnotized her. "We have much to discuss."

Climbing into the carriage, the door shutting behind her, she looked at the man's outline as it was too dark to see anything more. He wore a black cloak and top hat but the stark white of the scar on his face was even more pronounced in the darkness.

"I have heard this opera is going to be quite the sight," Moriarty said. "The third act, I'm told will be quite explosive."

Her stomach fell, then immediately twisted into knots. Not only the king, but Edmond was inside.

"I would have thought all of the theatrics of this case were too melodramatic for you, Professor," she said, proud her voice was strong.

He clicked his tongue. "Normally I would agree but I knew the rarity of the case would catch the Holmes' attention. And I knew you would be perfect to distract my grandson. Tell me, was Edmond completely taken in with you?"

Forgive me, Edmond. She thought. "More than you know."

"Good, good, I hated having to see you whore yourself out to him, but I am glad it worked in our favor. I was surprised when Mycroft asked you to do the same thing. But I always did admire his mind. So like my own. I want you to know, Arabella, I am not angry at you for betraying me."

"You're not?" she questioned.

"No, on the contrary, my dear," he stated. "It showed me how very like me you have become. Ruthless."

"What are you planning, Professor?" Arabella asked, hopeful he was in a talkative mood.

"At the moment, I am planning on watching as the opera house goes up in smoke." He began laughing. "A fitting end to all of them. Holmes, Percy, Edmond."

"And all the innocent people who are in there?"

"Innocent people are sacrificed in every war. And make no mistake, this is a war. A war I have been fighting for decades. And it has finally come to a close."

"You have never beat me, Moriarty, and you never will." Holmes' voice shocked Arabella as he yanked open the door. "I should have done this much sooner." Without hesitation, Holmes had pulled a gun and aiming at the professor, he fired. Arabella felt the spray of his blood across her face as the man who tormented her for years under the disguise of being a concerned guardian, slumped in the carriage. Holmes sneered and pulled the cloak back to reveal his face. The scar from Reichenbach still stark against the now deathly pale face. His eyes opened wide in shock as the blood from the hole in his head dribbled down between his brows.

Holmes took a deep breath and let it out slowly. "It's over." His voice was soft, and it sounded more like he was trying to convince himself of the fact. Then his eyes turned to her. "What are you doing here?"

"I had to help. I wanted to see if I could stop him."

"Edmond told you not to be here."

"I know, but I needed to. He made me live in fear for years and I had to see it come to an end."

"Then look," Holmes said turning back to the vacant eyes. "It's ended."

Arabella did look and took in the paleness of death, the stark red of the blood, the black of the gun powder burn, and the wide eyes of the man she hated. It was indeed over.

Holmes offered his hand to her and helped her out of the carriage. She then threw her arms around his neck.

"Thank you," she murmured.

"That is not necessary. You would have done the same. Now, give me the revolver," he said.

She pulled back and looked at him.

"Come now, I know why you came here, and it wasn't just to make sure Edmond was safe."

"Actually, it was," she answered but reached behind her and pulled out the revolver from the back of her trousers. "It was the only way to make sure he was safe, always. I would do anything to ensure his safety."

"I know you would." Holmes took a deep breath and let it out slowly as he looked up at the top of the carriage.

"What happened to the driver? Was there a driver?" Arabella questioned looking at the front where the horses pawed at the dirt.

"He's been taken care of," the way Holmes said the words made her know just how he had taken care of the driver. "I need to help Percy. We know where the bomb is."

"You won't be able to disarm it," she replied. "He would have a failsafe for it."

"I know," Holmes answered. "But if we can get it to the Thames…"

Arabella nodded. "Let's go then."

"No, you go back to Baker Street."

"Mr. Holmes, no," she answered. "I am here, use me. I can help. I know him just as well you do. I know what he would do and how."

Holmes thought for a moment.

"Dad?" Percy's voice called. "Are you— uh..." Percy appeared in the doorway and looked at Arabella up and down. "What are you doing here?"

"Immaterial, Percy. We need to stop the performance and get the king to safety while I find the bomb."

"Moriarty..."

"Dead," Holmes stated.

Percy's sharp intake of breath told Arabella just the how much hell they had gone through while hiding from their grandfather.

"Can't say I'm sorry to hear that," Percy said.

"Stay with the carriage and horses, Arabella," Holmes ordered.

"No, again Mr. Holmes, I know more about this than you do," she pushed passed Holmes and Percy and entered the opera house through the stage door.

The area was dark, but she didn't miss the outline of Edmond hurrying up the steps. He froze when he saw her.

"Ara?" he questioned. "What are you doing here?"

"I needed to see if I could help," she answered.

"I told you to stay away." Edmond placed his hands on his hips.

"And I told you no."

"If we could get back to the task at hand," Holmes broke in. "Moriarty is dead."

"What?" Edmond's gaze flew to his father's.

"He's dead. But the bomb is still very much alive. Beaumont and Brown under control?"

Edmond nodded but Arabella saw something in the shadow of his features. Looking down, she covered her mouth so she wouldn't screech. Edmond looked down at his waistcoat.

"Are you all right?" Holmes' voice was tight.

"Yes," Edmond answered. "But Brown shot Henri."

"What?" both Holmes and Arabella nearly shouted.

"Shh," one of the stagehands reprimanded them.

"He'll be all right. Terrey found a doctor. It's a flesh wound."

"Thank God," Arabella cried.

"We need to stop this opera and get the king to safety," Holmes said.

"I'm surprised they didn't hear the gunshot," Edmond answered.

"The lower area of the theater is soundproof," Holmes explained. "I'll find the stage manager. Percy, go to the king. Edmond..." Holmes looked around and found a cloak worn by Dogberry in the second act and handed it to him. "You can't go around with blood on you. Wear this and let's see if we can dispose of the bomb."

Edmond hurried to pull on the cloak and followed his brother out from behind the stage to the main lobby. Hurrying up the stairs, Edmond saw Yancy and Jakob standing guard just outside the king's box. Thanking them with a nod, Edmond, Percy, and Arabella entered the box. The king looked up, fear in his eyes.

"His highness is safe," Edmond whispered.

The king heaved a great sigh of relief. "Thank God," he

whispered then, looked at Arabella with confusion.

"But sire, you are not," Edmond went on before he could question her presence or attire. "Keep your eyes on the opera and let my brother and I find what we are looking for."

"What are you looking for?" he asked.

The brothers exchanged a look, but Percy nodded. "There is a bomb somewhere in the Royal Box. We need to find it."

All color drained from the king's face, but he nodded quickly and forced his eyes back on Benedick singing about his love of Beatrice. All three began searching.

After the walls were discovered sound with no hidden compartment, Edmond and Percy turned to see Arabella crawling around on her hands and knees, near the king's chair. Then, she turned on her back and wriggled her way under the chair. Edmond got down on his knees.

"It's here," she said taking the velvet, tacked on the underside of the chair. Edmond got on his back and looked underneath with her.

Sure enough, as soon as Arabella took the velvet off, the bomb was there. Edmond took in the various wires.

"How does this work?" Edmond whispered.

"You imagine I have bomb dismantling experience?" Arabella asked.

Edmond looked over at her. "Don't fail me now, Ara," he said.

"I'm flattered." But she turned back to bomb. She said nothing for a long moment as she traced some of the wires. "There needs to be a trigger but if this model is what I think it is..."

"What?"

"Don't let the king stand up."

Edmond breathed out quickly. "You mean..."

"The second he sat down; he triggered the mechanism. If he stands, the bomb will explode."

"Merde," Edmond cursed. "Can you disarm it?"

"Maybe," she answered. "But probably not in time."

"Let me see," Edmond crawled further under the chair. Arabella moved away for him to see better. Muttering to himself, Edmond followed the wires and tried to see where they all led. "This one attaches here," he said. "And this one attaches to that. So, if I pull this one..."

"It could trigger it," Arabella said.

"It could, or it could disarm it," Edmond replied.

"Do you really want to risk the king's life on a *could?*"

"Do you have a better idea?" he asked.

She looked desperate for a moment then shook her head. "No," she replied.

"All right, then," Edmond's heart sped as he reached for the wire.

"Wait!" Arabella stopped him. He looked over at her and she took his face in her hands and kissed him briefly but strongly. "I love you."

Edmond stared at her for a long moment. "I love you too." Staring into her eyes, Edmond tugged the wire loose.

Epilogue

September 1902

Terrey stood looking down at the grave. The flowers in his hand, English Roses, weighed heavily as he set them down in the family plot. Straightening, he took off his top hat and held it.

"I don't honestly know what to say," he said to the headstone. "You taught me so much about life and how to live it to the fullest. You were my best friend and someone I miss every day. Without your guidance I can't say where I'd be right now. I miss you so much." His wife's hand slipped into his. He glanced over and smiled at Grace. "And now that I'm a father, I need your guidance, Father."

"He would be so proud of you," Grace spoke softly leaning her head against his shoulder. "I know you miss him, my love."

"I'm just glad I have you and little Julian," he said. "Though why Edmond insisted on his second middle name when I wanted to name him after him, I'll not understand."

"Because Julian is much more English, Ter," Edmond stated, walking over to him, and pulling his top hat off as well. "And in a world where Englishmen are highly respected, it will give your little lord a leg up in society. Besides can you imagine Edmond Manson Terrey, Lord Beaumont? I shudder." He winked.

Terrey chuckled. "Well, I can understand. But still. Without you, Grace and I wouldn't be together. And our good name wouldn't have been restored. I owe you everything."

"Then, find me a new valet," Edmond winked. "Since I have to keep this Sir Edmond title, I need someone I can trust to dress me."

"I would be very happy to help you find someone suitable."

"I would be grateful. My wife keeps harping on it," Edmond stated.

"And speaking of the devil," Arabella walked over to him, their seven-month-old son in her arms. Edmond turned and grinned, opening his arms to them. Other members of his family gathered close.

"Arabella," Grace stepped forward to take her hand once Frederick was safely in Edmond's arms. "I cannot thank you and Edmond enough for agreeing to be godparents to our little Julian."

"Oh, my dear, we are honored," Arabella stated. "There is nothing we wouldn't do for you both."

"Thank you so much. And thank you, Edmond again for everything. You were instrumental in giving me the love of my life back," Grace said looking lovingly at her husband.

"It was my pleasure, Grace," Edmond replied then cooed down at his son. "And besides, without Terrey's help, I might never have pursued Arabella and added to my family."

"You needed little help from me, Edmond," Terrey smiled

at him. "But I am glad. *All's well that ends well*, as the old Bard says."

"Indeed," Grace replied. "But I think, my love we should head back. Our guests will be waiting."

"It was a lovely christening, Grace," Arabella stated as they hurried past. "Edmond and I will be up shortly."

Once they were alone, Edmond looked back at his wife.

"So," he began.

"So?" She raised an eyebrow.

"The king has asked me to accompany him on a quick tour to Germany," Edmond revealed.

"And you said yes, of course," Arabella stated.

"I did," Edmond agreed.

"Good," she replied. "He would be quite lost without you."

"I believe you mean without us, my love," Edmond said. "For if I recall correctly, you were instrumental in finding the bomb that nearly destroyed England as we know it."

"You recall correctly, husband," she answered with a teasing grin. "But you should hurry back."

"Well, of course, my love, I always do."

"And you know how much I love... celebrating, your returns."

Edmond's smile turned into a salacious grin. "All the more reason I go with his majesty when he needs me."

"I imagine that is true." Arabella laughed and took his hand as he shifted his son onto one arm. "But this time, you'll need to return for more reasons than my welcome home."

"Oh?" Edmond asked. "And why is that?"

"Well, Sir Edmond," she placed his hand on her stomach. "There just might be a reason."

Edmond's eyes grew as wide as his grin. "Are you certain?"

"I am," she answered. "So, you'll have to return for not only my sake, or Henri's and Frederick's but for this little one too."

Edmond let out a whoop of excitement and kissed her firmly. "I promise you, I will return in a month."

"You better," she said. "But I do not intend on letting you go just yet."

Edmond chuckled. "No indeed, my love. We do not leave for a fortnight."

"It is hard to believe how this all began," Arabella continued as they walked up the hill to Beaumont Estate where Terrey and Grace held the christening luncheon. "Even harder to believe how it all came about."

"After the bomb was diffused, and Moriarty's body was carted off to the morgue, Brown sung like a bird. Naming names and pointing fingers. Beaumont did himself no favors by spouting his priggish fantasies as they carted him off."

"Still, time in Bedlam," Arabella shook her head. "If anyone deserves to be there, it's him."

"Indeed, and the king granted Terrey's land and fortune back. His brother is managing the finances as Terrey settles in as caretaker for his son, the next Lord Beaumont."

They met his father, mother, brother, sister and their spouses, children, and Henri at the top of the hill. Marguerite offered to take her grandson from Edmond and little Frederick went willingly into his beloved grandmother's arms.

"Their wedding was very fine indeed," Arabella said.

"Not as fine as ours, my love," Edmond replied.

"I liked the wedding," Henri piped up as he walked with them. "It was... interesting."

"Yes, and profitable for you, son," Edmond laughed.

Henri's face turned bright red. "I don't know what you mean, *mon pere.* You forced me to give it all back."

"I did indeed. No more pickpocketing, we agreed," Edmond winked.

"It's all right, love," Arabella said. "I'll teach you my safe cracking skills while your father is off on his next task with the king."

"Ara," Edmond cautioned. She waved him off.

"You've been given another assignment by the king?" Mycroft asked. Edmond's relationship with his uncle had never returned to how it once had been, but he tolerated him and even spoke to him often.

"He asked me to join him on a trip to Germany," Edmond explained. "We leave in a fortnight."

"So soon after the coronation?" Alexandra asked.

"It was a month ago," Edmond reminded his sister-in-law. "I'm sure it won't be a long trip."

"Is he healthy enough for such a task?" Holmes asked.

"I believe so," Edmond answered. "He healed well after the appendectomy. I have consulted with the royal physician. He says all is well."

"Good then," Cedric replied. "Are you happy for another journey?"

"Not exactly," Edmond teased. "But I am happy to serve him. We have become sort of friends."

"After saving his life all those times, Edmond," Rebecca started. "Of course you are friends."

"And you know I can never retire," Edmond said.

"No, you'll wind up old and fat," Percy teased his brother.

"Deflecting, brother mine?" Edmond raised an eyebrow at Percy. Though his brother was hardly large, he had put on a good stone after his marriage.

The family chuckled at Percy's expense but soon Edmond spoke again.

"I will ask you to keep an eye on Arabella while I'm away."

"Why? Is everything all right?" Marguerite asked.

"Oh, never better, but since she is caring for my unborn son or daughter, I would hope you could check in on her."

Everyone cheered as they approached the front door. Marguerite kissed Arabella on both cheeks and Holmes, Percy, and Cedric slapped Edmond on the back.

"Your mother and I would be happy to stay with her," Holmes offered. "I think Baker Street can do without me for a short time. And besides, the home you were gifted by his majesty is stunning. The library and laboratory are my envy."

"Yes indeed, and in Autumn the Sussex Downs is beautiful," Marguerite said. "Have no fear, my love, we will look after them all."

"I know." He kissed his mother's cheek. "And be sure she doesn't teach Henri any of her safe cracking skills."

"No fair," Henri whined with a smile. Arabella laughed but took Edmond's hand.

Holmes, Percy, Cedric, Marguerite, Alexandra, Rebecca, and Dr. Watson all walked into the house while Edmond and Arabella stood together, Henri just inside the threshold. His family. Edmond motioned for Henri to come to them and wrapped an arm around his son's shoulders and held Arabella to him.

"Do you know how grateful I am for you all? My family? I never thought I would have this opportunity."

"Me neither, *Monsieur*," Henri rarely used that title any longer. But the nostalgia that it brought, made Edmond sigh in happiness.

"And together we can face anything. Right Henri?" Arabella asked.

"Right."

"Then there's only one other thing to say..." Edmond began.

"And what is that?"

"The life I carved out of pain and loss, became the life I never knew I wanted or needed. I am happy," Edmond explained. Then, after a beat, said, "I love you both."

"I love you too, *mon pere*," Henri replied.

"And I love you, Edmond, more than anything," Arabella stated.

Arabella squeezed his waist as he clutched Henri's shoulders. After a short embrace, Arabella followed Henri into the manor leaving Edmond outside watching them. After all, twenty-nine years of his life, he could finally say he was happy. Not that there wouldn't be more stories to tell, but for him at that moment, the rest was silence.

Finis

Acknowledgements

Thank you to everyone who loved *Soundless Silence* so much they clamored for a sequel! I never thought my *Sherlock Holmes Family* series needed a sequel but when I thought more about Edmond's story, I knew it would be a wonderfully fun ride to make Edmond do what he hates... fashion.

I hope you all enjoyed, and I hope you will join me for the third novel. Edmond Holmes receives information about Lei's death from China and not all is as it appears. There are also plans for a fourth novel in the series. Henri Holmes' quest for his real father begins after coming home from World War I, injured, angry, and desperate.

And a disclaimer: I always try to give my book as much true detail as possible, but for the sake of this novel, all events contained herein are fictious. The Prince and Princess of Wales were not in London for the season in 1901 as they were touring the British Empire but for the sake of this fictious story they had returned earlier than expected.

The history of King Edward VII is as true as I could make it. He did enjoy *Le Chabanais* and there was such a thing as his Sphinx bathtub and Love Seat. For more information, be sure to search both topics on your favorite search engine. It is... interesting to say the least!

If you enjoyed please consider leaving a review! Be sure to check out my website at www.mkatherineclark.net and follow me on social media!